THE FIRST BLACK PRESIDENT BLUES

By

David L. Dukes

ISBN: 0-7596-6565-6

This book is printed on acid free paper.

1stBooks - rev. 06/05/02

Chapter 1

It was to be my crowning achievement. After four years in office and an exhausting reelection campaign, my second round of inaugural activities would be the icing on the cake. Despite the pessimism of the nay sayers I'd remained fairly confident throughout the reelection run, that when January 20th, 2021, rolled around I'd be returning to the Oval Office. Confident enough, in fact, that I'd been contemplating a special addition to the inaugural ceremonies all along.

Sure the campaign got a bit hairy at times, every presidential race does. As expected my opponent focused his attacks in the domestic arena, my suprisingly strong track record in foreign affairs having left him little choice. My management of the Iranian Nuclear Crisis had certainly proven that I wasn't just a "home front" president. But it was my initiation of the U.S.-Russia Nuclear Nonproliferation Intelligence Exchange Treaty which solidified my place in foreign policy history. Thus, lacking credible alternatives, my opponent continued to rant about the "dictatorial" nature of my domestic agenda and its alleged "destruction of our social fabric." And of course he never missed an opportunity to attack me as the "anti-family president," a label which he had so eloquently coined. I guess the problem was that my opponent, so long on criticisms, was short on solutions, and the voters knew it.

The truth be known, the substantive issues of the reelection campaign were never my chief concern. In my initial bid for the presidency I'd hammered home the constant theme that I refused to conduct a quick fix administration. "Keep your vote," I'd said, "unless you're willing to walk with me to the dawn." For of one fact I was certain, my proposals for reform would require generational implementation, a continuity far beyond the two

David L. Dukes

short terms of an elective office or the brittle frailty of any single
life.

My first campaign was called radical and irresponsible and
worse things behind closed doors. Washington insiders mocked
the youthful naivete' of my forty-eight years as I refused to
participate in the time honored campaign traditions of promises
and compromise. But my priorities had been determined long
before I ever entered the race and no amount of resistance or
mockery could obscure the clarity of my vision. It was for the
people to decide. For I would walk into the great house with
their untainted invitation or I would not walk at all.

In the end, they say it was my uncompromising nature which
put me over the top. It seems that the electorate had become so
frustrated with the chameleon like positions of our country's
presidential hopefuls that my unwavering platform captivated
their attention. In fact, my unyielding resolve became the
cornerstone of my first campaign, perhaps even more so than the
obvious. No, the substantive issues were not of great concern to
me in my reelection bid. In truth, I was by far more concerned
with the color of my skin.

I must confess that all said and done, I believe the color issue
worked to my advantage in the first campaign. Although it was
never directly addressed one of my staunchest campaign allies
was the counsel of history softly whispering the question on
everyone's mind but no one's lips. When? When would a black
skin sit in that White House? In fact, I still can't help but believe
that it was this unspoken reckoning with the past, more than
anything else, which pulled enough election booth levers to
squeeze out my victory.

To be sure, even then the country still possessed its quota of
race haters. After all, in a country of three hundred million
people where everyone thinks it's their God given right to do
whatever they want, you have to expect a little diversity. But the
pure color haters were too few in number to pose any signifigant
threat to my election hopes. The hatred of the ignorant, whether
it be in skins of black, white, yellow or brown, generally just

tends to cancel itself out. It was the fence sitters that would turn the tide, that block of citizens Asian, Hispanic, and White who didn't mind a Black man getting an equal share of the pie just so long as equality didn't include that black skin telling them what to do.

Then again, it was the twenty-first century, and in the minds of many, wasn't it really time to let one of the blacks be president? Besides, maybe a black face could start fixing all the problems they'd caused. In the end, whatever their reasons, more fence sitters than not cast their ballots in my favor electing me the forty-sixth president of the United States of America. Oh, and of course, the first black president ever, because after all, wasn't that really the important thing.

But the reelection campaign was an entirely different matter, my greatest fear being that my first term had satisfied the country's voters for all the wrong reasons. In the minds of most, hadn't my election to our highest office served to right the past transgressions, fading away the blemish of our racial hypocrisy? But really wasn't once enough? After all this was the President of the United States we were talking about not the Miss America Pageant.

Somehow as election day raced toward us I just couldn't shake the feeling that the very thing which in all likelihood first placed me in office, my own black skin, might now serve to remove me before my work was done. For although the legislative accomplishments of my first term had made great progress, a final push was required to solidify the gains. I desperately needed to return to the remaining short sighted holdouts of Congress with the public's electoral directive firmly stated. Yet how ridiculously ironic it seemed that as I strode confidently toward my crowning glory, one fearful eye looked ever backward awaiting the moment when my color would catch up with me. Thus, I campaigned with a calm vigor, confident in my performance record, yet resigned to the fact that if fate had decreed I was to be defeated solely by my blackness, I was powerless to say otherwise.

3

As we anxiously awaited the election day returns it quickly became clear that my fears of skin color politics had been overstated. Taking forty-six states and sixty-three percent of the vote made it difficult for even my most vehement opponents to deny the sweeping nature of my triumph. The contrast with my narrow margin of victory four years earlier just served to make it all the more glorious. Imagine it, the people's overwhelming mandate to implement my vision for reform. But more than that an undeniable expression of their faith in my guidance.

Oh how gratifying the victory. For even though I'd always strove to conduct myself in a color blind manner, inevitably the cancer of distinction would rise in my conscience leaving my insecurities to wonder was it ever truly I they'd elected or merely the blackness of my skin. But how sweet the vindication of reelection proving emphatically to all the doubters, yes even to me, that I was no longer merely the first black president of these United States of America. I was forever more a president of the people.

Inauguration day, January 20th, 2021, and even despite the relative youth of my fifty-three years, the day had been a long one. The swearing in, my inaugural address, the traditional lunch with Congress, and a lengthy parade. Cap it off with visits to nine different inaugural balls spread all over Washington and the First Lady and I should have been ready to call it a night. But Rachel knew just how much this last inaugural party meant to me and as the helicopter sped us toward Baltimore, the rushing night air served to reenergize us both for what was to come.

To say the least, my surprise addition to the inaugural festivities had not been well received. Staff objections had been burning my ears ever since I first proposed the event, not to mention the displeased murmurings of dignitaries and political contributors, exceedingly miffed that I would cut into their time. The complaining got to the point where I finally had to put my foot down, informing everyone from the members of the Inaugural Committee to my security detail that my proposal was no longer a suggestion but an order. Decorum, tradition, logistics, security, image and approval ratings could all step aside, for this was to be my personal triumph.

As the helicopter set down in Baltimore I was positive my decision to end the celebration on the streets of my youth had been correct. For what better way to lead than by example, and what better case to exemplify the vision of my reform legislation than my own poverty to president tale. As with all presidents, I'd received my share of death threats by everything from tormented psychotics to international terrorists. In fact, I'm told that thanks to the large increase in threats of a racial tone, I'd long since surpassed JFK for the honor of greatest security risk.

Naturally, my security staff wasn't thrilled with the idea of an open invitation outdoor inaugural reception at the site of my childhood home. As far as they were concerned anything out of the ordinary routine was sinful conduct. But the threats had slowed to a trickle over the last few months and, as I pointed out to my security detail, it was highly unlikely that any "nigger haters" would be lurking in the segregated projects of my old Baltimore neighborhood. In the end, to appease my protectors, I agreed to limit my crowd mingling and of course to suit up in the ever present "iron underwear." For although I was never comfortable with the bulky appearance the vest gave me, I suppose it's far better to look portly on one's feet than cut a fine figure in the coffin.

As our motorcade sped through the crowds down Pratt Street I reached across the seat for Rachel's hand and, as her smile lit up the car, I couldn't help but wonder that it hadn't changed at all the past twenty plus years. Where would I have ever been without her? In fact, through all the debate regarding my proposed inaugural plans she was the sole supporting voice. For only she could truly appreciate just how very important I felt it was to return home.

As we crossed South President's Street I glanced to my right glimpsing a flurry of welcoming waves from the Little Italy crowds. What a difference the years had brought. But such loving greetings from the very neighborhood that had spurned me as a child brought a bitter taste to my lips so I quickly redirected my gaze to Pratt Street's other side. For I would allow nothing to spoil this moment.

The motorcade turned left into a protective corridor of police escorts bumping over the curb as we drove into the Flag House Public Housing Project. Funny the contrast between these dirty apartment buildings and the house for which they were named. I'm sure little Mary Pickersgill never imagined as she sewed that her star spangled flag would inspire the anthem of Francis Scott Key. How then could she have ever forecast the urban blight which now encircled her home. In fact, I used to envy so the well tended tranquil beauty of her Flag House Museum, on occasion even imagining it was the way that all of us should live. But despite my youthful musings I always knew it was nothing more than a star spangled dream.

Then looking to the north end of the block I saw that the old shot tower still stood, silently tending its ghetto flock. How many lead balls of shot had its solemn heights produced, sending them forth to drink of British blood. Yet in all fairness, how could its nineteenth century simplicity have ever predicted the pace at which urban bullets would fly. But then as quickly as it began my reminisce had ended and we merged into the crowd.

Even I was amazed as we pulled onto the basketball court, for with the exception of the cleared security area it was as if we'd been swallowed in a sea of blackness, my security detail and a few brave politicians the only whitecaps in its flawless majesty. The crowd's roar buffeted the limo, it's sheer force rocking our suspension and as I stepped through the door their waves of approval washed over me with the warmth and love of innumerable voices.

Weakened by a flood of childhood memories and the overwhelming beauty of their reception I allowed Rachel to escort me to the stage. Still, my prepared speech was quickly abandoned its prose so stiff and inappropriate to render in the face of such affection. Instead I toasted them with my gratitude challenging them all to eat and drink their fill, my attempt to convey the meaning of my return quickly drowned in the mist of my tears.

I was reduced to standing weak-kneed before them basking in the warmth of their love. But as my eyes cleared I suddenly became aware of the human fence of security personnel standing between me and my people, catapulting me back to the deprivations of my youth and taunting, "not for you, now or ever, not for you." It was at that moment that I at last truly understood why I'd come home. For in my own rise and the complexities of my vision I'd come dangerously close to losing sight of why I'd first begun. Then and there as I swept the faces of my people, those unfocused masses, I renewed my vow to guide them, to lead them, and finally make them whole.

I then turned briefly to whisper in Rachel's ear before I started down the stairs. Alarmed by my movements the chief of my security detail raced toward me in confusion.

"Mr. President sir. What are you doing?"

"I'm going down into the crowd to touch the people."

"But sir, you can't do that." He must have read my look because he quickly blurted out, "Excuse me Mr. President. It's just that we weren't prepared for that type of exposure sir."

"Well Agent Meyers my suggestion to you is to prepare as quickly as possible because here I go."

When the crowd realized what I was doing a jubilant roar echoed across the courtyard. But it wasn't enough to merely lap at the edges, I plunged straight into their midst and was immediately swallowed up in the human wave. I don't know how long I floated there, seconds, minutes, hours, buffeted about by the ebb and flow of that human tide. But the press of bodies soon began to ease and I heard the polite but commanding voices of my security personnel ushering people away as they encircled me with the open space they deemed to be so precious. Then, a buffer zone cleared, I stood alone once again, the President of these United States, operating at a distance, from the safety of my inner circle. Yet the important thing was that I'd touched them, felt their hopes and fears, their aspirations and desperation, and that once again I'd felt their love. Yes at last, at long last, I'd finally come home.

As I turned to go I heard a call, ever so faint against the din. Briefly scanning the crowd I heard it again, just barely, over there, somewhere to the right. Then I saw her, just another slender arm waving frantically in a forest of arms. Yet the face, although hollow and scant, had a vague familiarity, the name buried somewhere deep in my past, too hazy to recall. I reached for her hand, allowing our touch to linger despite her cold and clammy grip, and her eyes searched my own, pleading for recognition. But despite my efforts to remember I was forced to deny her, the name simply failing to come.

"I'm sorry dear. Please tell me your name."

"I'm Boncy, Reggie's daughter."

Reggie's daughter. Could it really be after so many years? I carefully studied her again. Surely no more than twenty-two but her face revealed just how hard the years had been. Yet despite her emaciated appearance she had the look of Reggie's eyes, almost as if I were seeing his own. Quickly I motioned one of my staff members foward.

"Look Boncy, I have to go now but give your name and address to this gentleman and I promise I'll get in touch with you. You know your father and I used to be very close."

"Yeah I know."

Then as I moved off through the crowd I noticed the tingling sensation. I'd just started back toward the stage when all of a sudden there it was, like a bee sting on my neck. But I couldn't lift my hand to touch the spot and my legs grew heavy and leaden. Then I was falling, down, down to the pavement so far below. I heard the screams and shouts, bodies closing in around me until I couldn't see anymore, and then there was only darkness.

8

Chapter 2

My vision cleared to the grainy pitch of blacktop, nose pressed flat against its biting edge. But deadened limbs spurned my efforts to rise and I discovered with great horror that my lips were as lifeless as the cold dead pavement which they kissed. Then, as a fit of panic rushed over me I heard the familiar voice of Agent Meyers.

"Clear the President on my go. Murphy. First Lady. Higgins. Keep that pressure constant. Go."

In a flash I was staring skyward, astral twinklings high above the inaugural party's hazy glare. I struggled to raise my head or wriggle a toe without success, for my body was as distant from me as the stars above, and strain as I might my eyes stayed locked in a straight forward stare denied the luxury of even a single swivel. Swiftly and effortlessly I flew through the night and confusion, passing into the depths of the waiting limo like bread into an oven or a coffin to its hearse. Then the doors slammed shut wrapping me in utter and total silence.

"Mr. President can you hear me sir? Talk to me Higgins what have we got? Mr. President it's Special Agent Meyers sir."

"Rear entry wound, upper left cranium, small caliber, probably a .22."

"Louis honey it's Rachel. Can you hear me?"

"Please Mrs. Hayes I know you're upset about your husband but we have to finish looking him over to assess the damage. Mr. President please acknowledge if you can hear me."

"No apparent exit wound, minor skull fragmentation, no visible brain matter, blood flow stable under pressure."

"Mr. President your eyes are open. If you can see me please acknowledge by blinking your eyes as I'm doing now."

"Respiration normal, lungs clear."

"Louis honey can you feel my hand? I'm here Louis."

"Please Mrs. Hayes just another minute. Mr. President sir. If you can acknowledge that you hear or see me in any way please do so at this time."

"Blood pressure steady ninety-eight over sixty, pulse 65. Should I start the oxygen?"

"Get it ready. Mr. President I have not registered your response. If you are able to hear me or see me please acknowledge so at this time." Jesus. Enough already Meyers. I know you boys are thorough but it must be pretty obvious by now that I'm not in condition to acknowledge anything so why don't, you just move out of the damn way and let me see my wife?

"Agent Meyers why do we continue to just sit here when my husband could be dying?"

Rachel. Rachel honey. Where are you?

"I'm sorry Mrs. Hayes but we're clearing the way right now. It'll just be another minute."

"Well how far is it to the hospital then?"

Rachel please come closer. I can't see you.

"Five to seven minutes maximum ma'am. Everything's just about cleared for us then we'll have a straight shot through to the Maryland Shock Trauma Unit. We've radioed ahead and they're already setting up for us."

Rachel where are you? Please come to me.

"How do you know he can't hear us?"

"Ma'am you saw what I just tried."

"Louis. Can you hear me Louis?"

Thank you God. Thank you. At least don't take those eyes away from me. Stay right there honey. Please stay right there. If I could just feel your touch.

"Hang in there Louis. Just stay with me. We're gonna make it honey. I know we will."

You're right Rachel, we'll make it, you and I.

"Higgins start up the oxygen."

"Oh Louis how could this have happened to you? I just can't believe it. Why did they have to pick today of all days? You were so happy. Higgins, are you sure you're holding that compress tight enough? There just seems to be so much blood."

"Yes ma'am it's plenty tight."

"How much longer Meyers? Why won't these fools get out of the way? Damn it. Don't they know he could be dying?"

Come on now honey don't worry. It's gonna be alright. It has to be.

"Things are clearing out now ma'am. Please just try and relax."

"Relax? You want me to relax? It's not your husband lying here. At least tell me you caught the person that did this. At least tell me that."

"Yes ma'am. We already have her in custody. It was the last person he spoke to before leaving, one Boncy Raines. She still had the gun and has already confessed."

"That tiny little thing? But she looked so frail. What on earth could she possibly have had against Louis?"

"I honestly don't know ma'am. There are alot of crazies out there."

As she leaned over me Rachel's eyes began to mist. Yet for all of my supposed accomplishments, there I lay in motionless agony, denied even the communication of a tear.

"I love you Louis. You know that honey. Please know that."

Lord if I could just give her a sign, anything at all to let her know I'm here. No it didn't make sense at all. Why would Boncy want to hurt one of her father's oldest friends? As I puzzled over the intentions of my would-be assassin the street lights began to flash by. Gratefully, I breathed a sigh of relief for at least I was on the way to the hospital with Rachel by my side, and I was still alive.

I guess the last time I saw Reggie was that big scene at my campaign headquarters way back when I was first running for Mayor. It's not that I hadn't tried my best to keep the friendship alive but like all things it's a two way street. I kept trying to call him even after our falling out that day. But despite my efforts to set things straight he just never seemed to show much interest. I guess I finally just gave up.

My buddy Reggie he used to come up with some of the strangest things like the name changes for instance. He used to sit around for hours making up nicknames for Reginald Emanuel Smith. Manny, Naldo, E Man, Reg. E. Smith, Double G. Almost as if he could have a different life just by changing his name. I remember how he showed up at my office a few weeks after I announced my mayoral bid, his cute little four year old daughter in tow. Come to think of it that must have been Boncy because as far as I know out of all those kids he had there was just the one girl.

In he walked, proclaiming once again how he'd finally seen the light and was set to go straight. It was love he said. All the other women had been just so many bitches but now he'd finally found a true soul mate. So he'd gotten married and had his baby girl or had his baby girl and gotten married. I never did quite get the story straight. He was so proud of his daughter proclaiming her to be a sign from God that after five sons with three different mothers he'd finally found his mate. In fact, when I asked about the boys he just shrugged it off muttering something about the sons of bitches. Kind of funny hearing that from the same man who used to boast his sperm was sanctified, guaranteed to spawn only males. But then again Reggie always did have a habit of adapting his principles to the circumstances.

I distinctly remember that it took quite a few "excuse me's" before I realized what Reggie was calling his daughter. Apparently, he and his latest soul mate had taken to referring to their new addition as their "bouncy" baby girl even though neither one of them could really pronounce the word or spell it. By the time I finally understood what he was talking about my response had been reduced to a forlorn sigh. As the minutes passed by I listened patiently to Reggie's speech about how things were gonna be different this time and all this brother needed was a chance. Hell, I'd heard it all so many times before it was all I could do to hold back the yawns. But Reggie and I went back a long way and he knew it just as much as I did so in the end I set him up with a job and promised we'd get together real soon.

I was busy as hell at the time trying to keep abreast of my work at the State's Attorney's Office as well as run a campaign but I still checked in on Reggie every so often to see how he was getting along. We never did have a chance to get together though. He always seemed to have something else to do. But I didn't mind. Lord knows I was busy enough, barely having time to spend with my own wife and kids. I was just happy that everything seemed to be going alright for Reggie. Maybe he really finally had turned over a new leaf.

But it wasn't enough for Reggie to just pass out leaflets and hang posters. He had a greater plan. After a month or so the bad news started to filter back to me. My campaign staff was well aware that Reggie and I were childhood friends so naturally there was some reluctance to tell me about the negative turn of events. But his behavior soon became unbearable not to mention a threat to my election hopes. Apparently, he'd been running around puffing out his chest announcing how I was his "main man" and he was "my boy." Talking to anyone who'd listen about the government positions I'd already promised him and how "set" he'd be once I won. But the last straw came with his bold predictions of my victory and how I couldn't lose because everything had already been "fixed."

Despite the objection of my staff I still wanted to give him another chance so I met with him at campaign headquarters one afternoon and tried to smooth things over. I don't know why he couldn't just listen to me when I tried to explain some of the political implications of his actions. But not Reggie. No one could ever tell him anything, not even me.

I guess things got a little out of hand and I'm the first to admit that it could have been handled better. But listening to all of his excuses and accusations just really rubbed me raw. There just wasn't any talking to him. In the end, I had no choice but to let him go. I simply couldn't allow myself to be treated that way in front of the other members of my staff and hope to maintain their loyalty and respect.

But the most pathetic thing about the whole incident was having to stand there in front of my multiracial campaign staff and listen to the insults Reggie threw at me. "Turncoat high yella", "sell out oreo", "stabbing my own people in the back." I was so shocked by the anger in Reggie's voice and the bitter hatred in his eyes that I could do no more than watch sadly as he stalked out the door. Yes, I guess that's the last time I saw Reggie. The funny thing is I still don't quite know what happened. How did we ever turn out to be so different?

Chapter 3

"Meyers what the hell is this? Two stinking blocks and another traffic jam. You said it would all be clear."

"I know Mrs. Hayes but apparently there's still some left over congestion from the parade. We're doing the best we can."

"Well why don't you get on that fancy radio of yours and do better? I'm not just gonna sit here and watch my husband die in the back seat of this damn limo."

"We're doing everything possible Mrs. Hayes. Believe me. Higgins how's he taking the oxygen?"

"Good. Nice even flow, he's looking steady."

Steady. That's right steady. Please everyone just stay calm. If anybody should be panicking it's me and Lord knows I don't think I can afford to panic right now. Trapped alone inside this vacuum, no outlet for my fear, what's to keep it from growing and growing until it consumes me? No I can't afford to panic. Not now.

"What about the side streets, another route? Can't we go around?"

"No ma'am we've already directed all our efforts toward clearing Lombard Street. It's the widest and most direct route to the hospital. We just have to be patient."

Patient. Patient. I guess I don't have much choice lying here in this lump of a shell. If someone could just know that I'm here. Dammit I'm here.

"Okay. There. It's clearing out. Here we go."

That's right. Let's keep moving, just keep moving. Please don't let me stop.

###

It seems like I've known Reggie forever. I don't even remember how or when we first met. He'd just always been there. I suppose it was because our mothers' apartments were both on the eighth floor of building 107 in the Flag House Public Housing Project, apartments 8-C and D. In fact, one of my first memories is that Reggie was never afraid of standing right next to the wire screen enclosing the open air hallways. As a shy and lonely four year old such feats of bravery were mighty impressive to me and I suppose Reggie's daring set the tone along which our relationship would develop. Because I have to admit that I was kind of intimidated by Reggie's boldness until the day I saw him crying next to the elevator door. Quickly confronting him as he tried to hide the tears I left him little choice but to reveal the source of his misery.

"My mommy don't love me today," he said.

The despair in his voice was of grave concern because at the time his mother was one of the few stable things in my life. She could drink and swear with the best of them and I'd felt her slaps more than once but she was generous with her hugs and kisses, something which meant a lot to a child like me.

"What do you mean Miss Grace don't love you today?"

He paused for a moment waiting for the quiver in his lip to subside.

"She...she letting Lamar hit me whenever he wants and she don't say nothin."

Lamar was Miss Grace's current live in lover and as I knew from the sounds that echoed through my bedroom wall he could be nasty when he got his high. Besides the sting of hand on flesh was not entirely unfamiliar to me as I'd felt the wrath of my mother's own live in "friend" on more than one occasion.

"Well where'd he hit you Rege? Is it bad?"

Briefly he hesitated, scanning me with suspicious eyes, before gently placing my hand upon his wound. The taut little knot at the base of his skull rose to greet me as I tried my best to conceal my suprise.

"Aw that ain't too bad Reggie but I know it hurts."

"Yeah man it hurts alright."

"Hey Rege. How bout we go down and play by the parking lot, just you and me."

"Naw Louis. I'm just gonna hang up here. I don't feel like doing nothin."

Having stood in his shoes before I ignored the refusal instead doing exactly what I'd always wished had been done for me. So when the elevator door opened I put my arm around his shoulders and pulled him along.

"Come on Rege. Don't worry about it. Hey, some days my mommy don't love me either."

Startled, he flashed me a questioning look.

"Serious Louis?"

"Yeah Rege you know it."

Then he locked his own arm across mine and I suppose it was as we descended through the darkened elevator shaft that day that we became brothers.

It just seemed like things were so much better after Reggie and I made our pact that day. I guess until then each of us in our own way had just been so alone. Of course Reggie didn't lack for siblings. He was the fifth and final child. But his four sisters were all more than a few years older leaving him as the odd man out in more ways than one.

I suppose it was around that time that Reggie became a more or less permanent fixture at our dinner table. It wasn't that my mother and I were wallowing in abundance, just that a lot more food actually made it to Reggie's belly when he wasn't competing with his sisters. The problem was Reggie's sisters had all taken after their mother in the girth department while Reggie was molded along somewhat slimmer lines. Not only was he the youngest in his household feeding hierarchy but at an overwhelming size disadvantage to boot. Needless to say, in his own kitchen Reggie generally got about as much to eat as a lamb in a buffalo herd.

As for me, I'd finally found someone I could count on. It's not that I didn't love my mother, just that even back then I had this sad sense that she was engaged in a constant struggle just to keep her head above water and when push came to shove my needs would inevitably get lost in the shuffle. I just accepted it as fact that when two people are drowning it's everyone for themself. It wasn't that she didn't care, just an instinctive feeling I had that no matter what my mother's intentions she would never be able to protect me.

But as far as I can remember neither Reggie or I ever discussed our plight. Besides at that age I doubt if either of us could have put words to what we felt. It was just understood between the two of us that all said and done neither of us had anyone to shield us from life's perils. I suppose that's why in the fall of 1973, when we were delivered into the arms of kindergarten, it was not the hands of our mothers which we held but each other's.

Wrenched from the embracing familiarity of our apartment building, Reggie and I clung tightly to each other in this strange new environment. But it was no time at all before we realized that this school thing wasn't half bad. Our greatest fear, that we'd be separated, was eliminated since we had the good fortune to be assigned to the same class. Thus secure in our comradery we plunged into discovering the wonders of this new world.

We quickly caught onto the many differences between school and the place we called home, the most readily apparent being our size.

Up to this point in our lives we'd lived each day as the smallest thing on the block. Our existence at the bottom of the slapping hierarchy in our respective apartments required that we each tread lightly or suffer the consequences. The playground at the base of our building was a no less dangerous place with angry and frustrated characters of all types just waiting for an excuse to vent their bitterness on confused and frightened little boys. So we'd both learned young to always keep a watchful eye for danger and never hesitate to flee at the first hint of trouble. But in a protected classroom of our peers we were no longer defenseless small fry. Thus, it was in public school we each

18

received our first taste of control. Coupling the strength of our brotherly alliance with the fact that Reggie was by far the most aggressive kid in the class granted us unquestionable supremacy. In kindergarten we were king.

As with any fiefdom our reign had its advantages. If there was a toy we wanted, we had it. If there was a game to be played we made up the rules, and of course were declared victors. When the time came for cookies and milk there was never a dispute as to who was first in line. In fact, absent the shrill shouts of our teacher and her talent for pointing out our mental, moral, and physical deficiencies, the place would have been perfect. But on that fateful occasion when Reggie's errant eraser throw struck her backside we both knew our wonderland had ended.

Slowly we trudged to the principal's office in fearful anticipation of the beating to come. Our anxieties grew as the lecture dragged onward for it was a well known fact that a beating's severity was always proportionally related to the length of verbal scolding. When we were then ordered back to class we made our way in a state of profound confusion and it was only as we neared the classroom door that the significance of the event revealed itself. We shrieked with glee as we realized the teachers couldn't hit us, for it was then we knew that we'd truly found heaven.

Of course, school was not without its bad points. Once thrust into the hallways, outside the safety of our classroom, we again became two frightened little boys. Try as we might to walk unnoticed through the older students' gauntlet, inevitably we were called upon to satisfy their demands, and although on occasion the encounters were friendly, more often than not we were stopped with no good intent. To this day I still don't believe it humanly possible to seclude a nickel's milk money from a school mate's searching eyes.

But most bothersome to me was that after a while I secretly wished my mother would stop walking me to school. Still in her early twenties at the time I suppose she cut quite a figure. But her beauty provided little buffer against the foul remarks of the older boys and although I was as yet unable to comprehend the meaning the stiffness in my mother's stride explained their nature. To my mind those walks were the only time I ever envied the insulating fat of Reggie's mom. For never before or since have I felt so defenseless.

Perhaps the most vivid memory of those first school days was the smell. My elementary school, old school 139, was the first building I'd ever set foot in that didn't carry the stench of vomit and urine. In fact, until I went to school I'd assumed that every place smelled just like my apartment building. But when my youthful mind recognized that the place where I lived smelled badly the effect was profound. Words are simply insufficient to describe my embarrassment and shame and I was never again able to walk into the building I called home without a bitter feeling of disgust.

By second grade we discovered what girls were for. We were both pretty confused that day when Tanya pulled us off to one side of the playground. But the shouts and screams of the other children quickly faded from our minds when her intentions were made clear. The truth be known, Tanya already had somewhat of a reputation around the school. For it was generally known that Tanya and her sisters were poor. That may sound like a strange label coming from a bunch of housing project kids but the way Tanya's family lived crossed that invisible line between poverty and desperation.

Television shows had made Reggie and I quite aware that we lacked many things other people had. Our clothes were generally well worn, food was always short, and the toys were never new. But our mothers still had standards. More days than not we took a bath and brushed our teeth sleeping securely in the knowledge that our mothers would not let the next day pass without finding us something to eat.

Tanya's family was different. Her mother had a wild look about her and often wandered the halls of our building muttering. As for Tanya, she and her sisters wore the same clothes day after day and were forever talking about food. In fact, Reggie and I used to marvel at the times our mothers refused us second helpings only to see them later hand the leftovers to Tanya.

Despite the fact we knew all about Tanya her offer still surprised us. Although we both boldly proclaimed that we'd touched lots of coochies our eyes spoke otherwise and after all her being in the third grade left little doubt as to who among us was the wiser. Thus, the deal was struck for the next day before school, as long of course as we brought our money.

The night passed restlessly in anticipation and my uncharacteristic eagerness to return to school the next morning caused a perplexed frown to crease my mother's brow. As agreed Reggie and I both appeared at the designated spot, nickels clutched tightly in sweaty little palms. Then, when it seemed that the first bell would ring at any second Tanya rounded the corner and led us behind the cafeteria dumpster.

As usual the boldest of us went first and try to look as I might Reggie's shoulder blocked my view. But then as the school bell rang Reggie pulled me forward. Taking my nickel Tanya quickly lifted her dress revealing pantyless hips. Paralyzed in my surprise I stood motionless, captivated by the naked folds of her girlhood. Until finally impatient with my delay Tanya grabbed my hand, briefly brushed it between her legs and in a flash was gone. Before I knew what was happening Reggie was dragging me out from behind the dumpster in a mad rush to beat the closing classroom door.

Our coochie touching escapades progressed rapidly as we quickly discovered that Tanya would let you touch her in a variety of ways. Rubbing, spreading, poking she didn't seem to really care, as long as she got her nickels. I must confess that from that day on I seldom had any milk with my lunch. But in retrospect, given the choice between my nickel going to Tanya or one of the older bullies the decision was an easy one.

It wasn't long before we found out there were other girls willing to play. In fact, Tanya dropped off our list as soon as we met Chiquita because playing with Chiquita made both Reggie and I painfully aware of just how badly Tanya smelled. As we grew wiser the challenge was to convince your playmate to let you touch her for free and it wasn't long thereafter that our interests turned to more than just touching. In hindsight, I guess I continued to play the coochie game until I met Rachel and got married. I suppose the only difference was that the rules changed a bit as well as the way you could touch.

Once we'd been playing with Tanya for a couple of weeks the three of us agreed to meet after school to give us more time. Naturally, we became pretty involved in our game the minutes flying by until I noticed that the shouts of the other children had all but died away. In a panic I pulled at Reggie's shirt and though he was engrossed in a particularly intimate form of touching he soon yielded to my frantic tugs.

"Reggie, come on man we gotta go."

For in our curiosity we'd forgotten that our mothers would be waiting in front of the school to walk us home. Our feet gave us wings as we scurried from our hiding place and fled across the playground. I still remember Tanya's confused expression as she sat pitifully upon the asphalt, dress about her waist, third grade legs naked and splayed. But as we rounded the building's corner our eyes searching frantically, no familiar face appeared. In a panic we assumed the worst, for had not our fingers been caught in a cookie jar of sorts, and the horrific realization closed in upon us. Our mothers had come and gone.

That we'd be beaten was without doubt, all that lay in question was the severity of the blows and as our little brains churned in search of a truthful sounding lie all options seemed to end with the unbearable sting of the belt. Unable to envision our salvation we resigned ourselves to the pain that was to come and fearfully made our way home. As trembling little fists knocked at our doors we flashed each other good luck signs before assuming our most pitiful expressions of remorse.

To my surprise, I was greeted by my mother's boyfriend Link who immediately shoved me toward my room with a scowl. But as I pressed my ear to the bedroom wall I was even more surprised by the silence. For by now I had fully expected to hear

Reggie's cries for mercy. Options nonexistent, I curled up on my bed in anxious confusion and awaited the worst.

It was long after dark when my mother awakened me for supper and apologized for not meeting me at school. Besides, she said since I wasn't far from eight years old it was time I started walking myself. Apparently, there'd been a fight and she'd taken Reggie's mother to the hospital in an effort to repair the damage Lamar had done. For their part the police had escorted Lamar off to a place more suitable for his abusive ways.

I wanted to see Reggie and let him know how sorry I was about his mother but it was already far past my bedtime. So as my mother ordered me to bed I pondered my new found freedom and all the things Reggie and I could now get into between our building and school. Yet as I drifted off to sleep I couldn't help but think how nice it would be if Link would finally hit my mother hard enough to put her in the hospital. Then, the police would come to take him away just like Lamar and my mommy and I could live happily ever after, just the two of us.

Chapter 4

For a while Reggie and I couldn't have been any more entertained. After years of tagging along behind our mothers walking to school by ourselves was a whole new world. The simple fact was that we thought we were so grown up. But by the middle of fourth grade the novelty had worn off. That's when we discovered hookey.

I suppose like most things Reggie found out about it first. But also like most things when Reggie wanted to try something new he came to me. It really wasn't such a bad thing. We'd just cut school and hang around the neighborhood or spend the day in the park. Nothing really special, a little wrestling, throwing rocks, playing cops and dealers or just staring down the sky. But everything you did seemed so much better when no one else was telling you what to do.

By far the funniest thing was that old man's fruit cart down in Little Italy. Sure, there were other street vendors to raid but none nearly as exciting. In fact, we probably wouldn't have bothered him as much if he didn't always get so upset. But we could always count on him to pepper us with a fiery mixture of Italian expletives and racial slurs. So we kept grabbing his fruit and he kept trying to chase us, the funny thing being that the more he chased, the better it tasted.

Near the end of fourth grade Reggie and I were skipping school and doing the usual when we decided to make a run over to Little Italy. Sure enough, when we turned onto Exeter Street, there was the old guy and his cart. We split up with Reggie coming from the right and me from the left converging on the cart in a dash. That poor old man never even saw us coming. Fruit in hand we happily raced toward safety, that is until we hit the wall. Our surprise was such that we offered zero resistance. But I seriously doubt if two ten year old boys could have freed themselves from the grip of those strong white hands. Only then did we raise our eyes to look upon the smiling face of Officer Randall.

"That's it. That's it. Arrest the thieves," the old man screamed, "they've been stealing my fruit for years."

As the fruit vendor approached, with fists clenched, Officer Randall calmly pulled us to his side.

"Now now Mr. Degallo how many times have these boys actually stolen your fruit? Once? Twice?"

"No more. Hundreds of times. I told you two little monkeys I'd get you. Now you'll pay."

"Just a second Mr. Degallo let's not get into name calling now. Why don't you let me talk to the boys alone for a minute."

"All right Officer but I want them punished. Do you hear me? Punished."

Officer Randall marched us up the block a ways before dropping to one knee in front of us.

"Now I'm going to ask you both one time and one time only and if I were you I wouldn't lie. Is this the only time you've stolen fruit from Mr. Degallo?"

I don't know why I said what I did. Reggie and I had already exchanged glances. But as Reggie uttered our agreed upon "yes" for some reason I told the truth. Reggie's eyes flashed me a quick look of betrayal but he had no time to speak before Officer Randall's pointed finger was sternly jabbing his chest.

"Now son, I know you're lying to me, because I saw the two of you down here stealing last month. I've half a mind to take you down to the station right now. But I'm gonna let you go with your friend here, because he told the truth. Now the both of you know that stealing's wrong so I'm giving you another chance. But if I catch you again you're not going to be happy with the results. Now get on along."

As Officer Randall turned to go I pulled out the two shiny red apples I still held. He looked at my offering and nodded with a smile.

"No son, that's alright. You two keep the apples and I'll pay for them. Just learn a lesson from this and don't let me catch you again."

Puzzled by the strangeness of his behavior I stared after him. But then Reggie was tugging at my shirt and off we ran.

In deference to Officer Randall we stayed clear of Little Italy for a while and I must admit that our brush with the law increased our school attendance for the rest of the year. But by the time summer rolled around the incident was all but forgotten. For like all ten year olds on vacation we had more important things to ponder.

The start of fifth grade saw us pick right up where we'd left off, spending more time out of school than in, and since neither of our mothers ever bothered with report cards, we thought our system was full proof.

As it turned out we were so skilled at hookey that both of us were left back to repeat the fifth grade. Needless to say, such a major accomplishment did not go unnoticed on the home front. My mother's rage struck out with hand, belt, brush and spoon, anything that came to reach. Eyes downcast, I bore it all silently, for I knew the fault was mine. But when her lover raised his hand my eyes gave challenge.

My mother had suffered me from birth and I suppose it was her right but he was no substitute for the father who'd left and his keeping of my mother's bed was to me of no consequence. For in my mind he was nothing and of this my eyes spoke. If anything my scorn fueled his wrath. Once, twice, a third time his angry slaps lashed out striking again and again until at last he'd had his fill. But each time I picked myself up growing stronger in my resolve that at the very least he'd never see my tears again.

As it turned out being left back wasn't so bad, regardless of the beatings. For it was in my second year of fifth grade that I met Dana. Naturally, Reggie wasn't to thrilled with my sudden shift in loyalty, but there was no reaching me. To me she was irresistible. The problem was that Dana lived in the opposite direction from school as we did, all the way in the Perkins

Homes Project. Everyone knew that people from Flag didn't go to Perkins and vice versa. But I paid no attention to such things, for in school I could see Dana every day and in no time I'd actually grown accustomed to going to class. My interest in classwork was still way below zero but it seemed that I could sit through anything as long as she was there.

In a way Dana had a double impact on Reggie and I. Even though Reggie had done his best to turn my head from her, pointing out that she was from Perkins, too tall, dark skinned, and above all a book worm, in the end he gave in to my affections with a tolerant annoyance. Left without his running mate, Reggie ended up hanging around the school nearly as much as I did.

A natural result of our increased attendance was that we became more involved in school social life. For Reggie and I that meant finally testing out our status as two of the school's bigger students. Since we'd put in our time being victimized by the older students it was now our turn to snatch the money, call the names, and slap the heads of those less fortunate.

Of course, our more aggressive attitude caused the occasional conflict when our victim's older relatives became involved but there was nothing the two of us and our extended network of friends couldn't handle. The fact was that a lot of the families in our building had been there for years. Being the only thing they knew, it was an extended family of sorts and while you might take advantage of or beat on someone in your own building, if an outsider crossed the line he better look out. For when push came to blood the fellas in our building were very loyal. I suppose in a way that's what broke up Dana and I.

Our puppy love romance had been blossoming all through the fall of that year when we finally started to explore each other's bodies more intimately. In fact, Dana was my very first kiss. For despite all the coochie games I'd played with girls like Tanya, for some reason I'd always viewed kissing as the most private of intimacies and though neither of us really knew what we were doing, clearly it was something special.

But like most young boys I was prone to exaggeration and thus when others inquired about our romantic exploits my rendition was far more risque than the truth. Evidently Dana's big brother Purnell didn't take to kindly to the circulating rumors and thus cornered alone in the school yard one day, I received a fierce beating. It mattered not that my own lying tongue had been the catalyst, for my pride had been challenged and with Reggie in tow we returned Purnell's favor a few days later. Purnell's original intent to protect his sister's honor was somehow lost in the shuffle and the stage was quickly set for an all out face off between the Flag House and Perkins faithful. But on that fateful day as our respective gangs stared each other down in prelude to combat Dana seized the spotlight.

"Me and Louis ain't nothing to be fighting over," she coldly announced. "I never wanted him anyway. Why would I want a dumb ghetto nigger that can't even read?"

As Dana stalked away, all expectantly awaited my retaliation but I was far to stunned to reply. In fact, I was not alone in my dismay, for to many in that gathering Dana had breached an unspoken rule of neighborhood etiquitte which protected the illiterate among us. For the truth be known, there were many. But that did little to ease the burn of my shame. It was I alone that stood in the open so branded.

I believe Dana moved away shortly thereafter because I never did see her again. But wherever she is I pray that she's happy and safe because I never did get a chance to thank her. It was the embarrassment I suffered that day which finally taught me to read, for although Reggie and I went back to skipping school, at my urging, it was with far less frequency. While Reggie's mind continued to wander aimlessly in restless boredom, for my part I tried something new, I listened. I suppose that Dana should also be credited with my promotion to the sixth grade, for I'd started going to school again to be near her and I continued going to spite her. The harsh words of the gauntlet she laid down had awakened something deep inside of me. For lack of a better word, I suppose you'd call it pride.

Even though I was starting to enjoy learning, old habits are hard to break, and while our skipping was much less frequent it had become by far more productive. By then we'd learned the joys of shoplifting and just how easy it was to snatch and run. For although it wasn't hard to spot us, catching us was an entirely different story.

Thus, by the fall of sixth grade we considered ourselves to be practiced thieves, displaying the grandness of our booty to friends and neighbors alike. For in the limited perspective of our twelve year old minds we were accumulating vast riches. In our youthful ignorance we never realized how unjust was the pittance we received for our labors, as unlike our older and wiser bretheren, we knew neither the value of our loot nor the risks we took. For their part, our mothers never questioned our flimsy lies of things found and gifts given by friends unnamed.

I believe it was October of that year when exalting in our good fortune we decided on another visit to the old man's fruit cart in Little Italy. We'd long since outgrown such pitiful prey but as we swept down upon him we reveled in nostalgic amusement. Our bounty snatched we dashed quickly away when suddenly Reggie disappeared from my shoulder. In a panic I whirled only to break into laughter at the ridiculous sight of my friend. A half block behind Reggie struggled toward me mimicking the old man's feeble pursuit. As if the sight of Reggie's pantomime wasn't silly enough the old man followed directly at his heels swinging a broom handle with each step. On they came, partners in their perverse dance, until they were almost upon me and as the old man's enraged eyes and blood flushed face came into focus the thought flashed that perhaps it really wasn't so funny.

Shouting, "I'm gone," I whirled to run but my shirt collar jerked me backward racing feet sprinting out from under me. I hit the pavement hard its surface jarring my bones and before I could focus was flipped face down hot breath ordering me to lie still. I raised my head as the sound of scuffling feet scraped my eardrums only to have my face shoved back down into the coarse black street. As things quieted I was not asked to stand but lifted and my confused eyes settled on the familiar sight of Officer Randall's meaty hand wrapped in Reggie's collar. Then my own captor's grip set equally tight dragged me toward Officer Randall's piercing gaze.

"Sorry to see you two boys didn't get the message the first time. I probably shouldn't have paid for the apples. Well come along, there are a few folks you need to meet."

As they pushed Reggie's head into the back seat of the patrol car I was surprised by the fear in his eyes. For I'd grown accustomed to hearing his bold pronouncements about "how the Man wasn't nothin to him" and how he'd "handle anything the po...lice could dish." Naturally, his loss of confidence concerned me. Thus, as the wheels of the patrol car picked up speed, so did those of my mind whirring ever faster through the countless rumors and stories about the dark places which awaited us. But to our surprise there were no dark rooms, no beatings, no torture. In fact, the police treated us exactly like what we were, two scared little twelve year old boys. Then, after the paperwork was completed and a brief phone call made, embarassingly, we were released to our mothers.

As our respective mothers ranted and slapped away we both listened for a change. For in two months time we would face the one they called the judge. Thus, we marked the time timidly careful to be on our best behavior in hopes that whoever was responsible for such things would somehow make note of our attonement. Then, on the day of judgement we did our best to stand stoically, all efforts focused on concealing our fears and when the old man in black uttered his strange words we quickly mumbled our agreement wanting nothing more than that it should all be over. As if we were an afterthought, we were rudely pushed from the courtroom, shuffling from the building in the wake of our mothers.

Only then, standing under the clear blue skies of day, did we realize that we were free. Sure, there had been some mention of a thing called community service but it was only a fleeting thought, quickly dismissed by all involved. For our punishment was behind us as soon as the courthouse door swung shut. Yet that was the last of my thieving. There were still to be many times ahead where I was needful or jealous of the things that everyone but me always seemed to have. But I guess I just figured I'd gotten off easy and was unwilling to further test my luck. As it turned out both of us learned a lesson that day, because where I never stole again, Reggie just got better at it.

Our larceny convictions served as a sort of approval stamp with the criminal element in our neighborhood as if we'd somehow been initiated into a special society. I suppose the way Reggie talked about the incident didn't hurt our reputations any either. In the short time it took us to walk home from the courthouse, Reggie had already begun expounding his distorted view of the facts. On and on he rambled to anyone that cared to listen about how the white cops had roughed him up and lied in court, how the white judge was such a "bitch" and what he'd do to "them" if he ever caught them in our neighborhood. Of course, Reggie preferred to exclude the fact that our crime had been the most heinous act of stealing four apples.

But I suppose he was merely parroting a popular litany in our neighborhood and since no one ever seemed to have much to do around our way, there were always plenty of people to listen. But the truth is after a while I just got sick of hearing it. So one day after his monologue had ended I pulled Reggie aside to remind him how Officer Randall had warned us the first time and even bought the fruit. But none of that seemed to matter to Reggie. He just looked at me with a hard stare before calling me a "know nothing nigger" like what Officer Randall did had never even happened. After that we never talked about it again. I suppose it was just one of those things better off left unsaid.

The good news was that thanks to Reggie's creative story telling our new found criminal status got us each running jobs for one of the neighborhood dealers. Weed, smack, lovely, the rock, he had it all and in my neighborhood it was the best paying job a fella could get. Besides, it wasn't as if it required a whole lot of effort. Just make yourself available, take what he told you where he told you, and keep your mouth shut.

Looking back on it all, my youthful sense of morality drew a clear distinction between thievery and running. As a runner, I was providing a service someone was willing to pay for and to be honest about the situation, it wasn't like we were shoving the stuff down anyone's throat. In my mind, anyone dumb enough to use the stuff deserved whatever hardship came their way. I just figured if they were bound and determined to throw their money away, some of it might as well fall into my pocket, where at least it could go to good use. All said and done I guess my basic thoughts on the matter still haven't changed.

As with everything else we did the brotherly competition which existed between Reggie and I extended to our new employment. Although the truth be known, Reggie was operating at a decided advantage. For while the money was tempting I was still determined to completely eliminate the blight of Dana's insult. Thus, while Reggie began devoting his full attention to running I continued to make it to school on a regular basis.

Naturally, Reggie pulled in a lot more cash, constantly reminding me that I was wasting my time by going to school. The funny thing was that the closer I got to graduation the more Reggie seemed to flaunt the money he made. But while I was of course jealous of his earnings at the time, redemption of my pride just seemed a hell of a lot more important. When I proudly walked across that graduation stage passing into seventh grade it left no doubt that the public taint of my illiteracy had been forever wiped away. As for Reggie he was a no show at the graduation program, as usual having something better to do. But he'd soon get another chance because of course the Board of Education invited him back to repeat the sixth grade.

Once summer arrived I was set to run again full time. But I quickly found out how much my employer had disapproved of my inconsistencies. In fact, only Reggie's pleading pulled me back into the fold. But once all thoughts of school were out of the way Reggie and I were again the best of friends.

One night toward the end of our thirteenth summer we were summoned to the fifth floor apartment of our employer Terry B. At the wise old age of nineteen Terry B had taken to viewing himself as a mentor to us of sorts. But we were well aware that he was easily angered and prone to exacting immediate revenge if crossed. Thus, as we hurried down the alley toward his building, we anxiously reviewed our recent runs and upon determining that everything checked clean, silently rode the unlit elevator to Terry's floor.

Met at the door by one of his stone faced lieutenants he patted us down before waving us through to Terry's darkened den. It was a grim faced and drunken Terry which lay splayed upon the couch before us, his scowl increasingly bitter with each swallow of cognac. Finally, after one particularly long pull on his bottle he peered up at us and spoke.

"Reggie. Louis. You boys been good to Terry B. Been doing a whole lotta runs, ain't been no fuck ups. Some a these dumb ass niggers can't do nothing right. So Terry B got something for you."

He pointed toward one of his men and gestured for us to follow. Warily we followed the broad back down a dimly lit hallway and timidly eased past the guard into a side room. His towering presence swallowed up the door frame as he unrolled one massive hand in our direction. To our surprise two fat marijuana cigarettes cut cleanly across his wide flat palm.

"Enjoy," he said.

As he shut the door we stared at each other in amazement. Yet we had no time to ponder before we were startled by the sound of her voice.

"Well are you boys gonna get over here and do your business or just stand there grinning."

When we turned to see one of Terry B's prime women stretched out nude across the bed we fully realized the magnitude of his gift. It was only then that she truly saw us grin.

I suppose my passage to manhood that summer inevitably led me to what happened next. For if anything my relationship with my mother's live in man had sunk to new depths of hatred. While I no longer personally suffered his fits of rage I all too often heard his slaps upon my mother's skin. For the life of me I couldn't understand her tolerance. Reggie's mother might have been fat and homely yet she'd already rid herself of four such men. But each time I confronted my mother with her passiveness the answers were the same.

"Link has no place to go" or "deep down inside he's a good man." "There's nothing the police can do," and occasionally the worst of all, "but he loves me." Always the same to the point I just stopped asking. For in the end I knew the real reason was none other than that she was afraid.

Then late one summer night as Reggie and I dropped by for a snack angry voices touched my ears. Unable to ignore the familiar sound I edged closer to their bedroom door.

"Come on Louis," Reggie said trying to pull me away. "Forget about it."

But my feet held fast awaiting the sound I knew would come. Silently there I stood, Reggie by my side. Raised voices then became shouts, harsh words profane and then the crack of palm on skin rang out, the thud of fist on flesh. Into the room I burst, the pent up hatred of years spewing forth.

My fists rained upward, vain attempts to maim my towering foe. At first the shock stayed Link's hand, briefly confused by the gall of his assailant. But then confusion turned to fury and fury turned to blows. Once, twice, faster and again, out lashed his fists in a blur. Yet dissatisfied with the meager results of the blows his claw like hands locked upon me, raising me, lifting me like some pathetic toy soldier and hurling me against the unforgiving surface of the concrete wall.

The impact showered me with flashes of bright and sparkling pain. But thankfully as I lay near the wall's base my agony quickly gave way to a soothing circle of darkness. The last thing

I saw as my eyelids slid slowly downward was my mother and Reggie, standing guard in front of me, continuing the fight.

In hindsight, I suppose the broken arm I received was a small price to pay for regaining my mother. She put the police on Link that very night and never spoke a word of him again. With Link gone from the scene my mother had more time for me and we actually started to act like a family of sorts. In fact, it was my mother who suggested I join the Teen Challenge Program when I got to seventh grade.

Chapter 5

"Higgins grab the code card from his pocket. Here's the drill. The President's military aide will meet us at the emergency room entrance with the "football". You'll carry the President's authorization card and the two of you will be choppered down to Vice President Johnson as soon as we reach the hospital."

"Hold it right there Meyers. What did you say?"

"Please Mrs. Hayes just move back and let Agent Higgins do his job. We're dealing with national security here."

"I know what you said. You want to take the nuclear codes away from him. Well he's not done with them yet."

"Hold up a second Higgins."

"You're damn well right you better hold up a second. That's my husband you're talking about there, the President of the United States. We don't know for sure he can't hear us, see us, feel us. We don't have the slightest idea what he's thinking. But I do know I'll not have you do one thing that might diminish his strength or will to fight."

"You're right ma'am. There's no way we can know for sure what's going on in there but one thing we do know is that right now, for whatever reason, the President's not responding to us out here. Please understand Mrs. Hayes we're just not in a position to take chances here. I have no choice."

"Choice. Like Louis has a choice. Like he's ever really had a choice."

"Look we're all under a lot of pressure here ma'am but I just want you to remember that your husband's my boss and I'd lay down my life for him in a second. You know what type of man he is and right now you just have to realize I'm doing exactly what he'd want."

"It's just so unfair Meyers. Why does Louis always have to be the one to suffer?"

"I don't know ma'am. I just don't know."

"Well go ahead and take it then. I'm not even sure I should stop you if I could. But it's just all so unfair."

That's right honey. Just let it go. Let them take it and good riddance. I've been carrying that damn little plastic card with me ever since my first day in office not to mention being constantly shadowed by the little black briefcase of Armageddon. Commander in Chief, Leader of the Free World, nuclear holocaust for my decision alone. But what good was any of this so called power? Could it stop my country's deterioration into a pit of spineless selfishness? Could it guarantee passage of legislation demanding accountabilty? Could it keep the bullet from my skull or even in this most desperate of moments grant my lips the strength to tell my wife how much I love her?

But then again maybe all these so seemingly simple things are still beyond our reach even though at our finger tips we hold the destructive force of the sun. Hell, maybe it's for the best. I could use a break. Pass all the damn codes and responsibilities and worries on over to Vice President Johnson for a while. Harlan can handle it. He's a good man. I can't believe this was ever my job in the first place. What ever made people think I was fit to safeguard the destiny of mankind?

The truth be known, by the time I reached seventh grade I'd pretty much satisfied the extent of my ambitions. Graduation had proven my point making me one of the more educated people in my building and I was already my family's chief interpreter of the public assistance notices which came our way. Seeing that the schools I was now to attend had long since deteriorated into undisciplined holding pens I figured the only thing I had to look forward to was an overview course in social ailments. It was the Teen Challenge Program that opened my eyes.

In fact, there really wasn't much of a program unless that's what you'd call one old guy with a limp. But Chester "Chet"

Robinson was all we had. Back in his day Chet had been a ball player of one kind or another, a star we were told. Football or basketball or both it didn't really matter, all we needed to know was that at some point in his life he'd been something special. He was forever talking about the future, how important it was to think ahead, as if doing so could actually make a difference, and it was easy to trust Chet because when he told you he'd do something it always got done. But the main thing about him was that while everyone else was always telling you what you ought to be Chet was showing you how to get there.

There wasn't much to joining Chet's program. If you were of a certain age you just showed up at his office and hung around. He seemed to have some running arrangement with the school that allotted him full time use of one of the smaller classrooms and though it never seemed very organized you always left feeling like you knew more than when you came in. I first started visiting Chet in the fall of seventh grade. My normal street activities still being restricted by the cast on my arm I suppose I had Link to thank for starting me off as a regular. For in those first days I viewed the whole set up with a great deal of scepticism. But after a few weeks my suspicions melted and in time I started to treat that cramped little classroom as a sort of second home.

Naturally, Reggie became curious as to where I was spending so much time, so despite the fact that Reggie was still in elementary school, I asked Chet if I could bring him on by. But the fact is Reggie wasn't very impressed. He showed up for a while but after a month or so it seemed like he always had something better to do. In the end, I guess it was the very thing I liked most about Chet's program that turned Reggie away.

In my eyes it seemed like Chet knew everyone in town. Not only was he known around the limited haunts of our neighborhood but downtown as well. He was always inviting people to drop by and talk with "his kids" as he called us and drop by they did. Politicians, government officials, businessmen, all kinds of people, even cops. Chet seemed to have an inexhaustible supply of people for us to meet. A lot of our visitors even went so far as to invite us to come see them at work. That was the part I liked best of all, the fact that such important people would actually take the time to see me. Somehow visiting them in their nice clean offices with everyone all dressed up and speaking to me so politely just made me feel different, like I was really someone special. But Reggie hated it, claiming they were just "slumming, preaching and looking down their noses at the ignorant ghetto niggers."

"You couldn't trust them," he said, "because the minute you believed a word they said they'd just turn around and stab you in the back. Besides, what did we need them for when we could learn everything we needed right here from our own peoples."

I tried to tell him that some of these people had grown up in the exact same kind of neighborhoods we had but he just never seemed interested. He figured he already knew enough to get by and damn sure didn't need any "stuck up whiteys" or "turncoat oreos" telling him what to do. In fact, I never could convince him to go along with me on any of the visits. But it occurred to me after one particularly heated discussion with Reggie pointing out how I was wasting my time being a "wanna be whitey" that it really made no difference who was doing the talking. Reggie's mind would be forever closed.

I have to admit that at first I was as intimidated by these strangers as Reggie. Of course, the fact that some of them were white did little to ease my apprehension. For up to that point my contact with whites had been minimal to say the least. But Chet had been straight with me on everything else so I figured the least I could do was give it a try. Besides, one fact stood out very clearly no matter what the skin color of the people who came to see us. They always showed up wearing nice clothes and driving a car. To my mind you just couldn't get any better advertisement that some of these folks must have something good to say.

At the start, I figured I was only meeting the lucky people in life, the rare and privileged few. Surely none of this could ever happen to me. Then one day after school Chet took me along on one of what he always called his "fishing trips" where he'd hit the streets in search of donations for his program. That particular afternoon we drove down to Annapolis to see a man named Martin Greenway who Chet called the Comptroller. If before I'd thought that Chet was an old man I now had to change my mind for as we walked into that gloomy inner office I came face to face with ancient. Introductions completed, we'd barely settled into our seats when our old as life host creaked to his feet and shuffled from the room.

Chet explained to me that this old white man was responsible for managing the finances of the entire state of Maryland. Of course, Chet had always introduced me to people with what I considered to be large sums of money, more than I could count, but at the time I never dreamed that one man could be in control of so much. Yet the most striking thing was how all of those people could entrust the control of something so precious to someone so utterly frail. Suddenly, it hit me that even though his body was weak and decrepit what mattered most was the power of his mind. Needless to say, not having placed much emphasis on matters of intellect to that point in life, the impact of my revelation was profound. As the old man slithered back into the room and handed us a check we rose to go. But before I could turn he pointed a single gnarled finger in my direction.

"Work hard Louis and everything else will fall in place."

I wouldn't see the Comptroller again for a long time and I really don't know what it was about him, all that money he controlled, his power, or just the fact that he was so very old, but for some reason his words kind of stuck.

Chet continued his parade of personalities and as the months flew by I ventured forth more frequently into the world beyond our projects. Gradually I realized that there were a whole hell of a lot more of them out there than there were of us. Then, as I lay awake one night, it came to me that, just like the Comptroller had said, there wasn't one damn reason why I couldn't become just like one of them. The very next afternoon I went by Chet's to find out how.

By the time I entered, high school it was apparent that I was no athlete. I wasn't exceptionally tall, strong or fast and after a few failed attempts I resigned myself to spectator status. Nor had I found my calling in music with both my instrumental skills and voice being decidedly deficient. In fact, the only thing that could be said about my physical attributes was that I was exceptionally mediocre. Not that the physical world was the all and end all of everything but if there was one thing Chet stressed it was to find something to be good at. The problem was there just weren't a whole lot of opportunities around my neighborhood to be good at something.

Rejected by athletics and the arts and having already turned away from the illicit economy of the streets I entered my sixteenth year as one very confused young man. Perhaps what hurt the most was that Reggie bested me in whatever we did. Sports, music, games, and even the girls, he always came out on top. Coupling this with the fact that Reggie was still pulling in all kinds of money from his drug runs tended to make life seem pretty unfair. I just couldn't understand how if I was supposedly walking the right path and Reggie the wrong why he was having all the fun. But as usual a few words from Chet helped to set me straight.

"Hey," he said, "if Reggie's pulling cash with the fellas, no problem. Let that be Reggie's thing. If Reggie's got the sweet J, don't sweat it. Let that be Reggie's thing. If Reggie's down with the fine young ladies. So what, let that be Reggie's thing. But don't you ever forget one thing. You ain't Reggie. You just worry about what your thing's gonna be. It doesn't matter what it is only that you find your thing. And once you find it you work at it, and work at it, and make it better."

Chet always was pretty cagey that way. He was never really worried about what you learned or how or when, only that you did. In fact, it was Chet who helped me fill out the job application for the corner McDonald's. Competition for the legal jobs around my neighborhood was always pretty stiff. The 7 Eleven was never replaced once it burned down and the jobs available to blacks in the restaurants of Little Italy were few and far between. Not to mention that the last thing any of the small Korean merchants wanted was a young black male on staff. But Chet knew the manager at the McDonald's and convinced him to give me a try. Once my foot was in the door I worked with a passion and when Reggie and his crew took to laughing at me for making chump change it just made me work all the harder. For although I was sure I hadn't yet found "my thing", at least I knew I'd found some thing.

I suppose it was my job at the McDonald's which started to change things between Ma and I. Up to that point in my life she'd paid for everything. Sure I'd made a little money stealing and running drugs but for the most part our apartment, food, medicine, clothes and everything else I had came out of public assistance checks with Ma's name on them. It didn't matter to me that my mother had never worked. I just always thought of it as her money.

Then I started working after school, maybe bringing home a hundred bucks a week or so. Ma kept telling me how proud she was of her "working man" and after a while she even started asking for money. Not that I cared. It wasn't much at first, maybe twenty or thirty dollars toward the rent or groceries. Besides, she'd lived in the middle of all that crime and filth and violence for so long I was just happy to be giving something back, trying to make things a little easier. But after a few months it seemed like the more hours I put in mopping floors and flipping burgers the more money she wanted. Then different things started showing up around the apartment like new clothes and make up and Ma's drinking got worse. Despite all the bad times we'd had I still loved my mother dearly and wanted her to be happy. Still, one bothersome fact kept grating on me. I went off to school bright and early each day returning home from work late. In contrast, my mother rarely left the apartment except for shopping or party sessions with her friends. My irritation brewed until one day when Ma asked for money I mentioned what was on my mind and told her about some adult education and job training programs she might want to check into.

I don't know what I was thinking, maybe that things had changed with the passage of time. But whatever I thought did nothing to prepare me for her reaction. Hostile eyes bore into me as clutching fingers gripped my arms. Violently she shook me with the screams of her rage.

"Who the hell are you? Thinking you so high and mighty now cause you flippin cheap ass hamburgers, parading around in your polyster blue suit like it means you somebody. Well you better take a good look at yourself boy and remember exactly who you is. You think you just gonna forget how good I been to you and all I done for you? You gonna be so low to deny me, your momma, who raised you, a few dollars? Who is you to think you so special, just taking and taking, never giving in return, thinking that leaving your own peoples behind just so easy as walking out the door."

Ma always did have a way of getting her point across and as her shouts increased I came to see the light. When her yelling stopped I mumbled an apology and found the door, quickly on my way before the mist in my eyes could turn to tears. My cash contributions to my mother were never discussed again. It was just understood that from time to time I would place a portion of my earnings in the cabinet drawer by the fridge. Yet, despite the mutuality of our understanding, I have to admit that my view of her was never again the same.

By the time I reached twelfth grade Reggie had already become a family man. He'd long since dropped out of school to make his way in alternative pursuits and I have to admit that at the time he seemed to have it all pretty well figured out. The combination of his girlfriend's public assistance checks and his "business" earnings would give them more than enough to live in style. I still remember hanging out together the night his second son was born. It was almost like old times, just the two of us. We were just hanging around and having a great time until Reggie made his offer.

"So I'm saying to you Louis you got to come back to your own man. This is Reggie talking at you, your brother. You know I always done right by you. Now look, I been talkin to Terry B and you know we been doing fine, pulling some serious cash, and Terry be knowing I'm his number one. So he been saying it's time I got myself some back up. Now look ain't dime one a this coming out a my thing. Terry's gonna cover it all. So what you say bro. You and me just like it used to be."

"Aw come on Reggie. Hey, you know you and me we'll always be brothers. Can't nothin break that up. And I appreciate what you're trying to do for me. But Rege you know I cut out a that a long time ago. That just ain't me no more."

"What you thinkin Louis. You think you just gonna smile nice and polite and jump through all the white man's hoops and he's gonna let you in his world. You too stupid to see he's just using your dumb black ass. Here you gonna go and get yourself educated, say a lotta yessum massers and work some slave job while the whole time you just keep on smiling your pretty masser boy smile. But it ain't gonna get you nothing bro, not one damn thing."

"Hey fine Rege, just leave it alone then. It ain't none of your problem."

"No. I ain't gonna just leave it. You always running around here talking all this high stuff about the future, repeatin that old man Chet like he's some kind a prophet or somethin. Well if he's so bad why don't he have nothin, not a goddamn thing. Listening to someone with nothin all the time you know exactly what you gonna get."

"Hey lay off a Chet, Rege. He ain't done nothing to you."

"Whoa boy, don't go bodying up on me. You know I'll fuck you up. Why you actin like I was talkin on your mamma or something. You so into the future. I'll tell you the future. You gonna work and work and still never have enough to live in the white man's world. Because even if you did ever make enough he still wouldn't let you in. Then one night when you're coming home to your shit little house in your all nigger neighborhood one of these crazy ignorant niggers out here is gonna blow your head off. And you just gonna lay in that dark ass street and bleed because ain't no one gonna care. There ain't but one future bro and you know it as well as I. It's these rocks and this gun."

"Well don't worry about it then Reggie. I'll just have to take care of myself."

"Shit Louis, you ain't gonna take care of nothin. I know you. You keep thinking that you gonna be just like the Man, that you gonna work his work, live in his house, and drive his cars. But you gotta remember what you are bro. You was born a ghetto nigger, you always been a ghetto nigger, and you gonna stay a ghetto nigger til the day you die. The Man ain't gonna let you in his world and you damn sure ain't never gonna make it out of ours. But you just gotta remember Louis, in our world you got to kill or be killed."

"Hey what do want me to say Rege. I'll just have to deal with it when it comes."

"I want you to say it's gonna be you and me again. Man I'm just trying to look out for you because the day's gonna come Louis. Ain't no dodging it. Your day's gonna come. Man fuck all this anyway we supposed to be celebratin. Let's fire some of this rock. I got it special just for us."

"Naw, but you go ahead Reggie. I'll just stay on this beer. Besides, I got school tomorrow."

"Oh, so now you too good even for this huh. Can't even celebrate my child with me. Dammit Louis, it's like you didn't hear one fuckin thing I said. Now hit the pipe man."

"I heard you Rege. I just don't want none. I know you don't understand but it's the whole damn thing. It's just ain't me anymore."

"Well if you ain't gonna hit just get the fuck out then. Give me a call when your head comes back down here with the rest of us."

I closed the door behind me as the first match flared, because there really wasn't much point to hanging around. When Reggie got in one of his moods there was just no talking. Despite what he thought I did listen to him, just as I tried to listen to my mother and everyone else around. But I had to wonder despite all his talk just who was really in charge. Was it Reggie or the guns and drugs or did he really even know? Lucky for me I suppose Chet's words generally carried the most weight. It was at Chet's suggestion that I applied for and received a college scholarship because as he pointed out, "if someone else was paying I'd be a fool not to try." While that seemed to make a lot of sense I must admit that the mere thought of college petrified me. For although Chet's words were usually of great impact, even they could not wash away my ingrained sense of inferiority. Thus, as I turned my thoughts toward college I focused on one and only one word. Failure.

Chapter 6

The word scholarship is probably a bit misleading. For while I'd successfully completed high school I could hardly be called a scholar. In actuality what I received was a tuition waiver through a state run assistance program. I was just one of the many so called economically disadvantaged students invited to Morgan State University each year. Neither the motivation behind this generosity or who would bear the cost really mattered to us. The only important thing was that the bill got paid. Yet even all logistical matters aside, I still couldn't help but recognize that the nature of my scholarship was by far more assistance than reward.

Nevertheless, that first morning of college I rolled out of bed and took the city bus from my mother's place in the projects to the hallowed halls of Afro-American academia, three transfers to be exact. In effect, I began a life which from then on would consist of two very different worlds. But of course, I was not alone. There were quite a few of us project scholars in attendance, in fact, far more than I'd expected, almost as if they had to take us. But in those first few months it mattered not at all to me the reasons behind our presence for the security blanket provided by my fellow ghetto classmates was truly the only thing that kept me going.

The fact was that although I'd tried to convince myself back in high school that I could make it I immediately encountered the gap between confidence and actually getting it done. The short bus ride from the projects to Morgan had taken me to a completely different level. It seemed that everyone was light years ahead of me. The professors, the administrators, even the paying students, all seemed to take for granted knowing about things I'd never even thought of. Back and forth I travelled each day between the contrast. They planned, worked, learned and

47

succeeded while each night I lay down among people who lived every day for a hand out, forever excusing their failure. Yet even though I knew I didn't want to remain as one of us I just couldn't imagine that I'd ever become one of them. Thus, in those early months I arrived home after work each night exhausted only to lie in bed awake and contemplate the things I'd never know.

When I started college in the fall of 87', there was a general consensus going around that the sciences were the way to go. Computers, biology, engineering, it didn't make a difference what just so long as you got yourself a "skill." Everywhere I went the preoccupation was with preparing for the future, anticipating what was to come. Yet I was still stumbling about campus painfully aware of my overwhelming ignorance. What good would it do me to look toward the future when I was so pitifully confused by the now? I suppose in the end I settled on history because it seemed like the only thing that wasn't in a constant state of change. I just figured that if I had to start learning the way of things the last thing I wanted was a moving target. Besides, unlike the threatening unknowns of the future it offered the eternally consistent facts of the past and at the time it was a comforting stability which I so desperately needed.

I took it all. Afro-American, U.S., World, European, African, Asian, Latin American, Medieval, Colonial, Urban, Islamic, Native American, Russian, even the History of Afro-American Women in the Feminist and Sexual Revolutions of the Twentieth Century. The funny thing was that the more I learned about the past the more I started applying it to the present. I found out pretty quickly that mostly everything happening in my fast paced crazy world had already occurred in one way or another in the past. And the more I learned about other times and places the easier it became for me to understand the here and now. But I suppose the most important thing was that contemplating the lives of all those thousands of other people, day after day after day tended to put my own life much more in perspective. Then it hit me just how very long it had been since I'd seen Chet.

I'd become so involved with college that I'd completely forgotten about the man that put me there. Sitting in the fall of my sophomore year I hadn't seen Chet for over nine months and I had yet to give him word one of thanks. Nine months might not seem like a lot in the normal scheme of things but this was a man I'd seen weekly if not daily for the past seven years. Amazed at how quickly the time had passed I resolved to visit Chet on my very next day off work.

Walking into Chet's old classroom seemed so very strange, like I'd just returned from a long, long journey yet absolutely nothing had changed. There he was sitting behind that beat up old desk with kids of all ages scattered about the room in a variety of positions. But the real surprise was that I'd come on a visiting day and as I looked toward the front of the room I saw none other than the Comptroller.

I slipped into a chair as the Comptroller continued to speak about finances, politics and responsibility. Then, when he'd finished I started to rise preparing to give my greetings. But Chet offered the Comptroller his chair and crossed the room to stand by my side. Arm about my shoulders Chet proceeded to tell the kids how proud he was of me and just how well I was doing with Morgan State and my job. On and on he went, like I was some kind of sports star or something, outlining my record in such detail that I knew he'd been checking up on me. Then, when he finished he pointed in turn at each and every face around the room, telling them all they should follow my fine example. It was really embarrassing.

As the others filed out I went to greet the Comptroller and compliment him on his talk. But he would hear nothing of it pointing out that I was the one that deserved the praise.

"Chet's been telling me all about your accomplishments Louis. It sounds like you're doing a fine job. When's graduation?"

"Oh I'm just a sophomore sir. Graduation's too far away for me to even think about right now."

"Not so far as you think maybe. Things have a way of moving pretty fast you know."

"Yes sir I guess they do."

"Well it looks like you remembered what I told you last time we met. Look Louis I don't need to tell you that life can get pretty confusing at times. It happens to all of us. But if I can ever be of assistance to you please give me a call. Well I have to run, now Chet and I are late for a meeting. Good luck son."

I tried to tell Chet how grateful I was but there was only time for a quick hug and my promise of future visits. Then they were gone.

The funny thing was the Comptroller hadn't seemed nearly so old to me this time, as if he'd somehow changed. When we first met in his office some five years ago my fifteen year old eyes thought he was the oldest thing in the world. I couldn't imagine that he wasn't already lying in his grave much less walking and talking. But today he'd seemed different. Still older than old to be sure but as if he somehow had more life. Maybe it was the fact that we weren't sitting in his dark and dusky office. Maybe it was the energy with which he'd addressed his young audience. I just couldn't seem to place it. For certain he wasn't getting any younger. I guess the trick of the matter was nothing more than that I'd just gotten a little older.

I took my time leaving, reaching the street only as the last children's shouts faded in the distance. Then I took a seat on the curb and watched the silence. How many years had Chet run his program? How many kids had he taught? Time after time he reached out touching child after child, his resources no more than the strength of his wisdom and love. But when had it ever become his job to bear the crosses let fall by others? In fact how many years of his life had Chet given to me? Was it seven and counting, then multiply that by the thousands.

Yet he was only one man, just one. All those children, so many lost children, surely they weren't me anymore. I'd come too far. Yet in a way wouldn't I forever be one of them, for could I ever truly just walk away? Besides, wouldn't it be foolish to think that it would ever just stop? For wasn't that just the way of things, on and on with never an end. Thus, as I rose to go I resolved to drop by more often, no matter what my work load. After all it was the least I could do. Then I let out a sigh and started a slow walk toward home.

In those days, despite the long hours at work and school, I was never in a rush to get home. For in my absence my mother had taken up with a new man and the more I was out of the apartment the more he was in. It wasn't that I expected my mother to live her life solely for me. It was just that I generally got the feeling she liked things best when I wasn't around. Despite my complaints his presence kept expanding until it became clear that eventually there'd be no room left for me. Of course, I knew my mother was lonely but after all we'd been through I could only view her actions as yet another betrayal. If she wanted a love or just a lover it was fine by me but I just couldn't forgive her for choosing another of the exact same type that had plagued our past.

For a change her friend was nowhere to be found when I arrived home that night. Instead we were graced with a much smaller visitor. Apparently Reggie had started yet another family, but as my mother explained his new mate had been jailed on possession charges before they ever actually got around to setting up house. Naturally, Reggie wanted to do right by his latest offspring so he'd brought the baby by for his mother to look after. Unfortunately, Reggie's mother being out, he'd left the baby with mine because as always he had "business" to do.

Even though Reggie and I had grown somewhat apart in recent years I still thought of him as my brother, so I eagerly took the infant from my mother's arms to have a look. But as I held the child my mind revolted against the idea that this baby was any form of kin to me. It's weak little body was a strange and sickly grayish brown. It's face and arms were intermittently speckled with reddened splotches and crusted scabs while a puss filled sore festered just below it's left ear. Worst of all, the child was extremely dirty, filthy, as if it hadn't been washed for days. I just couldn't believe what I was seeing. I quickly returned the child to my mother and crossed to the sink to draw some bathwater.

"What are you doing Louis?"

"I'm gonna give the kid a bath. How long's it been here anyway?"

"Oh don't go worrying about that, just leave it until Miss Grace gets home. That no good Reggie, expecting his mama to take care of his chilluns like she ain't got nothing better to do."

"But Ma you can see the kid. It's filthy. We can't just leave it like that until Miss Grace comes back. That's the trouble around here in the first place, everybody's always waiting for someone else to take care of things."

"Now hold on a minute boy. Don't go forgettin who washed your dirty little behind all those years and kept your belly fed."

"I wasn't talking about you Ma. I can't believe Reggie just left the kid here like it was a sack of dirty laundry or something. That's why none of the kids out here are even getting a chance. People bring them into the world and then treat em like just so many dirty drawers. I'm sick of it."

"Well I don't see you out here being anybody's daddy. If you so sick of it why don't you do something about it?"

"But look at this kid Ma. You never just up and dumped me like that."

"Don't make such a damn big thing out of it boy. The child ain't so bad off. Plenty a babies been a whole lot worse. You got to realize that sometimes life has a way a gettin you down, things start to slide a bit and you can't always do for your children like you want. But you'll learn someday, once you get your own."

"Not that bad? How can you say the kid's not that bad?"

"Well I can remember a time or two when folks seemed to think I wasn't doing right by you but you done come out just fine. It's hard to make a way in this world Louis. No one out there gonna give a body nothing."

"No Ma that's not it. That isn't it at all. It takes more than that. People at least have to put up the effort. No one's ever going to get anything just sitting around waiting for it."

"Well don't you have the demons today, sitting so high and mighty. But don't you go talking to me about effort."

"I wasn't talking about you Ma. I'm talking about people in general."

"I worked plenty in this world. You forgettin who carried you and bore you, who made you a man."

"Just forget it Ma, forget about it."

"No I ain't just gonna forget it. You sitting here in my house talking this way after I've paid every cent I've had for you. Sitting there talking like you to good for me or somethin. Well you just shut your mouth."

"Ma just..."

"I said shut your mouth. You just don't know all the troubles I had raising you Louis, making sure I done right by you. You just don't know the times. Things ain't always so plain and simple in this world. Just cause you the college boy now you thinking you somethin big and special. But don't you ever go forgettin who you is. You still just a ghetto nigger like the rest of us and you can't ever go turning your back on your own kind."

"Look Ma you just gotta..."

"I said shut your mouth."

"Ma all I'm saying is..."

"I said shut your mouth."

"Ma you just don't understand that..."

And then she slapped me. Holding that pathetic little creature in the cradle of her left arm she slapped me. I don't know what happened but I lost it, screaming at her.

"No Ma, you haven't paid a cent for me because you never worked for nothing."

Her hand lashed out again but I caught it.

"And what have you taught me Ma, how to take a handout and survive in the ghetto. No wonder we never made it out of here. You're always high on talking about respect. But all you ever did was spread your legs and make a baby. Well that's just not good enough. You want respect from me Ma, you want respect from your child, well you gotta earn it. You want me to listen to you then do something worth listening to, set an example worth following for a change. What have you done in life Ma? I'll tell you what. Nothing. You never even cared enough to try and pay the bill. No Ma, you never taught me a damn thing."

I slammed the door on my way out but I'll never forget the horrified look on her face as if the knife was stuck deep inside of her still twisting.

After that it was kind of like we weren't parent and child anymore. We went our separate ways and rarely spoke. I moved out during Christmas break finding both a dorm room and a job on campus. The strange thing was that as I carried the last of my belongings from my home of some twenty years my dominant feeling was of relief. But I still stopped by occasionally to place a little money in the cabinet drawer by the fridge and as far as I know my mother never did try to get a job, even to the day she died.

The transition to living on campus was a lot easier than I'd expected. My roomates were nice, I liked my job, and freedom from the daily bus routes between home, work, and school meant I now actually had some free time to spend. Still, I kept my promise to Chet, visiting every week or so to tutor and talk with his kids. I was just trying to set a good example and give a little something back. But on the nights I made my way from Chet's back to the campus, I couldn't help but feel grateful that I was now just visiting.

I guess all those years I'd lived in the projects I never realized how much they wore on me. The poverty, the crime, the rudeness, the violence, even the trash. It all just kept coming and coming like a never ending flood, and there wasn't a damn thing you could do about it. But once I escaped I could finally let down my barriers and walk free. The truth is once I left I never wanted to go back. Now Morgan wasn't heaven by a long shot.

But it's amazing what clean buildings, some manners and a little grass could do for the spirits. The weeks just flew by and for the first time in my life I was really happy.

The funny thing was that the more I learned the more I realized how little other people knew. Thus, where I'd first stepped on campus in a kind of awestruck wonder, I now strode the pathways with a somewhat belligerent cynicism. My chief frustration was that most people were only concerned with their own little societal niche and never the workings of the whole. Not that I had everything all figured out. It was just that I seemed to be surrounded by people who chose to live in an academic and racial fishbowl as if all they had to do was step in and pull the dark curtain closed.

But my years with Chet had already taught me different. It was a big old world out there with all kinds of people and none of us could operate in a vacuum. I just couldn't understand how most of the people at Morgan could content themselves with the tiny microcosm that was our school almost as if they believed that by simply denying the truth enough reality would eventually change.

University budget discussions were a prime example. A majority of the faculty and staff spent a great deal of time complaining about our state funding. There was a constant buzz about how the legislature was playing political games and trying to stifle the strength and growth of the University. Honestly sometimes it seemed as if the majority of the campus believed that no one ever actually had to pay for anything. Like it was always someone else's responsibility to provide us with the means and the supply of money was inexhaustible.

Naturally, some of the fiscal commentary focused on racial issues and our supposed mistreatment by the predominantly white legislature. One of the most amazing things to me being the complete agreement from our limited number of white staff members as if everyone were well aware of the grand conspiracy to keep the black man down. The white politicians were doing this and the white business community was doing that all with an eye to making sure we never got too much.

For the most part I found it hard to believe all these white people were spending so much time thinking about me. In fact, the whites I'd met through Chet generally seemed just the opposite, like they spent as little time as possible thinking about blacks. In the end, I guess that most of us sat around all the time worrying about what the white folks were doing when all the white folks were really doing was flat out ignoring us.

Perhaps what impressed me the most was the way that everyone always talked about how much they knew but did nothing about it. They all kept telling me this is the way the white man works and this is the way the white man thinks. Yet no one ever stepped out of our little black world to go and get what the white man had. How in the hell did they ever expect to teach me if they were afraid to go themselves? Then it finally occurred to me that Chet was the only black person I'd ever known who moved as easily in the white man's world as his own. But then he went and died.

One of his older students called to let me know a couple of days before my April fourth birthday, the day I was to turn twenty-three. It was one hell of a birthday present and on the date of my birth, which also marked the death of Martin Luther King, I couldn't help but think that surely he'd died for more than this.

Chet was just leaving work when it happened, eight bullets in all, one for each dollar they took from him. Just the wrong place at the wrong time I suppose, a couple of confused, frustrated adolescents. The exact same kind he'd spent his life trying to save. I attended the funeral as one of the pall bearers but the saddest thing was that out of the hundreds, even thousands of kids he'd helped over the years only about forty people showed. A tribute like that kind of made me wonder if he hadn't been wasting his time all along.

It didn't hit me until a few days after the funeral just exactly how much Chet had meant to me. But by then of course it was way too late. Without a doubt he'd been the strongest thing in my life those ten years we'd been together, something steady when all else was muddled, and deep down inside I knew that even though he was already gone it would be a long time before I'd fully understand just how much he'd done for me. It was my senior spring and as exam period rushed down upon me I tried my best to concentrate on my studies, to complete the degree that I knew would have made him so proud. But something inside me lay empty and I felt it all starting to slip away. So late one night, despite the pain, I forced myself to come to grips with my grief. I finally allowed myself to admit that Chester "Chet" Robinson had been the only father I ever had, and now he was gone.

Things got better after that and though I was still in a great deal of pain at least I could concentrate again. Yet as I turned my eyes toward my future there was no Chet to consult and I came to realize just how much I'd relied on him through the years without ever even knowing it. In my confusion I sought the counsel of many but all came up short. I even paid a visit to Reggie in hopes that he could somehow help me to find the way. But still floating in his world of drugs and guns, women and fun, he turned out to be nothing more than another dead end.

On and on he rambled about "being on his own again and how he'd had it with all these crying ass kids and bitches. Never should a tied myself down in the first place," he said. "But I done seen the error of my ways. From now on it's strictly business and the party. No more of that daddy shit for me. Besides, too many fine bitches after my stuff to stay with just one ho. I'm telling you Louis now I'm the man. Got the money, got the bitches, I got it all. Ain't nothing stopping Reg E. G. When you gonna get wise bro and get back with me? You had to have learned by now that you on the slow road to nothing."

He didn't even care that Chet had died or what the loss had meant to me, flipping off some comment about how, "that old man shouldn't a been sticking his nose in everybody's business no way. Just like I done said Louis, that old man went a bleeding and a dying in some dark old alley and no one gave a damn."

I was still too numb to react so I just gave it up. Reggie would have never understood anyway, even if he tried.

I guess it happened right after I left Reggie's that night. I'd gone no more than a few blocks when two of them slipped from the shadows. They were thin and wiry, neither of them more than fifteen, their only claim to adulthood the glint of gold capped teeth.

"Yo bro, give up the cash."

As they circled me up I wondered if this was how it had happened to Chet, anonymous faces in the darkness. Perhaps his killers were the same, lost children out to prove their manhood, pronouncing their disrespect for any and everything, even themselves. It probably never even occurred to them that the true source of their power was not the guns they clutched but their own pathetic societal insignifigance. For they contributed nothing, owned nothing, controlled nothing, and were nothing in society's eyes. Thus, unlike more responsible citizens who could somehow be held accountable, these and their kind were ever free in their complete and utter anonymity to pull the trigger and scurry back into the sewers they called home.

"Yo I ain't fuckin wit you man. Give it up o you gon be dead."

Had Reggie been right all along, was this my day, my time? Was it now my turn to quench the gutter's thirst for blood?

"Man don't be playing this shit wit me. I start pullin this trigger you be one dead nigger. What you doing down here anyway. You should a done stayed up where you belong."

What had Chet died for anyway, merely to feed the ignorance of a manchild such as this, all of it meaningless and for nothing. No. Chet had lived for more than that. His life must have meant more than that.

"Last chance bitch you better give it up o I gonna take it."

"You know something?"

"Don't wanna know nothing cept bout yo cash. Now shut up bitch."

"Fuck you."

"What you say?"

"You heard me. I said fuck you. You want to be the big man, little boy with the gun. Well pull it."

"Nigger, I ain't playing wit you. You a dead mother fucker. Now you dead."

"Pull it then. Go ahead."

"Come on Flip this nigger's stupid crazy. He ain't got no money no way."

"Naw fuck that. Ain't nobody gonna talk to me like that. He dead."

"Well I'm gone then Flip ain't none a my thing."

As his friend raced down the alley I stared into Flip's raging eyes. Gun muzzle locked to my chest I watched the frenzy of his mind spinning through the frustration, anger, and rage to gunshots, blood, and death. But then what? Satisfaction, relief, pride, or regret, fear, an outcast. Then, like a flash the uncertainty surfaced, bubbling up through the rage and he ran. Breathlessly, I watched him go, my heartbeat a thunder, just barely able to stay the trembling until he disappeared from sight.

Once I'd collected myself and made it to the bus stop I couldn't help but wonder if there was any point to it all. Chet lay dead while I lived but there wasn't one damn reason why it couldn't have been reversed. There alone in the darkness I struggled to make some sense of it all only to have the confusion close in around me and strangely enough at that very moment the Comptroller popped into my head. Having nowhere else to turn I decided to pay him a visit the very next day.

I'd not set foot in his office for nine long years, yet inside the gloomy interior of his inner sanctum it seemed as if nothing had changed, as if he'd always sat there and always would.

"Louis I'm terribly sorry to hear about Chet, I know the two of you were very close. In fact, he always spoke of you like a son. But I guess the reality of things is that those of us left behind have to carry on even though at times it might seem terribly unfair. Now what can I do for you?"

"Well to be honest about it, you told me to give you a call if things ever got confusing so here I am."

"What seems to be the trouble then?"

I don't know quite what it was about the Comptroller but it just seemed like at one time or another he'd seen everything. Like for years and years or even forever he'd seen it all come and go so many times until for his eyes nothing was new. Yet he had this way about him, the way he talked, so it was never as if he were judging you or preaching. It was merely the recognition of the fact that he knew and you didn't and as someone that knew it was his responsibility, even duty, to pass it on. That's just the way it was.

What did I have to hide from a man like that. So I told him. I told him everything. I told him about my mother and Chet and the father I never knew, about living in the projects, my frustrations with Morgan, and my confusion about why white people always seemed to have everything I didn't. I even told him about just how hard I'd worked to get to a place that looked a lot like nowhere. He just sat there patiently and listened absorbing every word I said and when I'd finally finished he turned to me with a smile.

"Louis," he said, "I think you're just a little confused on one aspect. You don't just want to learn about the white man's world. That's really a fiction. The fact is that no society ever exists without someone in control. What you really want to learn about is the control and the place for that is with the people that make the rules. Every society has its sheep and its shepherds Louis, you just have to decide which one you want to be. Law school son, that's the place for you. Why don't you just let me make a few calls."

We bid our goodbyes and I started for the door but before I could open it he stopped me.

"Don't be such a stranger in the future Louis, oh and please call me Martin."

I was interviewed, processed, and admitted to the University of Maryland School of Law within the month.

Chapter 7

"I've lost it."

"What?"

"Hell Meyers. I've lost the pulse."

"No. Not now. Louis baby come on don't let it go."

"Oxygen mask. Higgins pull off the mask. I'll do chest compressions you take the ventilations."

"Louis honey come on now you've come to far. You can't just let it slip away.

"Ready. One and two and three and four and five, breathe. One and two and three and four and five, breathe."

"Stay with us baby. Come on stay with us."

"One and two and three and four and five, breathe. One and two and three and..."

"How much farther to the hospital Meyers? How much farther? Louis, you've got to fight it baby, come on now you've always been a fighter."

"One and two and three and four and five, breathe. One and two and three and four and five, breathe."

"How much farther to the hospital? Dammit Meyers answer me."

"One and two and three and four and..."

"Come on Louis, just one breath, just take that first one honey."

"One and two and three and four and five, breathe. One and two and..."

"Dammit Louis, what are you doing? You at least have to try."

"One and two and three and four and five, breathe."

"Please honey, please stay with me. You can't just leave."

"One and two and three and four and five, breathe. One and two and three and...hold it Higgins. There it is. He's back."

Sweet Jesus what was that?

"Oh thank God. I knew you could do it honey. I knew you could do it."

"45...50 he's getting stronger."

What? What the hell did I do?

"Pulse 60, respiration good, blood pressure 90 over 60 and stabilizing. He's back alright but we almost lost him."

Oh. Christ, not that. I can't believe I almost did that. All those life after death television specials and what do I get, a big fat nothing. No lights, no angels, no revelations or long lost friends, only darkness, the void, nothing but black.

"Meyers. Higgins. Thank you both. Thank you with all my heart. You brought him back to me. You brought my Louis back to me."

"It's ok ma'am, it's ok. We're gonna make it. We're all gonna make it just fine."

"What street are we on Meyers? How much farther?"

"We just crossed Light. Eight more blocks to Greene Street and we're there. The Shock Trauma entrance is just west of Greene. Don't you worry ma'am we're gonna make it."

Greene Street. Greene and Lombard, right by my old law school apartment. What ever happened to the years? Everything was so simple back then, so very simple. How in the hell did I ever get into this anyway? Why couldn't I have just gone along with things like everyone else minding my own business and living the good life? But no, I had to go and try and solve the world's problems.

When the hell did I ever start thinking I was some kind of saviour, and look at me now lying here in a pool of my own dribble. Well they can take all their hopes and dreams, their criticisms and expectations and shove 'em deep cause I'm in no position to help anybody anymore. Hell, no strength, no voice, not even the barest semblance of control, I might as well be dead. No wait. Hold it. I didn't mean that. I really didn't mean that at all. Please don't let it happen again. It was so easy to just slip away, didn't even know I was going. Rachel honey where's your hand. Even if I can't feel your touch please just hold me and take me home. Don't let me cross over there all alone. God I'm so alone.

Martin was right because I learned a hell of a lot more in law school than just about white folks. It started with the U.S. Constitution and kept right on going. Like how everyone looked to that little piece of paper as the all and end all of societal guidance, as if it were a more contemporary replacement for the ten commandments of the good book. The sad fact was that as soon as you picked it up you got the feeling that you were joining some kind of exclusive club, forever more to be part of a distinct minority that actually understood the principles upon which the society was based. Perhaps sadder still was the well intentioned benevolence which flowed throughout its pages as if its drafters truly believed that people were inherently responsible. But then again, along with the sanctity the unspoken message of our instructors was abundantly clear. Everything in life was subject to interpretation. The challenge was making sure that things were interpreted to suit your needs.

Before I got to law school I used to always think the trick was knowing there was a way to get around any rule. It was only once there I learned how childish my previous thinking had been. I realized that only fools spent all their time trying to get around the rules. The real trick of the matter was to put yourself in the position to make them. But even beyond that, here were the people at the top, the rulemakers, telling me that nothing was ever sacred. Society was nothing more than a grand perpetual struggle with all of us forever trapped in its flux like just so many rats in a cage. Plus, they all seemed to know the very thing that people I'd grown up with didn't, the sweeter the prize the tougher the competition. Because nothing worth anything is ever given away for free. In fact, my classmates were driven, prepared to slave away for years and years to achieve their goals.

Almost without exception they possessed a quality which at the time to me seemed so very foreign. Call it foresight or perhaps vision, no matter its name it was clearly apparent that they were looking years and sometimes lifetimes ahead when my greatest concern was reaching Christmas break.

Yes, it was definitely a three year seminar in control thinking, the building filled with people used to running the show. I on the other hand represented the distinct minority of us who were accustomed to being told what to do. Yet I sat there each day carefully listening and watching and learning until, ever so gradually, in time I became one of them. Still, my initial outsider status was not without benefit for I'd seen how they jumped at the professor's call, so eager to please and be approved and it was in those moments I realized the weakness of my classmates, so arrogant and opinionated, so self assured. If they could be controlled then anyone could.

But why did they jump? What did they have to fear? They were the people with everything. All they had to do was put in their time and like their fathers and grandfathers before them it would all come their way easily. Yet they well knew the danger, for whatever is gained may also be easily lost and it was in homage to this fact they were willing to scratch and claw and fight to protect their due.

Of course, there were also youthful aspirations of grandeur, of untold wealth and power far beyond their promised legacy. Yet to my classmates these thoughts were of little motivation for nothing drove them more than the attainment of their birthright. Still, as I came to know them I was incessantly bothered by one thing. If the only prevailing influence upon them was the threat of losing what they had, how could society ever hope to control those who had nothing?

Yes Martin was certainly right, but he'd also forgotten one crucial thing. It's impossible to think of control when you're still convinced of your own inferiority. For despite all the laws, court orders, and rhetoric, equality means nothing unless it exists in the mind. Then again, of course it wasn't important to Martin to learn about whites. He'd never been black.

In law school I learned all about white people. All those things that everyone from my Morgan professors down to the street corner yo's always thought they knew but could never really understand. Because they were always just watching white people from a distance never having the nerve to get inside. But it was in law school that I began to lay down with all kinds of white people and really find out what they were about. For three years I lived with them. My classes, my roommates, my social life, my successes and even my failures. We were separated by nothing, until the time came that they were no longer just white people to me. They'd become my friends.

In the end, once I'd really made it inside, I found out they were just like me. All my strengths and weaknesses, my hopes and fears, my past brutalizations. The white man had it all. For underneath that pale lilly exterior he was nothing but me. The only true difference was not between black and white or white and black but from one person's circumstance to the next.

To be sure, my black skin made me a distinct minority in this bastion of caucasia, but racial confrontation was minimal. After all it was 1991, and my classmates were for the most part sensitized to the commonality of the human predicament. Even so, it would have been naive not to realize that a few of them believed that I was as different from them as the color of my skin. But once I truly came to know my pale skinned bretheren I realized that it was those few and not I that were the true minority.

Come to think of it, it was my second semester of law school that I first slept with a white woman. I must confess that at first the very idea of it bore quite a mystique. But once I'd come and gone, frequently returning for more, I knew she was no different from any of a darker skin. She was a woman pure and simple, nothing more nothing less and my future interracial lovers would merely confirm for me what she'd taught. Our relationship was a beautiful thing both of body and mind, dispelling many of the

65

myths behind which we so often hide. In fact, she made it clear to me more than once that I could have been black or blue or yellow or green, it made no difference, to her I was still just a man. Yet thinking back on it all she did bear one striking difference from the sisters I'd known. My classmate was exceptionally talented in the oral pursuits and the truth be known, her talent had absolutely nothing to do with the color of her skin. I'm positive in fact, it was solely because she liked it.

Naturally, our relationship did not go completely without notice. In fact, I suppose that our contrast was a beacon of sorts. Thus, occasionally in the course of our time together we received racial comments of a somewhat negative tone. But all in all incidents of such a character were few. For at least at that level of society we were accepted with a quiet tolerance, our classmates capable of understanding that our similarities far exceeded our differences.

My scholastic efforts, combined in part I suspect with my color, were sufficient to land me a clerkship at one of the city's most prestigious law firms. The opportunity granted, I toiled as if there were no tomorrow, determined to prove my worth. Apparently my efforts drew notice, for just prior to returning to school for my third and final year they offered me a full time position. This meant that upon graduation I would begin to receive the unheard of salary of twelve hundred dollars a week. If ever there was confirmation this was it. I'd landed the best of jobs, none of my more privileged classmates doing better, and I could now rest assured that at the very least I was their equal, for I'd done the unbelievable. I'd made it.

Then, as the fall turned cold I got a call from Reggie late one night. Terry B was dead, shot down in the street, while Reggie waited in a jail cell, unable to make bail. Apparently, their drug operation had been taken over by those of a younger and more desperate breed, willing to stop at nothing for a piece of their due. Reggie's fast money and friends had quickly disappeared raising me once again to the top of his list for after all weren't we like brothers. In fact, he was sure that I could make it right.

I tried my best to help him out, arranging things with the Office of the Public Defender, making sure Reggie understood the legalities of the situation, and visiting him whenever I could. Still, I couldn't help but marvel at how after all those years that Reggie had readily walked the walk and talked the talk, showing no respect for the rights of others, how quick he was to complain about his mistreatment by the System and its failure to protect him from harm. But really there was nothing I could do, so by springtime he'd been convicted, a two year minimum I believe. My brother Reggie would simply have to do his time.

The whole thing kind of shook me but not because Reggie had finally taken a fall. Though I was sorry to see him in jail, I couldn't muster much sympathy for he'd walked on more than a few priors. What struck me was the role of the Baltimore City State's Attorney. From day one of law school I'd been positive my future lay in the private sector, nice clean offices, fancy suits, and above all the blessed security of big fat pay checks. But as I followed Reggie through his preliminary hearings and trial the one person that most drew my eye was the city prosecutor. There I was watching my oldest friend about to be sent away on drug charges yet I couldn't help but agree with the State's Attorney.

In fact, the more I listened to him talk the more I found what he was saying to be true, and what a job he had. The Baltimore City State's Attorney, the prosecutor, protector of the people. For all the laws in the world didn't mean a damn thing if there was no one to enforce them, and he was that someone. Yet standing there in a position of such responsibility he was still so very young. Taking the available information from the police and other citizens, it was his job to determine who'd be prosecuted, to determine what was right and what was wrong. Now that was a position of control.

The more I thought about it the more I questioned my acceptance of the firm's job offer. What would I be to them anyway, some trophy on their shelf, my primary purpose being to proclaim their stance on racial equity. In fact, would I ever be granted a true say so or forever doomed to some permanent underling status. Even if I made it to one of their coveted seats of power, just how very long would it take? In his typical fashion Martin remained behind the scenes until I called on him but the statement of his preference was clear.

"You can sell yourself to the highest bidder Louis but it's not always so easy to buy yourself back. Shepherd or sheep son, shepherd or sheep."

In the end, I listened to Martin instead of the dollar sign and submitted my resume to the Office of the State's Attorney of Baltimore City. Competition for the few available slots was extremely tight but the combination of my record and Martin's reference letter persuaded them to offer me a position for the following fall.

Even though the money was a lot less, I was convinced that I'd made the right move. Yet one fact continued to nag at me as I neared graduation day. Despite all our battles I still had my dream of someday freeing my mother from the hardships of my childhood home. Thus, I couldn't help but wonder if I wasn't somehow being too selfish by rejecting the big money job. For though I agreed with little of what my mother stood for there was no denying that she'd reared me, and in my mind at least I still had a debt to pay.

My government salary, though small in comparison to what I'd turned down, would still be enough to take her away from the projects which for so long had been her home. We'd get an apartment at first and after a few years of saving we'd be able to afford a moderate rowhouse. But somehow that just didn't do justice to my dream. Ever since I'd first laid eyes on The Flag House Museum I'd always pictured a free standing home with green green grass in the yard and a flower lined drive. I'd return home from work each evening and my mother and I would sit at the dinner table in a roach free kitchen talking and laughing over one of her home cooked meals. Because somehow the move would have changed her. She'd become happy and loving and things between us would be so beautiful. At last we'd finally be a family, forever and ever.

But her cerebral hemorrhage crushed my dream. She checked into the emergency room late one night just two weeks prior to graduation and before the sun rose she was gone. I don't know whether it was the drinking, the beatings or the life hurt that finally caught up with her. It didn't really seem to matter. The worst of it was that I was sure she'd died not knowing how much I loved her. As usual I was left alone to fend for myself. Thus, after the funeral I stuffed my feelings inside a dark little box and locked them deep inside. Then, I plunged into my new life and career, so ever alone.

Chapter 8

In those early days I really thought I could change things, would somehow make a difference. After all had I not been confirmed by one of the city's best law firms as well as hired by a powerful branch of city government? Didn't I have every right to be high on myself? For I'd reached a pinnacle of sorts, rising from the deprivations of my childhood to attain more than I'd ever dreamed. But as the days turned into weeks and the weeks passed into months, I came to realize what a bog I'd stepped into. Things weren't nearly so easy as I'd imagined. The entrenched system that was society paid deference to no one and if one thing held true it was that nothing ever changed quickly. But despite the frustrations I was enjoying my work and learning more each day. I should have been very happy.

Yet the loss of first Chet and then my mother had struck me deeply. Each day I awoke with an emptiness that could not be supressed. I surrounded myself with others arising early for work and often continuing into the night. Then, when the work was done I frequented the parties and get togethers, desperately extending them beyond the evening into night. Yet still dissatisfied, I took more than a few bedtime companions in the hope that they could somehow comfort me until the dawn. But inevitably in those rare moments when I was finally alone it all came rushing back to me. I was so very lonely and I feared it was to be my fate.

Then I met Rachel. We crossed only by chance, the most insincere of young black professional introductions. But to me she was a wonder, my rapture instantaneous. Many a time since I've been told that she's a beauty, yet it wasn't the physical which drew me. It was the unmistakable aura of purity which surrounded her. How I cursed our class differences in those early weeks believing that only they lay between us. But as I gradually came to know her I realized it wasn't our backgrounds that separated us at all, it was the contrary nature of our souls.

How many times since has she told me, "Louis you could find fault with an angel."

But who really could blame my cynicism with the rearing I'd had, witnessing again and again the greed, deceit and brutality of man's darker side, pounding my senses until no sliver of hope remained. How could I ever possibly overlook the base character which had been revealed to me? For man is first, last, and always, above all things, a preservationist and I or any man, yes every man without exception, will stop at nothing should he feel his existence threatened. When the lines of survival are truly drawn man knows no boundaries, no morality, no concept of natural law and no brutality or depravity is beyond his use. Instinctively we return to the beast that lies in all of us and to deny this truth of our nature is to unleash its awesome power.

But then there was she, holding near and dear the belief that all are good. Her belief much deeper, much more profound than the typical idealism of her priviledged background, where freedom from struggle so often begets the illusion of man's goodwill. But in truth, her upbringing mattered not for she looked upon the world both good things and bad without naivete'. In the spectrum of humanity she was a rarity, one who would have turned out the same no matter what her circumstance. She was pure and good to the very core of her nature. Her only flaw, if it could be called that, being her assumption that all others were the same.

Over time we grew to respect the contradiction of our natures, for in some strange way the opposites lent us a permanence of balance. It was unimportant that on this one thing we'd always disagree. All that mattered was my faith in the sincerity of her beliefs, for it was only through trusting in her unfailing goodness that I was ever able to pull down the barriers which confined me. It was my unequivocal faith in her that opened me and allowed us to become one. Thus, with her hand clasped tightly in mine, I turned my attention to making the family I'd never had.

As with many things my education at the law had done little to prepare me for the realities of practice. In those early months I of course had my good days and plenty of bad. But as I set about learning the nuts and bolts of prosecuting those that had gone astray my confidence seldom suffered. Even the worst of errors slipped from my back like water, for I rested securely in the arms of one who loved me and the awakening miracle of life which would soon bless us with two children.

Still, while my nights were filled with joy and beauty the days confronted me with the depressing reality of the deteriorating society in which we lived. Gradually, my work began to weigh on me and nowhere was this more apparent than when I prosecuted the youthful offenders of our city. Each morning I left the warm and loving bastion that was home to face a horrid parade of lost children crashing upon the shores of our system like the waves of an endless sea, and as if my job wasn't enough, the media confronted me daily with a bombardment of death and misery. "Youth Charged In Slaying, Sixth Grade Shootout: Two Killed, Fourteen Year Old Gang Raped By Brothers, Most Feared Face A Teen's, Violence Menace To Childhood, Twelve Year Old Convicted Of Contract Killing, Disturbing Viciousness Marks Juvenile Crime, Life's Just Too Short To Care."

Layer upon layer the suffering seemed to go on without end, growing and growing until my only hope was to scream away the tears.

Yet society's commitment remained so meager an effort in response to the flood. My days were filled with the sight of abused and floundering children jumping through the system's endless array of impotent hoops, each new dawn an aching reminder of my own painful youth. The starkest realization of all being that in my own childhood ignorance, I'd had absolutely no idea how pathetic I had been.

Then came the worst, the day Reggie called me in a panic because "They" were about to take away two of his kids. Apparently the mother had been found unfit and a custody hearing was scheduled for that very afternoon. Juggling my schedule as best I could, I made it to the courtroom just as the attorney for the Division of Child Protective Services began to read the record.

Two minors aged six and seven, three neglect complaints, physical abuse charges, four counts of sexual molestation, five evictions, six apartments in eight years, sporadic to nonexistent school attendance, exposure to drug abuse, prostitution, and periodic domestic violence. Background information complete the room grew quiet as the judge began to speak.

"Are there any interested parties present on behalf of these children?"

Reggie quickly scrambled to his feet and approached the front.

"Yes ma'am your honor, I've come to take my children home."

"And who might you be sir?"

"Reginald Emanuel Smith your honor, I'm their father."

"Oh I see. There's no record of any father being involved in this case. Well Mr. Smith what do you have to say for yourself?"

Reggie pulled himself up to his full height and began to speak.

"Your honor I came straight away as soon as I heard. I know things been tough on Lonnie and Tyrell and that mother a their's ain't done right by them, so I come today to set things straight. You see I love my kids, and if there's one thing I believe in, it's looking after my own."

"That all sounds very nice Mr. Smith, but there's no mention in the record of any visitation or child support payments whatsoever on your part as far as these two children are concerned. Frankly, I'm curious as to where you've been the last seven years."

"Well your honor I don't like to talk about it but I had to do a bit of time. But now I've changed. Now I'm not proud of it but..."

"When were you released Mr. Smith?"

"Three years ago, but that ain't got nothing to do with my kids."

"So what you're telling me Mr. Smith, is that Lonnie here is seven years old and Tyrell six, and that for the past seven years you've made no effort to be a part of their lives in any way, but that you love them and you want to make things right."

"Yes your honor that's exactly right. You see I been trying to get myself together so when I came back they'd have something to be proud of."

"Frankly Mr. Smith, as far as I can see it's not a question of your coming back or not, because other than depositing your seed you were never there in the first place."

Reggie glanced at me in confused frustration and I could see his eyes begin to turn bitter.

"Your honor I don't know what you talking all this stuff for. I love my boys and I come to get them and that's all there is to it."

"I'm sorry Mr. Smith but it's just not that simple. These children have been subjected to more harmful circumstances in their short lives than any of us ever has a reason to be. They've been exposed to drug activity, violent behavior patterns and a broad range of sexual and physical abuses living each day without consistent provision for even the barest of necessities. I'm sorry Mr. Smith, but in the opinion of this court if you loved them so much you would have done something about it long before now. The court hereby orders that in light of the absence of any fit guardian, that the children be turned over to the Division of Child Protective Services for placement in foster care. Further..."

In a frantic rage Reggie was tugging my arm.

"What she talking about Louis? They can't take my kids from me like that. They's my blood."

"Mr. Smith, I must ask you to contain yourself."

"No, I ain't gonna contain myself. They's my kids. You got no right to take my kids from me. No right."

"Mr. Smith, if you're not able to contain yourself I'll be forced to have you removed from the courtroom."

"Louis man, help me Louis. What they trying to do to me?"

"Settle down Reggie just settle down. She's already made her decision, we'll just have to try and get it changed."

"But Louis, we's family you can't just let them take my kids like that. We's family Louis those kids is like your own."

"This is your last warning Mr. Smith either contain yourself or I'll have you removed."

"Louis you take em. You can take em for me."

"Reggie wait a second."

"Your honor this here's my brother Louis. He's a government lawyer and everything and he can take my kids for me and give them a real good home."

"Excuse me."

"Louis here. Louis can look after my kids til I get things straight."

"Sir what is your name please?"

"Louis Hayes your honor, I'm with the Office of the State's Attorney."

"Is Mr. Smith correct Counselor Hayes are you offering to act as legal guardian on behalf of these two children?"

The circle of eyes bore down upon me, the judge, the clerk, Reggie, and his children. Staring back at their frightened little faces I was taunted by the fact that of course none of this was their doing. Their only crime was innocence.

Wasn't this the opportunity I'd been waiting for, my chance to step forward and finally make a difference. Pitifully they sat there abandoned and confused not even understanding that we were about to determine their fate. Couldn't I in fact provide them with the home they so badly needed, rear them, nuture them, love them and try to make up for all that they'd lacked.

Wasn't this my chance. Take them my heart screamed. Take them, protect them, love them and make them your own.

But wait. Wait. My mind raced forward. Six and seven years old, how many horrors had they already endured, how many scars did they bear? What painful legacy had they been gifted, what hidden dangers flowed through their veins? Would my home and teachings, my compassion ever be sufficient to make up for the damage already done, could my kindness ever wash away their pain and allow them to forget? Would my love be enough or were they too far gone to ever bring back?

And what of my own two children? What of all the dreams and aspirations I held for them? What if my love wasn't enough, what if I couldn't bring Lonnie and Tyrell back? Wouldn't the years of futile struggle and strain eat my own family alive, sinking us slowly but surely beneath the dark and lonely waters of their past? Was I now prepared to sacrifice my own children for the mistakes that others had made? No. I couldn't, I wouldn't, my answer had to be no. I would not forfeit the lives of my children to pay for other's sins.

"No your honor that's incorrect. Regretfully I will not be able to serve as guardian for the minors in question."

Reggie stared at me with confusion as if I'd just slapped him from the blue.

"I see well in the absence of any fit guardian I hereby bind the subject minors over to the custody of Child Protective Services for placement in an appropriate foster care situation."

"Not fit. Not fit. What you know about fit?"

"Mr. Smith I've warned you enough. My patience has run out."

"I'll tell you who's not fit. You not fit bitch. You ain't fit to judge me, you ain't fit to talk about my children, you ain't fit for nothing."

"Bailiff escort Mr. Smith from the courtroom and save me the trouble of doing the paperwork for a finding of contempt. He's not even worth the effort."

"Hey I'm gone, I'm gone, but that ain't the last of it. You better believe that ain't the last of it."

"In my opinion Mr. Smith it's a damn shame people like you ever have the capacity to make kids in the first place. Fifteen minute recess. Adjourned."

I watched the tear streaked faces of Reggie's kids as the social worker led them away, first steps in a sentence of foster homes, abusive caretakers, and lives as hopeless as any hell, and I couldn't help but think of the countless other children destined for the very same path. I'd had my chance and balked unwilling to subject my own to the very thing I'd worked so hard to protect them from. But shouldn't I have at least tried to stem the tide? Even if it was only two small children that no one else cared about, just two more lost little children named Lonnie and Tyrell. Yet, there I'd stood in all my idealistic impotency my inaction adding to the great mass of lost ones, its numbers growing and growing until inevitably there'd be no place left to hide, until it would swallow us all.

As I struggled home that evening I renewed my commitment to my own cherished offspring and somehow the mere act of walking through that front door faded away the bitterness of the day. Yet I knew it would all return with the dawn, opening my wounds afresh, again and again, building and thickening my scars, ugly marks never to heal. Thus, each day I relived my past through those lost and lonely faces, my bitterness and frustration welling up to near explosion only to be halted by day's end, the soothing tranquility of my family, and the coolness of the night.

Though I viewed my past as a haunting and desperately wished to forget, I must confess it was the savagery of my youth which propelled my rise through the ranks of the State's Attorney's Office. For although many of those from the old neighborhood viewed me as a turncoat, a traitor to my own, it was not unusual for my phone to ring deep in the dead of night. The very same people, whether due to some perverse sense of loyalty or just plain fear, which embraced the criminals by light of day, well knew my name once the sun went down. Inevitably it was to me they would call, imparting the darkest of their secrets before the growing guilt consumed them. Then, their own conscience cleansed they returned to anonymity content that I alone should wear the brand of traitor by the light of day.

The information garnered through this confessional of my past bore great value in my prosecutorial efforts, none of which went unnoticed by my superiors, and as is common in the give and take that is society I of course received my rewards in return. Yet even though I was well aware of the double role I played, a mere cog in the wheels of justice, I persisted with a vengeance, deaf ears toward the endless excuses of the accused. For I knew well of the countless others, despite similar circumstance, who never turned astray.

Thus, in the old neighborhood my efforts made me somewhat of an outcast, greeted by skeptical and malicious stares in the day and unable to venture there at night. For most I was the Judas twisting the knife in the back of my brother. Yet, armed with the information that sought me out and the instincts nurtured in my youth, I became a prosecutor extraordinaire and by my sixth year of employment I'd developed a lengthy record of convictions.

I suppose the culmination of my prosecutorial career occurred in my ninth year with the Flag Crew murders. The drug turf war that had developed in the Flag House Public Housing Project during the fall of 2001 became so vicious that despite an increased police presence the death rate for the four building complex was soaring. The highpoint, if one can call it that, was a rampage reminiscent of The Saint Valentine's Day Massacre which left sixteen people mutilated and in the morgue. As the then senior trial attorney in the homicide section the duty fell to me to right the injustice.

Despite the horrific nature of the crime I knew that to most people the real point of interest was the sheer numbers and brutality of it all. But I viewed the crime in a somewhat more personal context, it having taken place two floors below my childhood home. Still, even with the gruesome nature of the crime and perhaps because of it the police were coming up empty. But then late one night I got a call.

I suppose I should point out that the perpetrators viewed my investigation in at least as personal a regard and three potential witnesses were eliminated in rapid succession, each departing in the most grisly of fashions. But even the threats to myself and my family could not back me away for I viewed it as my opportunity to make some sort of a stand. Just to be on the safe side we were all assigned round the clock police protection and going one step further I began to carry a gun. Still, as the weight of its destructive force gradually became familiar at my side, I couldn't help but ponder how very little protection the average citizen had against the animals which stalked our nights.

The trial as I recall was a logistical nightmare, an exhausting affair with nine defendants and a myriad number of counts. But I'm certain that the greatest fatigue was generated not by the work itself, but by the constant stress that goes with waiting to hear the sound of gunshots and constantly wondering if your loved ones would be safe and alive when you came home.

But despite all the difficulties, convictions came down for all of the accused with for once the jury being sympathetic toward the State. Multiple life sentences were handed down to five of the defendants with the death penalty turned in for the two architects of the assault. Still, as the gavel rang out and court was dismissed I couldn't help but question the meaning behind my so called stand. The safety of my wife and children had been jeopardized and for what? In the end, my long sought after vindication seemed hollow and empty. For I knew that others were already waiting in line to replace those just sent away.

Yet across the city I was being congratulated on venting society's wrath, the lives of two of the defendants, at fifteen and sixteen respectively, over before they'd even begun. Yet in fact, should I or anyone pity them for if they'd stooped to such an act weren't they already far beyond salvation? But then my past called out to me, for what had I been at their age if not just as confused and lost, perhaps to have followed the exact same path without the protection of Chet's strong hand. Thus, in my confusion I desperately searched their adolescent eyes for some meaning but plunged only deeper into my misery with the answer I found. For their eyes revealed a complete and utter lack of remorse forcing me to admit that they were already far beyond what I'd ever been.

At some point they'd crossed over to the other side never to return and I had to accept that for them there was no hope of ever coming back. For what would it take to right the wrongs of their past pains, to bring them back into our arms, a year of love and nurturing or even two or three for every one of pain they'd endured, and how small were the odds that society would ever grant them such a chance at redemption or even want to try. Of course, the answer to their needs could only be no and lacking such an effort they were as hopeless as the sentence they were about to serve.

But as low as their lost eyes took me it was the juvenile hearings of the youngest two defendants which propelled me into utter despair. A couple of eleven year olds, it was impossible to try them as adults, though their crime had been the same. Yet even despite their "tender years" their eyes bore the same callous indifference, a reflection of their misery, one I thought I'd known so well, when the only way to stop the pain is simply not to feel. But how had we lost them in such a few short years? What deprivations and influences could have taken them away from us so soon? And then the harshest thought of all slapped me to awareness, if eleven was already too late, just how early would we have to begin?

But despite my own misgivings, city officials and the press heralded my results as a grand victory, a new beginning. It was then with my name flashing brightly across the full spectrum of the media that Martin called me to his house and suggested I run for mayor.

As a Baltimore city native and the Comptroller of the State of Maryland for some thirty years Martin was a powerful force in city life. Financial, political, or social it seemed to make no difference, Martin always knew exactly what was going on and more often than not could tell you about it before it even happened. The elected officials of our city came and went like just so many seasons but Martin and his statewide network of cronies had been there forever and would always be.

Since I'd taken Martin's advice on both law school and job choice, contact between the two of us had been sparse to say the least. For despite the fact that we were both involved in city life and frequently roamed the same hallways, our encounters were limited to the exchange of a few pleasantries and occasional queries as to the status of my family and career. In fact, to date the longest conversation I'd ever had with Martin was the day I turned to him as a somewhat confused twenty-three year old college senior. But as the years flew by and my career blossomed I never forgot Martin's guidance and the successes it had brought.

It's funny, but as I sat in his house and listened to his proposal, I never for a second doubted that things would go exactly as he said. It was just the feel of the house, the scent of control, the uninterrupted quiet of his study where no sound was ever made unless invited. Of course, I well knew the city grapevine on Martin, what little of it there was. For despite all the people that thought they knew him not many really did. Because in fact the world where Martin did the bulk of his work was a secretive place where the doors were always closed.

No doubt he'd seen thousands pass arrogantly before him, so sure of their direction, only in the end to revolve aimlessly about him once they'd lost their way. Thus, sitting there across from this wrinkled old white man I had no doubt that we were discussing what would be, if only I wanted it. For it was a rare day when Martin didn't have what he desired.

Out rolled his vision in that dry and whispery voice, like a plush red carpet, complete to the minutest detail. For in fact, wasn't the city still anxious over the latest murmurs of political corruption, its trail possibly leading to the Mayor himself? And despite the Mayor's optimism that it would all blow over, Martin was certain there would soon be a vaccum to be filled.

Ordinarily, the natural succession in the city hierarchy would fall to Manson Bates, the President of the City Council, that is of course, if he didn't happen to be white. For Baltimore with its sixty-six percent and growing black population hadn't elected a white mayor in years. The truth being, that Council President Bates never would have won the city wide election in the first place if he hadn't had the support of three term incumbent Mayor C. C. Barnes. C. C. figured, and rightly so, that the surest way to protect his hold on the Mayor's chair was to ensure that the next in line was unacceptable to replace him in the voter's eyes and who better to protect his political back than a council president whose skin color had already hit the glass ceiling.

The truth is, the city's existing white power structure had long since moved underground in a manner of speaking, preferring to control through the pocketbook as opposed to the mayoral gavel and having long since viewed the elective offices of the city not so much as political prizes but no win penal sentences to be avoided at all costs. What was the good of wasting time, the thinking went, listening to the constant cries of racial inequities, when the whole dilemna could be circumvented by merely keeping a black face in the front row.

But Martin had it through the grapevine that Councilman Bates viewed the corruption rumors as his golden opportunity, his one and only chance to take the Mayor's chair. Bates figured that the Mayor would be running for his fourth term without serious challenge, no one willing to waste the resources in a lost cause campaign. But if the Mayor's true colors were finally revealed the electorate would spurn him like so much over ripe cheese and if someone, like a certain interested councilmanic president, timed the release of incriminating information just right it would be too late for another plausible black candidate to surface before the election. As the virtuous whistle blower and the second highest ranking political force in the city Bates might just be able to swing some of the color conscious black vote in his favor. Coupling that with his coalition of liberal biracial voters and the fact that the working class whites would certainly vote for skin, and Bates could waltz into the Mayor's office in 2004.

But Bates hadn't counted on Martin forseeing his plans and preferring to implement one of his own. In Martin's view, there was no one better better to replace a corrupt incumbent than the straight talking prosecutor that had just cleaned up the city's worst ever homicide. If I'd only announce Martin could guarantee that Bates would never enter the fray. For while Bates was a schemer he'd certainly back down from the threat that my untainted black face posed. In fact, Martin guaranteed that a few carefully placed innuendos about the Mayor's dirt would have Bates so worried about protecting his own seat he'd be coming to us trying to cut a deal.

The way Martin laid it out it all sounded so simple, like there was only one possible way it would go. Still, when he'd finished outlining his plan with all its scheming twists and turns my first thoughts were of a less personal nature. What about my boss Douglas Paren, the city's current State's Attorney? Wouldn't I be stabbing him in the back by attempting to leap frog past him? Hadn't it been Douglas in fact that put me where I was by resting his faith in my judgments all those years, rapidly advancing me through the ranks? And was I to now repay that trust by supplanting his own aspirations with my own?

But Martin revealed to me a part of Douglas, that as his underling, I'd never seen. As Martin put it Douglas had lost the fire in his own failed bid for the Mayor's office some twelve years ago and in Martin's words, "didn't have the stomach to go it again. Trust me Louis, or ask Douglas himself if you want, all that talking he does about running for Mayor again is just for show. Talking about it makes him feel like a bigger man than he is, like he still has a chance to do better than he's done.

But he's comfortable where he is Louis and doesn't want anything to do with going higher. Mark my words on this. When the time comes for Douglas to choose between you and C. C.

don't expect Douglas to show you the same kind of loyalty you're putting up for him. Despite all the battles you've won for him he'll sit the fence. Because he's only concerned with one thing and that's holding onto what he's got."

In the end, Martin's plan was so convincing that there appeared to be only one logical choice, only one way for me to go, and that was up.

But as I discussed the matter with Rachel things became somewhat muddled for we were not just deciding for one. What about the future of our own family and children? Was I willing to risk the loss of all I'd worked for, including the rank and security? Furthermore, if I'd found the recent public scrutiny as a high profile State's Attorney to be intrusive what would my family be forced to endure in the office of Mayor? Was I really willing to subject my family to the bitterness and insecurity of public life, the unending criticisms and scrutiny, living under the constant threat of being turned out at the masses next election year whim? And where was the sense in all the sacrifice and struggle when the other road could be so secure?

Yet in my contemplations the lessons and memories flooded back to me. Was I ever to lead or merely be led, destined to remain for all time a faceless nonentity? The first step lay before me a path Martin had so clearly marked, if only I were willing to take the leap. Maybe I could still really make a difference, somehow help the children. At least I would finally be in a position to make the rules after all those years of watching child after child float endlessly by, so close but yet just beyond my reach where I was powerless to do anything but cry.

Didn't someone have to do it? Didn't someone have to speak for all those lost, a cycle never ending, destined to become lost adults and spawning more lost generations on and on to nothingness? Someone had to try and save them from the pain I'd endured. Someone had to help them before it was too late, too late for them, too late for all of us.

Chapter 9

Wait a minute, I can't die yet. What about my children? I've put my whole damn life into everybody else's kids and just when I'm finally going to have the chance to really start doing for my own God decides to take me. Well that's not gonna happen. That can't happen. I can't just up and leave my babies now. They need me.

Whoa Louis. Hold on a minute. Are they really your babies anymore? Mike's been working at the bank now going on three years and Jenna's graduating from law school this May with a job already sewn up. Sure there's still a lot I could teach them but then again I guess there's more than a few things they could teach me by now. Sooner or later they're going to have to go it alone, everyone does. The truth is they've both been doing just fine for quite a few years now without any help from me. Do they really still need me or maybe the fact is that now I need them.

But I was just getting to know them. He can't take me away now. Christ at least get rid of the damn sirens. Shouldn't we have been there by now? How long's it been anyway, five minutes, ten, an eternity? If I have to die like this right here, right now, at least it should be in peace and quiet. I guess I should just be grateful they both grew up so strong and independent, able to take care of themselves in this strange harsh world. I wonder if they even know how proud I am of them, how much I love them. Will they ever know Lord or will they just remember all the times I wasn't there, requiring that they sacrifice for my crusade? God knows I tried my best to give them discipline and values, to nurture and educate, to make them strong. God knows I tried. I just pray it was enough.

###

All things said and done my initial bid for the Mayor's office turned out to be a no contest. But I have to admit the victory was by far more Martin's doing than my own. Just as Martin predicted Councilman Bates shelved any ideas he had of making a run as soon as I announced, his years of political savvy making him well aware that my black face would be his downfall. That left the race between myself and the somewhat tainted image of our twelve year mayor the honorable C.C. Barnes.

In fact, the race was shaping up to be a close one, with the early polls showing Mayor Barnes running well in his traditionally strong poorer districts of the city even despite the rumors of his corrupt dealings. In his strongholds, which he'd fought for so long and hard, slowly winning them over through the years, their faith in him was unyielding. For Mayor Clarence Cecil or C.C. Barnes had come out of a working class east side home, and despite his somewhat questionable activities over the years, if there was one thing he knew how to do, it was work.

Starting as a precinct worker back in the dark days of Baltimore's political bosses it had been his responsibility to mobilize the precincts poorer voters, a job which he'd thrown himself into and carried out with great success. The project dwellers respected him as a black man with money and influence to throw their way instead of the usual rhetoric and even though he hadn't exactly started off as one of them they quickly adopted him as their own. C.C. gradually expanded his voter control to other precincts, and then across the district, until eventually even my old neighborhood came under his wing. Then, consolidating his power base, he rose first to a position on the City Council and eventually to Mayor. But he never forgot the first principle of politics, that the surest votes are the ones most securely bought.

Perhaps his biggest success was expanding his black voter base city wide and cutting across the traditional political division between west side and east side blacks. In fact, C. C. was the first to successfully unify the old church and civil rights west side blacks with the poorer political boss black voters of the east side. It was the strength of this unifcation which carried him to three successive terms in the Mayor's office and what he hoped would be a fourth. No, C. C. definitely didn't lack for work ethic, and he knew exactly how to say what people wanted to hear and exactly how to give them what they wanted. Then, once they'd been bought and paid for he welcomed them as his own. The problem was that the whole time C. C. was giving away the goodies he never thought about minding the store.

It came to the point C. C. thought things were so locked up that he could do whatever he wanted, so naturally he got sloppy. I guess that's when his hand got caught in the city's cookie jar. But in fairness to C. C., aside from his slip up, he was just giving people what they wanted. For his only goal was to keep his seat as Mayor and as long as people kept voting for him he figured things were running just fine. The problem was, C. C. had a way of surrounding himself with people he'd bought and paid for, so I suppose you can't really blame him for being a bit confused. For although he heard the distant complaints of crime and poverty, failing businesses and schools, his entourage continued to assure him that everything was going just fine. So C. C. kept doing the natural thing, just giving people what they wanted, and in all honesty if it hadn't been for his mistake I'm not so sure he wouldn't still be sitting in the Mayor's chair.

For our part, Martin had gone to work immediately after my acceptance, arranging my campaign manager and headquarters within the week. Calling on his connections my campaign staff developed in a blur. My campaign manager being followed with a press secretary, an issues coordinator, a voter analyst, a coordinator of special events, a volunteer coordinator, and my treasurer, all without my ever so much as lifting a finger. My campaign organization established they turned to fund raising and again with Martin's built in infrastructure it seemed almost as if the dollars materialized without effort. But where organization and finance appeared as if by magic, my personal appearance obligations were an entirely different matter.

Even with Martin's ace in the hole he was well aware that I was challenging an entrenched three time incumbent and wanted to take no chances. So despite the fact that I was the city's most recent favorite son I quickly had a campaign agenda which kept me occupied from dawn to midnight. Television and radio spots, civic meetings, business groups, law firms, employee unions, school events, press conferences, church groups, street corner waving, photo opportunities, sporting events, fund raisers, and the worst of all a series of one hundred and sixty-four straight early morning coffees. Anyone who's ever fancied a life in politics should try waking up after three hours of sleep and being energetic and articulate about city waste collection policies. The initial novelty quickly wore off and I realized just how big a grind it was going to be.

Since I'd gained my notoriety as a hard nosed prosecutor my mayoral campaign naturally carried a tough on crime focus and in keeping with Martin's plan I was marketed as a man of the streets who'd made good. For I was the welfare child who beat the odds, defeating an impoverished background to walk at the highest level of city government. Yet despite my success, I could still mingle comfortably with the people of my youth, a man of two worlds if you will. It didn't seem to bother anyone that I seldom visited the projects of my youth and then only for work related matters. In fact, it just seemed a natural assumption that no one who had a choice was really ever expected to return.

But though I fully believed in his capabilities I never realized the extent of Martin's connections until that first campaign breakfast meeting. To be honest, I was expecting a gathering of white businessmen not a room full of black preachers. But Martin well knew that a failure to split up C. C.'s black working and lower class voting block might spell the end of my political aspirations before they ever began. Thus, recognizing the nature of C. C.'s power base, Martin went straight for the black working class vote. He targeted the black clergy as the most crucial aspect of the campaign from the very start in recognition that nobody could turn out the black working class vote like their preachers. For as a general rule if a black pastor gave you his nod the votes of his flock would surely follow.

In fact, gathering their support turned out to be not nearly so hard as I'd imagined. For beside the fact that their political connections with Martin ran long and deep a split had started to emerge in the formerly solid black vote. Resentment toward Mayor Barnes and his constant pandering to what they viewed as the ignorant lower class blacks had since reached a boiling point and those people that viewed themselves as hard working and responsible had finally just gotten fed up. For back when attaining black political power had been the chief issue all recognized the need to vote with color. But now that it was time and again one black face against another the black block that C. C. had solidified was starting to crack. So I covered the black churches campaigning from the pulpits, preachers by my side, begging for votes as I praised the Lord. Then, on the flip side, I met with the bar association and business groups asking for votes as I quoted the law, and so it went back and forth day after day from teacher to drop out, social worker to welfare mother, industrialist to factory worker, riding across the spectrum that was our city.

In fact, I seemed to flip with ease from one class of voter to the next. The whites, whether they be wealthy, middle class or poor soaked up my prosecutorial successes and applauded my tough stance on crime. I was their champion and little mention was made of my ghetto upbringing. It was as if somehow through law school and my profession I had passed over to their side of things and become one of them. For despite my past didn't I speak as one of them, act as one of them and secretly didn't we really agree as to who was truly causing all the city's problems. Yet despite their smiles, the unspoken thought was always there, that no matter what my actions or speech, no matter what my record, my skin would never change.

Then, in the black sections of town, I was likewise heralded as a champion, my rise from the misery of our ghettos through the ranks of white society allowing them all to take some vicarious pride in my achievements. Of course, there was never as much mention of my success in prosecuting my fellow brothers and sisters, the preference being to focus on my rise from poverty success story as a beacon to all those of my kind. Yet despite their smiles, I felt their unspoken skepticism as well. The feeling radiated from the poor most of all, as if they all recognized that I was no longer quite one of them, for somewhere along the way I'd crossed the line forever leaving them far behind.

Despite the fact that no outright hostility was ever voiced, whether it be in crowds of black or white, it continued to weigh upon me. For still fresh in my mind were the vicious threats I'd received as a prosecutor. Thus, even though my trust in my security detail was complete, and I campaigned with unabashed freedom, my eyes continued to search the crowds for the glare of hatred or the cold eyes of the hunter, and I never stopped looking back.

But for all my dark inner thoughts it was clear I was the media's darling. Long since having tired of C. C.'s boorishness I was a fresh face with new ideas and by far a more attractive personna to cover. They praised my prosecutorial successes and speculated as to how my professionalism would cleanse the streets of our city. With three months to go until the election I appeared to be the favorite of the majority of those in power with Martin having secured endorsements from a slew of civic groups, the City Comptroller, two local congressmen, as well as the all important Sun Papers. Yet despite all our efforts C. C.'s iron grip on the city's poor still had us running neck and neck.

Yes, I was the man, we claimed, to turn our city around, our fine city of Baltimore long since having become the crime capital of the State and many would argue the country. For I both knew the problems of the streets and with my prosecutorial experience exactly what to do about them. I was heralded as the champion of the city, fearless in my confrontation with its darker element. Yet how ironic it seemed to me that I whose total career was vested in the very system that created the problem was now being held up to the populous as their salvation. For in the back of my mind all along the rhetoric of my campaign had a somewhat hollow ring and I couldn't help but think that the solutions I voiced at the urgings of my advisors were somehow far too shallow to solve the problem.

Despite all the campaign study and debate I realized that my head had been largely buried in the sand. For although I couldn't quite enumerate the answers I knew that this whole grand charade was somehow missing the problem's very root. Yet I held my tongue for what was I but a political rookie who'd been given a chance and in silence I watched and listened as my strategists churned ahead.

Still, as election day neared I couldn't help but wonder if I was truly the man as we claimed, for with less than a month to the vote the polls had us in a dead heat. Was it solely the power of incumbency, C. C.'s twelve year lock on power, or something more? For despite the rumors of ill dealings, despite the city's continuing decline on C. C.'s watch, the downtrodden still clung to him, unwilling to forsake their own personal brand of champion. Perhaps the answer lay not in me but in C. C. for wasn't he in his own way as much a man of two worlds as I. For even though I didn't agree with his views or the manipulations he practiced I had to admit, that as the polls showed, at least as many people as not still rested their faith in him and despite divisions of class were not those of the downtrodden at least as entitled to decide as the rest of us.

But then, at Martin's direction, the incriminatng documentation was leaked to the press. The media had a field day, the public crucifixion a massacre. The worst of it for C. C. being that he'd taken his kick backs through a public housing voucher scam. His constituent base, so hard fought for and so long loyal could forgive a lot of things, his womanizing, his drinking, his broken promises, but they would never, ever, put up with anyone, not even their beloved C. C., tampering with their entitlements.

The campaign was a downhill slope after that turning into a landslide as I defeated Mayor Barnes with an overwhelming 68% of the vote. The results were far better than I'd ever hoped for even with Martin running the show. Yet there was one crushing disappointment. One of the few precincts I lost was the very one which held my childhood home the vote going to C. C. in an extremely low voter turnout. My campaign advisors tried to console me pointing out that my home precinct was one of C. C.'s oldest and had a strong reputation for being anti-law enforcement. But no amount of rationalizing could serve to comfort me. I was completely disheartened that the place where I'd grown up and endured so much hardship over the years would now spurn their own son.

I swept the Republican challenger in the general election by an even greater margin of victory and set about preparing to govern the city. With Martin's assistance and connections the transition period flowed smoothly, my political appointments being made and my staff assembled in the smoothest of fashions. In fact, I don't know what I would have done without him. Governing a city of some 960,000 people and 30,000 employees with a two billion dollar budget can get pretty confusing in a hurry and it seemed I had a thousand questions each day. But Martin had an answer for all of them and in timely fashion I took my seat in the Mayor's chair.

I suppose that in my political naivete' I just always assumed that once the campaign was over and victory won, that I'd start calling the shots. I couldn't have been more wrong. For it was only once I sat in the executive's chair that the pressure really began. There wasn't a single one of my so called supporters, although I'm certain that contributors would be a more apt description, that wasn't screaming for my ear eager to obtain priority for their request. I suppose in some perverted way my time as a prosecutor had adequately trained me for one rather unpleasant aspect of my new job. For although I was shocked by the multitude and variety of threats I received from my so called friends and contributors even the most vicious of them seemed rather insignifigant in comparison with the death threats I'd received in my former employ.

I must confess that my first year in office was a total loss save for one hard earned lesson. For though I'd thought I was previously aware of the amount and variety of pressures that elected officials were subjected to it was not until I took my place in the seat of power that I realized just how little I'd understood. Thus, those first months passed with me being buffeted about by the demands, restrictions and influences of others. But thanks to the experience I emerged firmly in command of myself and the future. For it was near the end of my first year in office when I determined that I was tired of being a glorified spokesperson for others. I resolved then and there that reelection was no longer important to me. Henceforth, I would conduct my office exclusively under my own agenda and mine alone. Everyone else be damned.

Chapter 10

It was upon resolving to conduct my own agenda that I first realized I had none. For up to that point I had been a mere automaton absorbing information and responding but entirely lacking in my own vision. So I neared my second year in office exactly as I had my first with for the most part other people running the show. But there was one clear exception. Instead of concerning myself with meeting the goals of others I now began to formulate my own.

Upon taking an honest look at the accomplishments of my administration I had to admit that there weren't any. I was the chief executive of a government that was merely repeating the unsuccessful efforts of those that had gone before. Crime was still rampant and getting worse, as were our schools. Our public housing and city services were deteriorating at an even more rapid rate. The city was literally falling apart. Thus, as I reviewed my brief political career I was again struck by the futile nature of the campaign promises I'd parroted from the lips of my advisors, the words pledging merely a few more fingers to plug the dike. More policemen, longer sentences, increased security in our schools, summer job programs, drug rehabilitation programs, teen parent education. The list went on and on, a collection of just so many after the fact measures which qualified as far too little too late. Was I to continue merely pruning when my city demanded that I uproot.

Naturally as I perused the myriad problems of our social decay events from my own life leapt forward as striking examples of both the good and bad. For had I not indeed seen my fair share of both. But as I racked my brain for what I imagined to be mystical and evasive answers the days and weeks flew by in a blur. Thus, it was in beleagured confusion that I trudged home each night fearing that I was on the brink of inevitable failure.

Then one evening as I applied a much needed disciplinary hand to the soft and tender backside of my son my governmental role crystalized before me. Wasn't my vision for my family's future a mere microcosm of the city? In fact, was my elective role anything different than that of a temporary patriarch appointed to watch over my electors? Just as I monitored and settled the disputes of my children it was now my job to safeguard the day to day life of my citizenry and though individual freedoms and liberties were all well and good it was my chief responsibility, nay duty, to ensure the beneficial interaction of the populous. Thus, I realized that I'd been receiving instruction regarding my governmental agenda since the date of my birth and that a complete societal framework could be espoused in a mere three words, carrot and stick.

For somewhere along the way we'd become a leaderless society void of direction as well as lacking anyone with the mandate to point the way. Hadn't I myself been left as a youth to float aimlessly in a familial vaccum and hadn't my own childhood misadventures been prompted by a lack of parental guidance and restraint? Yet I'd been saved so to speak by the stop gap parenting of Chet and Martin. Where my own creators had allowed me to slip through the cracks destined for a life of misery, good fortune had smiled upon me colliding me with those who were willing and able to pick up the slack.

But what of all my childhood playmates and friends that weren't so lucky and the countless faceless others who slipped quietly away forever. Were we as a society to continue allowing an ever increasing percentage of our population to float aimlessly in a dismal sea of ignorance only to be eventually swallowed up by the same miserable masses which our inattention created? Or could the cycle be broken, our societal capacity to nurture and guide be adapted and rebuilt? What was needed was a system of benevolent indoctrination with sufficient vision and strength not only to recapture the lost generations but instruct those of the future as well. Still, even the grandest of visions is but the most fleeting without implementation.

But as I searched for solutions it seemed at every turn there was another valid reason why things had to remain exactly as they were. It seemed that we were locked in a downhill race to self destruction, a mired confusion of political rationals, judicial idealism, city ordinances, and governmental regulations twisting and turning without end. Truly, if I were to have any hope at all I must somehow get my head above the paralyzing confusion.

Thus, the next night I took home a copy of the Baltimore City Charter and as I crawled into bed next to Rachel's sleeping form I felt so very, very tired, wondering how on earth things had ever become such a grand mess. But after a few minutes of mournful self pity I expended the tremendous effort that it took to pry open the cover of my city's governing document and I started to read at what seemed to be the most logical point, page one.

As I poured through its pages studying the intended structure of our government, layer after layer of excuses began to fall away and I began to sense that things didn't have to be the way they were. Right there in the Charters's dusty pages it told me that I was the Chief Executive and it was my responsibility to provide for, in fact to ensure, the public good. I was charged by the people not to follow but to direct and permitting anything to stand in my way could only be seen as my own personal failure. When at last I'd finished, notes carefully taken, I felt a renewed sense of energy as powerful as the rising sun for though the Charter hadn't necessarily given me the answers it had at least pointed the way. Thus, as my first year in office raced to a close I turned my attention to implementation, straining the capabilities of my staff with my informational queries. And as the old year gave way to the new I resolved that ready or not it was time to act.

Standard operating procedure in the budget process dictated that each December the various city agencies send their budget requests for the coming fiscal year to the Department of Finance and the Planning Commission, respectively, and eventually the requests would trickle up for the Mayor's review when they'd reached the Board of Estimates. Thus, the budget process could be summed up as more or less a bottoms up procedure. Naturally, in the scheme of things everyone always asked for more than they needed under the tried and true assumption that no budget request was ever granted in full. Yet as far as I could see such a bottoms up procedure generally swallowed up any capacity for mayoral initiatives before the chief executive got to take his first look. Thus, I determined to approach the budget process from a top down fashion for a change putting the city on notice of my plans from the very start and preempting their priorities with my own.

When I first revealed the outline of my budget initiatives for the coming fiscal year the shock of my staff was complete to say the least. In fact, I suspect that many of them assumed I'd called the staff wide meeting to discuss preliminary strategy for my reelection campaign. The reaction was immediate. A credit to staff loyalty, fact and rumor flew about City Hall, carrying the news of my agenda outward like a water ripple across the city. But I absorbed the panic without comment determined that I would not fall prey to defending my agenda against the initial frenzied rush. For I was certain that my proposal's only chance of acceptance lay in a calm and careful consideration. Yet I must confess that as the clamor grew I had to struggle against the urge to lash out in response for I sat isolated and alone in my vision. Then, just when the shouting grew loudest Martin paid me the rarest of visits.

Since his retirement from state government Martin had made a conscious effort to spend as little time as possible in and about government buildings preferring to wield his influence from more comfortable locales. His standard retort being that the halls of government had already seen far too much of his life. Thus, in general when I sought his counsel or necessity demanded that we confer it was I who travelled to meet him, Mayor or not. When he quietly appeared at my office door late one evening I was surprised to say the least. But despite the rarity of the occasion he wasted no time in revealing the purpose of his visit, that he'd heard about my plans quite clear.

"Louis what are you trying to do? Why didn't you come to me first?"

"I thought you told me I'd make an excellent Mayor Martin. According to the City Charter I'm just doing what the chief executive's supposed to do."

"Of course you'll make an excellent Mayor Louis. I didn't mean that. But you've got to give it some time. You can't just go running off on your own like this. That's just not the way things work."

"You're the one that's always been telling me to think ahead Martin. Remember? Nothing's more important than thinking ahead."

"But what about your political career son? Do you even know the risks you're taking?"

"What political career Martin? What about the city, our society? Aren't those risks just a bit more important?"

"Louis I'm just not sure you know where you're going with this off the cuff idealism. Do you realize you might destroy everything I've worked for?"

"You've worked for? What do you mean you've worked for?"

My surprise at his visit was nothing compared to my surprise at what he next imparted. For it was there in the darkness, as most of the city slept, that he finally imparted to me his own long sheltered vision. It had not been by chance that Chet had introduced me to Martin that first day long ago. As with all things over the years Martin had constantly directed one eye toward the future, his own longevity being no exception. He and Chet had long had an understanding that Chet would bring Martin any children he came across with future promise.

Because Martin foresaw that the time for the likes of him to stand in the forefront of urban government had passed, the horror of his war having long since been forgotten, and respect for the depravity of the human beast having long since been shelved. In Martin's mind society now slept blindly, insufficiently wary and guarded against the baseness that is man and Martin knew that in an idealistic society such as ours only a product of the latest, most recent underclass could possess sufficient callousness and public mandate to purge society's ailments and regain control. For in Martin's view only an intimate and personal knowledge of the depths to which society could sink would provide sufficient armor to ward off the falsified pleas for compassion and pity. But his was no mere "My Fair Lady" experiment. For through the years Martin's net had been extended far and wide in search of future leaders and like the rest I'd received no more than a passing interest until such time as I'd proved my worth.

Then he confessed to me that even he had been surprised at the rapidity of my ascendancy and the seemingly naive ease with which I avoided the pitfalls of others, until it became starkly apparent to him that I was the one. He openly admitted that upon my acceptance of his guiding hand that he'd experienced a profound sense of, not happiness or satisfaction, but relief. For in his plans I would become the vehicle with which to extend his ever shrinking longevity into the future's darkness. I would be the one to ensure that his hard gained position of influence wouldn't merely dissipate with the exhalation of his final breath. I would serve the role of his reincarnation poised to carry out his vision far into the future and beyond me another and another all spawned from his creation into infinity. Amen.

Speechless, I sat there. Had I been nothing but a pawn. Here all this time I'd been celebrating my independence, relishing my success, yet I'd been nothing more than the peon of this used up old man. That couldn't be so, he'd just lost it somehow, somewhere in his years or loneliness, and was now willing to say anything to maintain his station. Yet as my mind raced backward I saw that it was so, that his words however despicable rang true, and I began to rage, to boil, to hate. Imagine the arrogance of this shriveled old shell of a man trying to make me his slave. My eyes burned across at him with the hatred of centuries, everything I thought I'd defeated, all that I prided myself on having risen above, closing in about me. For here the two of us sat on opposite sides of the table, just like we always had, as if absolutely nothing had ever changed.

But wait. Sure he'd put me in law school, but had he taken the exams, and yes he'd placed me in the State's Attorney's office, but had he won the trials, and maybe he had given me the Mayor's chair, but had the people voted for him? Then it occurred to me that even if he did believe it was all completely his doing the only important thing was that I knew it wasn't. Forget his intentions, his manipulations, his arrogance, for hadn't in fact he done for me, trained me, raised me, and in all truth didn't I owe this seat of power to him. Besides, I could well see how he sat there so old and withered, his best days long since done. How confused and bewildered was his expression so mystified at how he ever lost control. Thus, I resolved that the very least I could do was acknowledge his past assistance and if for that alone and nothing else I decided to show him some pity. My anger then calmed I took a longer and second look at this used up old man, that I called friend.

"Martin it will work you know. Besides isn't that really why you made me Mayor in the first place?"

Then as he raised his tired old eyes toward mine I set forth my plan, testing it on wisened ears. And for the first time ever he permitted his eyes to reveal his thoughts as I spoke. Then, when I'd finished he nodded approval and though he went on to point out a number of flaws by the time he'd finished we both clearly saw the way.

As we prepared to leave, Martin candidly admitted that he now realized why he'd been drawn to me this night, for while all along he believed he'd been molding me to become his successor somewhere along the way I'd surpassed him, sailing off into my own uncharted waters. It was in absolute recognition of this fact that he now pledged to me his unfailing support and there is no doubt in my stating that his unequivocal backing in the years that followed was a necessity of the most absolute in nature. For without the supportive strength of this old and withered white man there would have been no question that I would have failed.

Once people's initial shock had passed I'm told the general consensus was that my plan was either some form of political ploy or perhaps I'd just lost it all together. I can only imagine the surprise of the nay sayers when I began to act. For with Martin firmly by my side, I was no longer isolated, and could now begin to implement my plans in earnest. Although, at Martin's suggestion, I went about it in a dramatically different fashion than I'd originally intended.

In my studies of city government I'd gradually come to realize just how much power the Mayor possessed. For among other things I controlled the policy making body of the city, the Board of Estimates, possessed a budgetary line item veto, and was the chief executive of the various city agencies and departments. But still, I was well aware that I couldn't just order people to believe in my vision, and despite my new found awareness of my power it took the voice of Martin's experience to show me how to use it.

Where my natural inclination had been to leap to the offensive, Martin convinced me that the trick was not to fight unnecessary battles. Besides, if there was one thing we wanted to avoid it was giving potential opponents time to prepare their attack. He assured me that the implementation of my vision would be difficult enough and there would be plenty of battles to fight. Paramount, was that we conserve our resources and energy for times most needed.

Martin's biggest concern was that, since I'd already let the cat out of the bag so to speak, that we not divulge any further information. Thus, at Martin's suggestion, I had my staff pacify the various city agencies by directing them to go about their budget submissions as usual and disregard my proposed initiatives. As Martin pointed out, it was far better to back off in the short term than to fuel potential resistance, for if we used it wisely time would be on our side. If in the mean time others wanted to believe that their Mayor was confused or even incompetent so be it. Let them think what they will.

I couldn't believe it was so very simple but to my amazement Martin's strategy actually worked. Just tell people not to worry and go about business as usual and things would go away. I simply couldn't believe that people cared so very little. But that's the way it was. The minute they felt secure again, their personal interests no longer threatened, the apathy returned. Thus, by April, when it came time for the Department of Finance and the Board of Finance to recommend their budgets to the Board of Estimates, concern over the budget initiatives I'd proposed four months earlier had all but died away.

But while the rest of the city had conveniently forgotten my proposals, Martin and I had been hard at work, turning my ideas into feasible reality. Quietly, we gathered the necessary information from the various divisions of city government, more than once calling in favors that Martin was long since owed in exchange for silence. Cautiously, we pieced together the logistical needs of my agenda, ever so careful to obtain what we needed without revealing why. Then, once the factual base had been accumulated, we plotted the strategy by which City Council passage could be obtained. Thus, when the Board of Estimates hearings regarding the fiscal year 2006 budget began, we were more than ready.

The months of preparation paid immediate dividends for my proposed amendments, meshed intimately with the recommended budget, leaving no loopholes or inconsistencies. Thus, our planning and preparation immediately moved us beyond the failing point of most visions which merely point out where they want to go but fail to specify how to get there. Yet despite the concreteness of my plan, its well reasoned rationality, the predominant reaction was not of critical analysis but of shock. Just who in the hell did I think I was to propose such change, to suddenly depart from accepted ways, as if my mere election as Mayor bestowed upon me some visionary right. Well I had better damn well think again if I thought things would be so easy. For this city'd been doing just fine without me for quite a few years and would still be here long after I was gone.

The inital shock quickly passed through indignation to outrage and in a turbulent cacaphony the city began to voice its complaints. By far more interested in speaking than in listening my citizens hurled their objections, from agency head to civic activist all freely took their shots. While for my part, I watched face after scornful face turn befuddled at the ease with which I answered their harshest objections. And though I patiently addressed each complaint as it arose I refused to allow the Board's budget hearings to bog down, completing our review and calling for a final vote by the first week in May.

The five member Board of Estimates being the policy making body of the city Martin and I had both hoped for unity. For a unanimous vote by the Board would certainly go a long way toward getting my budget through the City Council. Thus, I wasted no time in informing my two appointees to the Board, the City Solicitor and the Director of Public Works, that I expected their full support of my budget initiatives, of course including their votes. In turn, Martin brought us the vote of the City Comptroller, his long time friend and political ally having not yet forgotten that it was Martin who first placed him in office.

But the one thing we hadn't expected was the still fuming resentment of Councilmanic President Bates. The Councilman's potential for bitterness that I'd stolen his one chance at the Mayor's chair had not escaped us, and it was in anticipation of just such a thing that we'd tried to soothe any anger by fully backing his own city wide reelection bid. But apparently even our political backing had failed to cool his fires and the introduction of my aggressive agenda so early in my term was if anything just more salt in the wound. It quickly became apparent that Councilman Bates carried the mindset that if he couldn't have the Mayor's office then I damn sure wasn't going to enjoy it, and he was prepared to do everything in his power to make sure I stayed there for as little time as possible.

Thus, any hopes of taking a unanimous Board of Estimates vote to the Council quickly fell by the wayside my budget being sent on with a count of four to one. I clearly remember that the City Council budget hearings started on a rainy Thursday, May the fifteenth, and it was that morning that the real storm broke.

Chapter 11

As Martin had predicted, by holding off until the Board of Estimates hearings to introduce my full agenda we'd taken the city somewhat by surprise, thus far avoiding any well organized opposition. But now that my planned iniatives were fully out in the open, opposition groups quickly began to form with perhaps our greatest disappointment being that none other than Councilmanic President Bates was leading the charge. While as Mayor I had full control of submitting the budget and its amounts the City Council could still exercise its purse powers and while they could not increase the amounts that I'd requested or shift the use of funds they could still reduce requested amounts via the budgetary ax. Although it was a power rarely used by the City Council it was just this budget ax that I sought to avoid.

Perhaps my greatest surprise was that no one seemed interested in discussing the underlying rationale behind my plans. It was as if the very basis of my agenda was just so much superfluous garbage undeserving of even the slightest consideration. Here we lived in the most crime plagued metropolis in the country yet despite the daily complaints about the circumstances of our collective home no one was willing to face the truth as to why. No one seemed willing to admit that somewhere along the way our city had reached a pinnacle of sorts and begun forsaking the most basic requirement of a collective society, personal responsibility.

In our own high opinion of mankind's enlightenment, we'd ever expanded the exercise of our desires while decreasing our restraints, thus permitting the unchecked propagation of man's most destructive characteristics. The greed, the selfishness, the mistrust, the irrational self serving hatred, all were running rampant through our society, growing unchecked and tearing the society apart at a far faster rate than any of our well meaning social programs could stitch it back together. Yet still, no one seemed prepared to accept responsibility for our collective decline. Certainly, all were eager to point the blame, but only so long as they bore no responsibility for its burden. But what good is blame by those who lack the moral conviction to point the accusatory finger at themselves. For who but a fool would accept the empty leadership of one who can't even lead himself.

Thus, our society continued its downward spiral where no man was held accountable for his actions and all could freely disclaim their responsibility merely by pointing to some other guilty circumstance which had stolen their self control. For in our mire of post World War II intellectualism and search for human motivations we'd granted far greater respect and complexity to the human beast than he was due. In our boundless passion to understand ourselves we'd discarded the one tried and true safeguard against the very worst of our natures. That every man must bear responsibility for his actions.

But if I were to stand any chance at halting the decay I must somehow halt the trend, could accept no more excuses, no more slippery slopes. As a well intentioned society caught up in its own evolution we'd already intellectualized more than enough uplifting standards of human goodness. Already in place were more than enough laws and structure for any society to live and thrive by. Yet of what value was a societal code of conduct if no man saw fit to apply it or demand that it be enforced. In fact, all that was truly needed was for someone to finally acknowledge the inherent nature that was our beast and have the moral strength to restrain it. But never mind my broader vision of civic duty and responsibility. My citizens did not concern themselves with that. For in truth their only interest was that they continued to get paid.

Yet though the concerns of my fellow citizens focused chiefly on their enjoyments the necessity for the first aspect of my plan was to me so readily apparent. Perhaps W. E. B. DuBois stated it best in pointing out the need for the "talented tenth" to lead the post emancipation black population on its evolution from slave status to that of free men. But if DuBois were correct that every society has its "talented tenth" then didn't it stand to reason that each society has its "tainted tenth" as well. The truth being that there will always be a percentage of the population that runs outside society's normal course, rejecting constraints for a multitude of reasons, including everything from mental instability to deprivation to greed. For the stark reality is that the existence of society's "tainted tenth" is nothing more than a demographic fact.

Thus, in my city of one million, whether one worshiped the laws of mathematics, nature, or God, it was a given that a certain percentage would stray in even the most perfect of circumstances, not to mention in our state of societal decay. The danger of course being that as with all things in life society has a certain amount of symmetry and if the "talented tenth" was capable of leading society in one direction then certainly the "tainted tenth" was capable of leading it in the other.

For in our enlightened arrogance and search for ourselves we'd been foolish enough to elevate individual needs over the common good, not only accepting the flimsiest of excuses for the most heinous of acts but even devoting a great deal of societal effort to eliminating all vestiges of personal accountability. Thus, we'd not only relinquished our moral standing to keep the "tainted tenth" in check but created the atmosphere by which they could flourish and spread until inevitably the good would be not so much as overwhelmed by the bad but that we'd gradually all become a part of them.

Thus, of course the first part of my agenda was to create the means by which society could regain control of "the tenth" and not vice versa. For once a society lost its capacity to control itself, truly, what hope remained? Hence, my amended budget provided for the creation of a system of prison annexes by freezing the proposed capital budgets for the Office of the State's Attorney, the Police Department, the Department of Social Services, and the City Jail for fiscal year 2006. The freed funds would then be siphoned into a construction fund and operations fund for my proposed prison annexes. In addition, I'd drawn up a personnel reallocation plan for the Baltimore City Jail and Police Department to cover the requisite staffing requirements.

Thus, coupled with the capacity of the Baltimore City Jail the completion of my prison annexes would triple our prisoner holding capacity with space being provided for if necessary a full tenth of the city's population. Truly if our federal government could house tens of thousands of foreign refugees seemingly at the snap of a finger at least our city should be capable of keeping the irresponsible off the streets. For the grim fact was that our continued failure to act would only ensure that not they but the good people of our city became the true refugees.

My plan provided for three levels of incarceration with one for the petty criminal, one for the hard core, and one for those beyond salvation, with the increasing harshness of each successive level providing all the more incentive to avoid their depths. Of course, it must be noted that city resources being tight the new jail space would hardly be up to the usual standard of inmate expectation.

The four antiquated city owned wharf warehouses which I'd selected for conversion into the Baltimore City Detention Center Annexes could probably best be described as gigantic holding pens. But then my chief concern was hardly the comfort of the inmates, for no matter how bad the conditions of their confinement might be when the choice lay between the daily comfort of the law abiding citizen and that of the criminal element for me it was an easy one. In fact, my only concern regarding the prisoner accommodations was that there be sufficient room, enough in fact to reempower the enforcement authority of my government, and ensure that once a prisoner entered the jail they stayed there.

Naturally, the rather different approach of my proposals drew a great deal of attention which if anything served to make the members of our City Council all the more cautious. Councilman Bates in the forefront, the attacks came from all sides. The majority all the more willing to lash out in criticism due to the overwhelming consensus that I didn't stand a shot in hell of getting my budget through the Council. The procession of city Department heads through my office seemed unending, each in turn more stunned and horrified by the budget changes which I sought to impose. The police and corrections employees were up in arms as well and my phone on constant ring as each councilmember in turn tried to convince me of the error of my ways.

Nor was it necessary that I concern myself with prisoner well being for there were plenty of people to champion their cause. Prisoners, their families, rights activists, and even some of the jailers themselves popped out at me from all angles to bemoan the plight of the incarcerated. In fact, one of the most difficult things for me to believe was our society's overwhelming compassion and that those who so preyed on others could still be so loved. For in my mind the hardships of incarceration, whether due to fiscal constraints or not, were by the prisoners richly deserved. If anything I was of the opinion that their punishment would still be far too light. Yet such was the state of my city that the rape of a woman or child or the taking of an innocent's life could still be paid for by forfeiting a few years of freedom.

But perhaps the worst complaint of all stung my ears from the City Solicitor, who I myself had appointed, when he informed me that my intended actions would infringe upon prisoner's rights granted by the very document I'd come to hold so dear, the United States Constitution. But what of the constitutional rights of the good citizens, I had to ask? Did they have none? In the end, despite the uproar, despite the criticisms, my response was the same to all, firm and unyielding. This was the way things were going to be and they could either give me their support or get the hell out of the way.

If I'd thought the resistance to my proposed prison annexes was great it was nothing compared to the reaction against my youth home. But if I saw the reality of the "tainted tenth" and acknowledged that society could survive no longer without the resources to contain them, I had to also acknowledge exactly where they came from. Didn't it all necessarily have to start with the most fragile among us for in truth is any of us ever really stronger than the weakest we must protect? How could we as a society ever hope to regain control if we continued to throw our future citizens, the children, to the wolves?

The Baltimore City Department of Education spent well over half of the city's budget each year, some 1.2 billion dollars, and for what? The large majority of the money might as well have been flushed down the toilet for all the good it was doing. Our schools were in a shambles, having deteriorated to the point that to send a child there was a by far more detrimental influence than gain. For even the most innocent of babes could enter the evils of such an environment, enduring the verbal, physical, and sexual abuse of those that society had already lost, and within no time become just as hopeless as their tormentors.

There was one and only one solution and it was no different than the rational behind my prison annexes. The city must be given sufficient vehicle by which it could regain its authority and rid the public schools of their taint. Thus, I selected the long abandoned shell of Memorial Stadium as the site for my new youth home and again proposed an across the board freeze on all Department of Education capital projects for the coming fiscal year. The capital projects freeze would free up the funds for the conversion and renovation of the stadium into my new home for youth and renovate abandoned Eastern High School across the street as their new school. Again, I outlined a detailed reallocation plan from existing Department of Education personnel in order to meet the staffing needs for my new youth home and school. For in all honesty there were plenty of resources with which to get the job done all that was needed was that they be better applied.

Thus, within twelve months of the start of construction my youth home would be open for as many as six thousand troubled students with their school right across the street. One of the finest touches being the beautiful playground area which the youth home would have as its heart, right on top of the old Baltimore Orioles ball field. But aside from providing the children with the necessary recreation facility, the youth playground in contrast to my prison annexes carried a symbolic purpose as well. For if there was one thing that had to be abundantly clear it was that those who stayed in line would benefit while those who went astray would surely suffer.

But again the complaints raged the affected Department heads parading through my office, my phone ringing off the hook, teachers, social workers, parents groups, child advocates, all up in arms and marching against me. Still, amidst all the uproar I couldn't help but be surprised by the utter silence and lack of support from all those that had previously criticized the city's failure to make use of the stadium since its shutdown in 92' or still even more bizarre the public's disappointment that I would dare to use grand old Memorial Stadium for such a purpose when it should be obvious to all that its majesty should be reserved for the game of baseball.

Despite the fact that I was growing used to the turmoil it quickly became apparent that the media, with the public in tow, drew a grand distinction beween government aggressively putting more criminals in jail and an intrusion into the sanctified and hallowed ground of parental control. It seemed unimportant that through a more centralized approach my rerouting of educational and public assistance funds would provide the children far better housing, supervision, health care, and education at a reduced cost to the city. For the trumpet of parental rights blared loud and clear to the exclusion of all other considerations.

I was branded a would be dictator thoughtlessly spewing forth Draconian measures in a prophetic doomsday panic. Yet throughout the bleeting I refused to be distracted from the root of the problem and despite all attempts by my opponents to obscure the answer in a blur of moralistic and codified excuses I continued to focus on the origin of our deterioration, the inept societalization of our children.

Of what value was caging a thousand or even a million criminals only to have their paths in our streets refilled by a legion of mal instructed youth? When in fact had we as a people become so blindly arrogant as to abandon the collective nurturing of our children? As if to say by virtue of the mere possession of a penis or vagina that any lone individual would be fit to rear another. Ever so proudly we recited the mantra of our governmental system of checks and balances yet failed to apply similar safeguards to the rearing of our youth. So obsessed were we with the pursuit of our individual liberties that like a child in a candy store we became incapable of realizing when we'd finally had enough. But our riches made us blind to our deterioration and all the while we held our wealth forth like a shield obscuring the fact that perhaps more wasn't always better and that the less of our past might in fact still be the better path. For isn't there inevitably with all things a pinnacle between too much and not enough?

But as if I hadn't already heard enough I agreed to meet with a youth group director from one of the city's poorest neighborhoods, the self appointed role model for a group of some two hundred kids. Out of respect for his chosen work, but chiefly in memory of Chet, I made time to give him a private audience one evening in order to hear his views. Unfortunately inside of the first three minutes I realized I'd made a grave mistake for on and on he went about "my slave talk plans to ruin fine black children, and how I'd be giving them up to the power of the Man." For in his mind everything white or even remotely related was to be avoided at all costs, even if it meant the futures of the same "fine black children" he professed to so love.

Perhaps he really thought being black necessitated being contrary to everything white. But as far as I could see if blacks had to reject things simply because a white skin had already done them the future didn't hold much hope for my people. Then again, I did happen to notice that he'd so readily adopted a characteristic that many blacks view as peculiar to whites. That of course being his racism. If I'd been able to get a word in I might have reminded him just how close I'd come to being a slave of poverty and ignorance. But unfortunately his lips worked a hell of a lot better than his ears. Still, despite the idiocy of much that he said I was managing to hear him out, that is until he attempted to link the two of us.

"For you see Mayor Hayes we got to be sticking together or the Man gonna be riding over us just like he always done, cause as soon as you start thinking like the Man you gonna be one of him and go leaving your peoples behind. Now you and I both know where you come from and I's tellin you here and now you can't be forgettin who you is.

Now truth is Mayor Hayes I ain't got no real worry bout all this here cause we both knows that down deep inside, right here, we still just a couple a ghetto niggers. Always have been and always will be. But Mayor Hayes I'm just here to remind you that if you ever forget that fact there ain't gonna be no hope left for us all."

I have to admit that it had already been a long day so my temper was probably a bit short. But I'd come too far and worked too hard to put up with anyone coming into my office, at my invitation, and calling me that, no matter who he was or what he'd done. So politically sensitive or not I told him exactly what I'd thought.

"Mr. Causwell that might be the way you view yourself and I hope to God for the children you're supposedly teaching that it's not, but I am not now, never have been, and never will be a nigger by any definition. Now your time is up sir. Get out of my office."

Then just when it seemed as if there could be no more the City Solicitor again stood at my door, constitutional memoranda in hand, informing me that I was again astray of society's guiding rule. But again, I couldn't help but wonder about all the good parents and children out there and their protection, for surely they had rights too.

No, it didn't require much insight to see that as a society we'd been far too tolerant and idealistic for far too long. My city now required the very same practice tried and true by mankind throughout the centuries, the purging of bad from good. The cold fact was that our institutions and businesses, schools and families, and yes, even our individuals could never hope to escape the impending decline unless the cancers growing among them were finally cast out. For by its very nature any sore allowed to fester continues to grow until it consumes the whole. But as I was to soon find out by far my greatest challenge would be to maintain the focus on what must be done and not why it couldn't be.

Thus I held fast while all along behind the voice of protest I heard the displeased murmurs of the mighty state and federal bureacracies, quietly making their objections known through the voices of my citizens, content to remain behind the scenes ever so certain my agenda was doomed. For it seemed so sure to all concerned that Bates and his allies had the council locked up. But it was then that Martin and I truly went on the offensive with me leading the public charge while Martin worked his own special brand of magic behind closed doors.

It was Martin with his primary attention to finance that proposed we push my agenda in terms of taxpayer value. For as he pointed out there were only two types of voters, those who paid and those who rode for free. In Martin's view, for any agenda of social accountability to succeed it was a necessity to enlist the support of those who paid the bill for by their very nature those who rode for free cared nothing of responsibility but only that the gravy kept coming. Once the public was made aware of how much the societal blight was raping the paying citizen the usual apathy of societal haves would all but be eliminated. In fact, I agreed with Martin's point and it caused me to wonder where was the sense in a society that awarded people a political voice without first requiring them to contribute. For what type of judgment could be expected from those who couldn't even care for themselves. But for my part I saw civic value in a different sort of way.

Of course, I fully agreed with Martin that I had to offer my citizens something for their support. For in my experience no one ever did anything for free. But instead of appealing to their pocketbooks I targeted one of the most basic of human characteristics and embraced it as my ally. I appealed to their pride. Bypassing the more traditional routes of communicating mayoral directives through the city's various agencies I called a mass meeting in the Baltimore City Convention Center of what were at the time my greatest detractors. As the individuals that would be chiefly affected by my agenda, the police, social workers, teachers, and jailers of our city naturally viewed my plans with a fair measure of hostility. Thus, it was to they that I went directly to assure them I heard their voices and to convince them, that in the final analysis, this was not a struggle of city bureaucrats and department heads but their own.

As they gathered before me on that overcast Sunday afternoon it was clear that they were more than ready to shout me down. But I immediately captured their attention by announcing that should my plans fail I would not be seeking a second term. For my whole agenda was about accountability and if it didn't start at the very top then we had absolutely no chance of success. I could not order them to support me. Nor could I order them to care and I assured them that I would never ask them to do more than I was willing to do myself. Then and there I made it completely clear to all of them that I and my family, yes even my children, were prepared to make the sacrifice.

I stood before them in a last ditch effort for the life of our city, my path chosen only after long and hard consideration where no other choices appeared. Yet as I looked out upon them it quickly became apparent that the faces of my harshest critics were those in black. The scorn in their eyes clearly stating that only those who still wallowed in hardship were entitled to claim our lineage. Still, I spoke to them all directly from my heart and recounted the days of my youth, my personal deprivations. For I was not appealing to them with the force of lofty idealism but with that of my own personal suffering.

How were we ever to take back our streets if we as citizens were unwilling to enforce the rules and just how long could we expect to drink of society's benefits when no one was willing to pay the price. No. It had to stop and stop now, and if I were willing to make the sacrifice then it was my duty as their Mayor to at the very least stand up and ask that they do the same. No more could the wrongs, the selfishness, the greed be tolerated and from this moment on all citizens were on notice that if they chose to stray their punishment would be swift and harsh. But beyond the wrong doers I spoke of our children, floundering, lost, and hopeless. It was as one of these children that I stood here before them begging them to recognize that truly each of us was a parent and every child the responsibility of us all.

But I was fully aware as I looked out upon the supposed protectors of our city just how very long they'd been asked to do their jobs lacking the tools to get them done. For I'd often seen their hopeless look in my own reflection, so much to do and no hope it could be done. I knew exactly how their chosen professions had slipped ever so subtly into seemingly purposeless labor. Forced for so long to wage an ever more futile war I could feel their pent up frustrations, seeking any target upon which to vent. For these were the people who confronted the ugly face of our decline on a day to day basis, no buffer to soothe their pain.

But I was here to give them back their power, to wipe away their days of impotence. My agenda would return them to their former positions of power and allow them to take our city back for all of us. To my great joy their faces showed they actually heard my words and by the time their applause escorted me from the hall, that they believed.

Their support behind me the tide began to change but still I continued to preach the evils of the lawless and undisciplined tide. Yet for every ear I won another would turn away with my greatest foe, apathy, posing a powerful force. When citizens stood by me in the streets my words bore down upon them, but barricaded once again behind the falsely secure walls of offices, stores, and homes, my voice became a whisper, fears quickly subdued. For what fool would sacrifice the known comforts of today to guard against tomorrow's uncertainties.

Thus, when push came to shove it was necessary that I shove, the fact that so many agreed my political career already over only strengthening my resolve. Despite council member protestations I continued my media blitz, taking every opportunity to lambast their foot dragging. And if people scoffed at my so called "alarmist" methods when I declared a city wide state of emergency, then full realization of my committment hit home with my threatened shut down of city payroll services. But my greatest attention getter by far was my threatened organization of a city wide police and teacher strike. For after all if the city was destined to go down why not let it be now.

As June neared it appeared the Council was not so locked up as we thought and as Martin pointed out every councilmember had something they wanted to protect. All we had to do was find it. In fact, Martin and I met privately with each member of the City Council earnestly discussing which of their budgetary plums my line item veto would cut should my own initiatives fail. Not a threat to be sure but I wanted it clearly understood that I viewed my prison annexes and youth home as of paramount importance. Yet despite our efforts and the population's general agreement with my ominous prediction for the future with only a week until the Council vote it seemed we still might meet defeat. For if anything was more powerful than people's fear it was their reluctance to change. It was then that the Governor called.

The timing of my first personal call from Governor Dixon raised my hopes for his last minute support. Instead, Governor Dixon jumped right to the point dealing me yet another disappointment.

"Hello there Mayor Hayes. Governor Miles Dixon here calling to ask you a favor. Now I hear you're raising quite a ruckus down there in Baltimore and quite frankly you've got a few people kind of upset."

"Well Governor Dixon I..."

"Now now hear me out son. Hear me out. Now I'm not asking you to scratch all your proposals I'm just suggesting that you might want to slow things down a bit. So what do you say my friend?"

"Well frankly sir I just can't do that. We've worked too hard to get to where we are."

"Now look here, Louis, isn't it, I don't know what you think you're doing down there but you're upsetting people and I'm suggesting you better take a break before things get out of hand."

"Actually Governor, I was kind of hoping for your support from the start of this thing, but you never returned my calls. The fact is sir that things were already way out of hand before I ever came on the scene. I'm just doing the best I can to make it right."

"Now Louis, I don't think you're getting the point here. Now I may be new to the Governor's mansion but not to Maryland politics, and believe me I've seen a lot of faces come and go in the last thirty-five years. Now I'm asking you to hold this thing up so just take care of it. Okay. Good-bye."

Despite the Governor's pleasantries we kept pressing right up to the hour of the vote and all said and done I must confess that it was probably the very root of the problem which allowed us to pass the solution. For the majority of our citizenry was so accustomed to languishing free of accountability that most assumed my agenda would bear no personal effect for them. Somewhere along the way our collective consciousness had drifted from self-scrutiny to satisfaction and it was just this complacency which prevented my opposition from carrying the day. I truly doubt if the victory ever could have been won if people really understood just how accountable they'd become.

In the end, council members being what they are they saw the logic of my thinking. Most of them figured, that as long as they protected their districts, they could point the failure my way. Thus, the budget was passed 12-6 and forwarded for my signature, prison annexes and youth home intact. The calls started up again as soon as the vote was concluded with all of those that had previously laughed at the ridiculousness of my agenda now burning to get me on the phone. The State Department of Social Services, State Board of Prisons, the Justice Department, the ACLU, NAACP, you name it, everyone seemed to have a well reasoned prohibition for my plans.

"Things aren't so simple they claimed, far more complex than I knew. Illegal, unhumanitarian, unconstitutional, simply couldn't be done." Politely I listened to all of their pleadings, requests, demands, and threats in the end responding to each the same. Thank you for your concern but the City of Baltimore would be going ahead with its plans. But just when I'd thought I'd made it through the rounds and the morning finally came for me to sign the budget into reality Governor Dixon graced me with one last call.

"Now look Louis, I tried to be cordial the first time but apparently you didn't get the message. Perhaps your not fully aware of where Baltimore gets its money."

Finally fed up with the months of threats, criticisms, and complaints this time it was I that cut right to the point.

"No sir Governor Dixon, I believe I'm aware of exactly how much Baltimore receives in state appropriations each year."

"Well if you are then you better understand this. I asked you once nicely to back off of this thing and now I'm telling you. Don't sign that budget." It was all I could do to hold my tongue but in the interest of intergovernmental relations I struggled to remain calm.

"I'm sorry Governor but the budget's going through and there's nothing that can be done to stop it."

"Dammit son don't you realize the heat I'm getting from the state and national party on this. Hell, they think I can't even run my own state, not to mention the federal people breathing down my neck. Now I'm ordering you to back off. Don't you realize that both of our political futures are at stake?"

"It's not like there isn't a little heat down here as well sir. But to be honest, I hardly think our political futures take priority here."

"Well dammit if you don't beat all. That's it. When you fall on your ass you just remember that I tried, and don't bother looking my way the next time your city needs some help. Oh, and by the way, get ready to find yourself a new job come election day." I was on my way to sign the budget before the ring of the Governor's shouts even left my ears and with the ink from my signature still moist I directed my staff to proceed ahead without delay.

Chapter 12

Thus, it was in the summer of 2006 that we set about the renovations necessary for my envisioned prison annexes and youth home. I placed an absolute priority on having the facilities operational in time for the start of the 2007 school year. For with slightly more than two years to go in my term I was well aware that my license from the voters was short. Under my watchful eye, the drafting and negotiation of the construction contracts moved along in the most expedient of fashions. But as with all things the process began to lose momentum as the hindrances of our institutional and governmental bureaucracies began to wield their mysterious powers. Problems were proclaimed across the spectrum from architectural and engineering concerns to materials acquisition to the seemingly most meaningless administrative and legal details, with of course the ever present cry of insufficient funding constantly being bleated far and wide. In fact, it took the best that Martin and I could muster just to keep the project on track, expecting daily that the next dilemna would signal our defeat.

I marveled at how the construction of a new sports complex or commercial center never lacked for enthusiasm while the nurturing of future generations was seen as throwing good money after bad. But in all honesty I understood why society had reached such a state, the assessment in fact being brutally correct. For ever since our children's training had been so complacently yielded to a supposedly higher, more detached authority, ever increasing resource mismanagement had become not an exception but the rule. The blatant reality of any mass society being that no man's personalized compassion can withstand its sensory assault. Thus continued our decline with each step the "Great Society" gained washing out yet another of civic concern until eventually our fellow citizens became nothing more than passing ships in the night.

But despite all the headaches, the constant tightrope walk, as spring turned again to summer construction was almost complete. Then, with the hill nearly crested I received some assistance from a most unexpected source, my Uncle, Sam. Throughout the struggle my would be Federal protectors had been less than supportive to say the least, by far more interested in telling me what I couldn't do than in assisting my well intentioned goal. Why they now saw fit to lend a hand to say the least escaped me. I can only speculate that there was some curiosity as to our "little experiment" or that it was the seed of future Federal disclaimers should my efforts fail. But whatever big brother's motivation, once he unlocked his war chest the result was instantaneous, with a flood of beds, clothes, linens, and foodstuffs immediately coming our way.

The end result was that by August 30th, 2007, we had in place a six thousand bed dormitory for troubled youth with of course plenty of restrooms and an operational school directly across the street. Lest anyone should miss the point my multi-tiered, prison annexes were also ready and waiting with, in my mind, unlimited capacity. For if my reforms were to have any chance of success all must clearly understand that the right path would bring them success and pleasure while the wrong offered only suffering and misery.

The city would no longer offer a confusing and ambiguous guidance system to our citizens and youth. Only a fool believes people should possess rights they cannot responsibly use. Should an infant drive a car or a child be given a gun. Clearly no. For any freedom beyond one's capacity becomes not a benefit but a curse. Like all things wisdom is most often gained through a series of small progressions, the learned experience of success and failure, and it was in recognition of this human truth that henceforth in our city there would be clearly marked paths of right and wrong. All that was left for our citizens to do was make their choice.

Tools in place the battle was won. Now it was time to start the war. My only regret was that the bulk of reform would have to come from the harshness of the stick and not the nourishment of the carrot for I firmly believed that the human animal responded equally to both. But the reality of the time was that extracting societal support for a punitive program was hair raising enough, making a more costly program of positive incentives simply out of the question. I suppose though in the end analysis, which was used or what combination thereof was unimportant, for just as the hardened carrot may become the stick or the stick may sprout into carrot all things mesh and intertwine into one. Thus, as such the duality of the carrot and stick is a reflection of us all, both the good and bad, which inherently define our natures.

My personnel reallocations ensured that each of the new facilities would possess an operating staff. But while I had zero concern for the reduction in prisoner comforts that staff limitations might impose the youth home was an entirely different matter. I envisioned the youth home, although it might be for troubled children, as a transitional place where far more children than not would exit to productive lives instead of the prison annexes' harsh existence. Yet I was well aware of past attempts to nurture our cast off youth, with both the orphanages of yesteryear and the foster home programs of current day exhibiting a similar flaw. For instead of being sincere efforts to fill the parental void inevitably their efforts dwindled to merely removing the unwanted from view. And having been threatened with removal to such a place in my own troubled youth I was determined not to duplicate their mistakes.

I knew, that like all things, the success of my youth home depended upon the level of esteem with which it was viewed by both its occupants and staff. I had no illusions, that if left insufficiently supervised, my high hopes for the home would end in miserable failure. For although the staff members were excited about their new assignments, enthusiasm inevitably wanes, and since their charges, without exception, would be coming from the most deprived of backgrounds there could be no backsliding.

Thus, I hand picked the home's chief administrator, secure that he believed in my vision. In addition, I shuffled the budget to ensure that he and his principal lieutenants would be well paid, thus insulating them from corruption's threat, ever so near. Then, In recognition of the job's difficulty and the high standards which his employees must meet, I gave him absolute power over staff terminations. For if our charges were to stand any chance one thing was sure, their guardian role models must remain committed and pure. Finally, I armed them not only with the support of my words but of my presence as I committed to visit the home each morning as they awoke and each night as they prepared for sleep. My probing eyes thus watching the watchers, a clear message to all that the commitment was complete.

Still somehow dissatisfied I took one further step, and though many scoffed at the idea, I put out a general call for volunteers. For to stand any chance of success the children that would occupy the home needed an overabundance of guidance and supervision, the very lack of which had brought them there in the first place. Despite my impassioned plea the call for volunteers was not well received with only a smattering of people willing to pledge their time. Yet despite the poor response, staff numbers on opening day were still more than sufficient because when the doors of my prison annexes and youth home first opened their number of occupants was exactly zero.

For I had pledged that with this new beginning all citizens, and particularly the youth of our city, would in effect receive a clean slate. Thus, on that first day of September, 2007, I walked the silent halls of both the prison annexes and youth home addressing the staff members and advising them to enjoy the quiet for their work would soon enough be upon them. Then, I returned to the youth home that evening for my second visit, as I would do each day for the next three years, and though my visits

were generally brief, the point was clear, I would expect no one
to do what I would not.

My commitment was not without sacrifice as I in effect
became the father of my city often to the exclusion of my own
dear children. In fact, were it not for Rachel I have no doubt that
my perseverance would have waned. But Rachel tapped her
inner strengths becoming both mother and father in our home
and in retrospect I can only pray that my own children did not
suffer.

Fortunately, my efforts didn't pass without notice. For with
each day that I demonstrated my unwavering personal
involvement, my actions energized the beliefs of others, so that
by the end of October the volunteer rolls had tripled. People
quickly began to realize that this was not just another exercise in
political lip service and with their active support government
could actually do some good. The increase in volunteers came
largely from the school teachers, social workers, jailers, and
police of the city for as the front line fighters they were the first
to see the results. In fact, as their ranks grew, what had appeared
at first overwhelming became quite doable, for their collective
strength made no task too large.

The volunteers quickly turned out to be of the utmost
necessity. For old habits die hard and the facilities' first
occupants were on the way before the first night was done and
just as my opponents had threatened their law suits were right
behind. Thus, on September 2nd, as the first transfers were
processed, the United States Constitution was waved in both
state and Federal courts. The State Board of Prisons, the
Department of Justice, and the A. C. L. U. among others
bombarded us with their legal idealism shouting about the Fifth
Amendment, prisoner's rights, and punishments unusual and
cruel. But what did they in their clean white shirts know of the
streets of my city and what of the other provisions of this blessed
document guaranteeing life, liberty, happiness, and justice?

For the majority of my citizens were more often than not
barricaded in their homes for fear of the irresponsible few,

certain that their government offered no protection. Were not these citizens' rights of equal importance? And what perversion of societal thought had so desensitized us to the horrors of wrongdoers as if our constitution guaranteed them the right to wreak havoc with immunity. Even beyond that, far from punishing them we rewarded them with clean warm beds, health care, three meals a day, recreation, and cable T.V., the law abiding citizen sacrificing ever more and more for the comforts of his victimizer. This I could not accept. For of one thing I was certain, it was the perpetrator, not the victim, who must bear the brunt.

Yet the defenders of societal idealism continued with their clamor, trumpeting the alarm of my unjust transgressions. For how easy it is to pass judgment from afar never the necessity to lie amongst those you judge. But despite all their rantings I moved ahead calmly well aware that in the end none of my lofty opponents was truly prepared to take my city's tainted element as their own.

As with my prison annexes the youth home received the same, my opponents filing a bevy of state and federal law suits as the first children stepped through its doors. The accusations and threats flew with enough intensity to break even the strongest of resolves, the constitution was waved both in support of parental rights and those of their troubled spawn. Out rang the shouts of injustice with the Justice Department, the State Division of Child Protective Services, the National Coalition for Parental Rights, and the Save Our Children Fund, among a host of others leading the charge.

But what did they, sitting on their lofty pedestals, know of my city's children, so concerned with protecting parents that had long since abandoned their own. Yes of course each child no matter its past deserves some kind of chance. But at what point did chances turn to excuses, a cycle to the detriment of all? For what of those thousands of parents and children struggling so desperately to make a good life only to be dragged ever backward by the irresponsible few. Should the needs of those parents and children be ignored simply because they lived by the rules?

There, as the hot flames of defeat encircled me, the City Solicitor stood before me once again proclaiming all was lost.

"Louis, you know I hate to keep being the bearer of bad news but I've been warning you all along this was going to happen. Now I think it's time for us to admit that the game is finally up. There just don't seem to be a lot of options anymore. Each of the actions being brought against us is based on solid constitutional precedent and they're all seeking immediate injunctions against the operation of our facilities and heavy fines for each day of noncompliance. I guess I don't have to tell you the city's facing potential insolvency not to mention the end of our careers. Now in my opinion Louis there's only one way to go."

"John hold up a second."

"But Louis the Department of Justice..."

"John I said hold it a second."

"But Louis the State Board of Prisons..."

"John hold it."

"But Louis..."

"John shut up. Just be quiet and listen. Now I figured you'd be running back up here the next time things hit the fan telling me what I can't do. But I'm tired of hearing what can't be done. Now you probably know I've read the constitution a time or two myself..."

"But Louis..."

"John I said be quiet. Now I figure most people, including me, are sick and tired of hearing about the rights of the irresponsible few, about their victimization and their pain. I want to hear about the good people's rights for a change. So here's what you're going to do.

Now first take this petition of citizen taxpayers and file a response to all the prison suits naming these citizens as the city's codefendants. Then, when our opponents start gabbing about prisoner's rights we're going to tell these judges just how much the good people of this city have suffered and will continue to suffer if we're forced to put these criminals back on the street.

Then, you take this petition of public school children and their taxpaying parents and name them as our codefendants in response to all the youth home actions. Then when our opponents start going on about parental and child rights we're going to tell those judges just exactly how much all of these responsible children and parents have suffered at the hands of the troubled few. And John don't forget to note that my name's at the top of the list both as a parent and as the Mayor. Because any judge that doesn't realize just how much government has gotten into the job of parenting just isn't thinking clearly. Hell, maybe you and I didn't take on all of this governmental parenting in the first place but just because I didn't start it doesn't mean I can't finish it.

I've made it pretty easy on you John, the law and argument are all pretty much laid out. Now we're going to see just how much all these folks want to talk about responsibility. Hell, wouldn't I love to see the look on their faces if the judge turned around and ordered them to actually take responsibility for running our schools and jails for awhile. Then we'd see just how responsible they were alright. Oh and one other thing John. You and I are going to be arguing this one together so I expect us to start prepping for argument tommorrow afternoon. Now you have a nice night."

Evidently, the novelty of our legal positions was not so shocking as to muddle the judicial branch's thinking. For within the week the courts stifled each enjoining action against us keeping our facilities open for business and running full steam. I suppose all the judges had been waiting for was for someone to give them a way. Apparently, my replacement of more traditional thinking, where the individual's rights are viewed in an intellectual vacuum of constitutional ideals, with contrasting the rights of respective citizens in the context of societal realities was sufficient to fit the bill. For in truth, the constitution was not intended as commandments from on high but as societal guidelines from our peers, guidelines not in stone but adaptable to the realities of the day. Thus necessarily, any interpretation of its guidance required not just consideration of the impact as to any one citizen or single group but as to us all.

Perhaps the greatest surprise to any of us was that when we actually set about enforcing society's rules they worked. For people had become so ingrained with governmental ineptitude that compromise had become not the exception but the rule. But then who can truly blame them when their government seemed more concerned with making new laws than enforcing the ones they already had. It seems that our collective consciousness had become so used to compromising society's rules they'd become all but worthless. Yet the only necessity all along had been that once a law was made it be carried out. Thus, as we started to actually enforce our rules most societal problems began to be corrected. All that had been necessary was a return to people being held accountable for their actions.

When the judges realized that a convicted person would serve time they sentenced them. When the prosecutors realized that the judges would sentence a guilty defendant they prosecuted them and when the police realized that a person convicted of a crime would actually be punished they arrested them. In turn, when the teachers realized that students had to behave and pay attention or be removed they taught them and when the social workers realized their clients had to take some reponsibility or lose their benefits they helped them.

Across the board, in our courts, government, businesses, schools, homes and streets people began to live by and enforce the rules. The uproar was immense as all those who'd become so accustomed to life without restraint, taking and taking never giving in return, quickly found out that things had changed. Still, despite the progress by mid-November I began to have my doubts, wondering if perhaps I'd been wrong all along. For the jails were close to full, the youth home near capacity, and more and more public housing violation evictions were living in the streets. It seemed as if all were destined for collapse.

But then around the first of the new year a funny thing began to happen. The crime rates decreased dramatically as did problems in our schools. It was then that I realized with the rest of the city that what I'd been preaching all along had been so true. That there were by far more people in the city who wanted an ordered and responsible society and were willing to put forth the effort to have one. The truly unruly and irresponsible among us had been a decided minority all along with the only necessity being that the majority finally put its foot down.

By February a funny transition had occurred. Gone was the talk of insurmountable social dilemnas and hopeless decay. It had been replaced by a flurry of pledges and ideas as to how to correct existing problems and build for the future. Our prisons remained full as they would for years to come but there was no more talk of leniency, only the firm commitment of the City Council to build more prison space should the need arise. The youth home was a stunning success with the young people housed there learning and adjusting at an astonishing rate. A notable by-product of the mass removal of troubled youth from our public schools was that the school system once again began to function as a place of development and learning and not some grandiose holding pen of youth.

Of course, even despite the best efforts of the youth home teachers and counselors, a certain percentage of young people were never able to make the adjustment, eventually moving on to prison annex life. It's over their dismal futures that I still occasionally lose sleep, my only consolation being that no matter what society's effort, some will always be lost.

As for me personally my political opponents and critics seemed to all but disappear. In fact, Governor Dixon now openly applauded the success of my reform and humbly pointed out the risks he'd taken to allow me to go through with my agenda. The police, jailers, teachers, and social workers of our city were still among my staunchest supporters, even despite the house cleaning I'd done, for there was now a general consensus that all the short term pain had been quite necessary. In fact, it appeared that as my first term rapidly neared its close that I was the overwhelming choice of the people for a second term, there being no further mention of my performance based one term pledge.

I have to admit that the praise was a pleasant change to ears that had endured so much criticism, so I tried to soak it up well aware how quickly opinions could change. There, basking in the limelight, I realized that I was once again at a pinnacle of sorts, poised at a crossroads of future and past. Yet it was only upon stepping back for a moment that I saw what a strain the last few years had been upon both myself and my family. The threats, criticisms, and insults, the long hours and constant stress had all caused my eyes to carry a far older look than my thirty-nine years and the true irony was that my eleven and twelve year old children could to this point only have looked upon me as an absentee father.

I must admit that as I reviewed the furious pace of the last few years my better instinct screamed out that it was time to call it quits, just get smart and walk away. In fact, I'd already received more than a few private sector feelers leaving no doubt that I could do better by my family in another job. Besides, if as I'd said so often, that my performance would be the final measure, hadn't I already done what I set out to do.

But as the coming mayoral election began to heat up moments for personal contemplation were few, with political supporters, the media, and admiring citizens all anxiously awaiting the announcement of my reelection bid. The sheer volume of attention I was getting began to press upon me as if somehow I alone were responsible for our city. Not to mention the fact that each inquiry inevitably was accompanied by the unsolicited advice of those who professed to know best for my future.

It was as I struggled to blot out the din of unsolicited advice that Martin gave me another call. Despite his protestations that he would come to me I insisted on making the pilgrimage to his house for in fact I was eager to confer with what I knew to be my oldest friend. Seated once again in the confines of his dark and musty office I realized why I'd so wanted to come. For here in the secure recesses of his study, sheltered by my aging mentor, the clamor finally began to fall away, leaving me at last to think in peace.

Seated across from Martin it came to me that so many of my life's decisions had been made in just this setting, the intellectual products of our distinctly different backgrounds directed toward a common goal. But then again, for each of our contrasts some other aspect was the same and though our paths to these respective chairs had certainly been different, the commonality of our society had long since bridged the gap.

That my social vision had surpassed him we both agreed. Yet also known was that my vison would have failed lacking the knowledge of his years. It was in recognition of these facts that I now confided in him my immense fatigue and contemplation of an early exit from public life. Martin sat pensively for a while his wrinkled lemon squeeze face studying my own. Then, as I started to speak he merely held up his hand.

"Please Louis, let's just sit here a few minutes more and think." There in the silence as I obliged his request a tranquility descended upon me and for the first time in months I actually began to relax. Yet I enjoyed it no more than a moment before Martin began to speak and where I'd shocked him just two years before with my proposals for reform he now returned the favor in kind.

"I never picked you for a quitter Louis. The way you used to talk about this thing had me convinced you'd see it through. But I guess I was wrong."

"Now wait a minute Martin."

But his raised finger stayed my tongue as he reminded me of my own long espoused theory that the salvation of any person once tainted required at least as much nurturing as the sufferings of their past. Surely I'd made great progress but it would disappear like the wind with my departure. For the gains as yet were still tenuously based on stop gap funding and the volunteers who followed my example.

"You and I both know Louis how quickly people tire of a cause, no matter how important. What's going to happen when you go Louis? Are you willing to let it all go right down the toilet? Because you know as well as I that the battle's only half way won. Hell son, there's no long range system, no future appropriations. You have to realize Louis that until this thing gets institutionalized its only hanging on by a thread. Oh sure, now Governor Dixon's trying to take credit for your plans. But he doesn't have the moral license son, the vision. Only you have that. He'll just adopt some watered down version and sit the fence like he always does. It has to be you Louis, for the society, for the children.

Now I recognize how wrong I was before to think I was making some personalized monument. But you set me straight. Believe me I well know now that none of this is for me. I'll be long dead and gone. But what about the others Louis? Someone has to look after them. Can you sit there and honestly tell me that you've made things right, that you've done enough to cleanse our past? But even if you could have you so quickly forgotten that you're societal property bought and paid for?"

Martin had to say no more to remind me of our countless discussions as to the duties and rights of man. For it was true. I'd been a "public child," housed, clothed and cared for by the state. Just like any welfare bred rapper, athelete, or drug dealer, I'd passed my youth for free, taking all state gifts for granted as if by birth they'd been my right. But beyond that I'd dipped further, willingly accepting state hand outs for university and the law. Then finally, I'd pocketed the pay of both prosecutor and Mayor, laboring to be sure but paid for by the state. Yes, truly I was a child of the public more than most and all that remained to be seen was if I'd repay my debt.

But in truth, weren't we all public children in one sense or another, accepting society's collective benefits as our own. For what was society but nothing more than one great never ending cycle of receipt and reciprocation, the validity of its very existence relying upon the circulation of its wealth amongst the whole. Still, well knowing this fact man struggled incessantly with his greed, senselessly hoarding to the deprivation of his brother, while one eye stayed ever watchful for society's collapse.

The stark truth of Martin's words surrounded me, pressing in upon me, returning all my fatigue and weariness, until all I could think of was to curl up and hide. Yet I knew every word he spoke was true and that his was not a desire to hurt but only to remind me of what I'd originally set out to do. For Martin was right. Despite all the public vocal support I had yet to see dollar one of state commitment and without long term funding all the hard work would soon be just another memory of failed reform. Long term commitment was the key and as past experience had shown, to get it, someone had to lead the way. Yes, Martin was right. It was my responsibility to finish what I'd begun and fiscal necessity required that I turn to the purse of the state. It was then as I began to resign myself to the rigors of a second term that Martin dropped his bomb.

"I know you're worn out Louis. Believe me I"m tired too. But maybe this will reinvigorate you a bit. How about if I said that I see you in the Governor's mansion in 2010?"

My surprise was complete and I could do nothing but sit in a speechless stupor overwhelmed by the deja vu. For it was a mere four years earlier, with Martin and I sitting in these exact same chairs, that he'd outlined the steps required for my successful mayoral bid. Though our relationship had changed dramatically over the last four years I had to admit that I once again felt like a naive' little child as Martin spewed forth his gubernatorial scheme.

He confessed to me that it was only my own visionary radicalism that first sparked his idea. For what was I but a thirty-nine year old one time Mayor and a black one at that. No one skipped a certain second term as Mayor on a long shot bid for the Governor's mansion. But as I listened to the old Comptroller's plan it all seemed to fall perfectly into place.

The state was now thirty-eight percent black and though my reform programs had alienated a signifigant portion of the black constituency its success level had won the overwhelming support of the majority of voters. There was no doubt that the large increase in black votership over the past twenty years had left many in a state of mind that a black governor was just a matter of time. In fact, it was certain that with my aggressive track record and successful results I would definitely not be viewed as a mere skin color candidate.

The incumbent Governor Dixon would be coming to the close of an extremely unpopular term with a multitude of campaign promises unfulfilled. In fact, much of the voting public seemed to be clammoring for a change. The combination of Governor Dixon's current political unpopularity and my recent success made it virtually certain that we could at least make it a race. But above all taking the Governor's mansion would place me in the best possible position to procure statewide funding for my social agenda and ensure that what progress had been made thus far could be seen through to fruition.

As with all my decisions I discussed the matter with Rachel and she urged me to follow Martin's plan, her primary reasoning being because society needed it and even more simply because I could. So there was little surprise when I announced my reelection bid for Mayor of Baltimore with most people in the state, except perhaps for Councilman Bates and Governor Dixon, enthusiastically in favor of my choice. The real surprise came less than ten months into my second term when I held a press conference to announce my run for governor. The reaction was one of shock to say the least.

Chapter 13

Rachel. What about Rachel? Honey, I'm so very sorry. All those years of marriage through all the prosecutions, the campaigns, the politics, the pressure and instability, always chasing the dream trying to turn vision into reality. Prosecutor, Mayor, Governor, President, all the attention on me. Everyone always so concerned with my plans, my views, my well being, my accomplishments, my success or failure. But what about you honey? Weren't you always the one?

All those years of frantic racing, the obsession, forever chasing my crusade, all the preaching for children yet so absent from my own. Weren't you really the one getting the job done. All the times you felt the loneliness, when your heart suffered the ache, where was I but off crusading, not for you but for others, leaving you to bear the pain alone. Haven't you always been the one Rachel, for our children, for our family, for me. Honey what would I ever have done without you? And here now, in all my ignorance, I've waited until this, waited and waited until its too late.

But still there you sit even now, ever so patiently, by my side, just as you've always been, even before we first met. Oh what's going to happen to you my love, my soul. How can I just leave you behind. Must I always race out ahead of you, even now, in this. Hasn't our life together just started, haven't we just begun to live. This can't be our repayment for all the sacrifice, just trying to do what we both thought was decent and good and clean. Oh Rachel, I'm so sorry. I just couldn't see far enough ahead. I always just assumed we'd have more time. But no I had to go and waste the years, thinking you'd always be there, that the two of us would always be. How could I have been so stupid honey, so arrogant, to think the work was almost done, that it would ever be done. Oh God, dear God, please just give me one more minute, one last touch. I know its within your power Lord, to grant me one last chance. Please just let me show her how very much I love her.

"What street was that Meyers? Shouldn't we have been there by now?"

"We're just right around the corner Mrs. Hayes. Just another two blocks. Don't you worry now, everything's going to be just fine."

Wait a second, see there, just around the corner. Get a grip Louis. You're not dead yet, no sir, you see just minutes away from the best surgeons you can find, the miracles of modern day medicine. They'll plug up the holes and have you back to the Oval Office in no time. Oh no, this isn't over by a long shot. No. This just can't be over yet.

My bid for the Governor's Mansion in 2010 held two major surprises for me, neither of which was at all related to the issues. The first was that my blackness was now of paramount importance. For in Baltimore with black mayors having long since been accepted and the political scene possessing at least as many black faces as white, I'd almost forgotten that skin color could make a difference. But if the political importance of race had somehow temporarily slipped my mind, the gubernatorial campaign slapped me back to awareness.

Percentage wise Maryland had become the blackest state in the Union with some thirty-eight percent of its population being of African-American descent. In fact, combining the black population with other minority groups had actually turned Maryland into the country's first majority-minority state. Yet despite the demographics I was campaigning to become only the third black governor in the history of the United States, with only my two predecessors in Virginia leading the way. For the political reality was that Maryland still possessed a great deal of remote farm land and mountain country the political views of which had changed little over the past hundred years. Thus standing in juxtaposition was a loud call for a black chief executive against those that viewed a black face in the Governor's mansion as the end of all they held near and dear. Needless to say, the campaign received a signifigant amount of media attention from the very start.

The second surprise was that Martin began to take on a far more agitated edge than I was accustomed to. Though to most he appeared his same old unflappable self as the campaign heated up I couldn't help but notice his increased anxiety. I'd been aware of Martin's long standing feud with Governor Dixon ever since the last gubernatorial campaign in 2006. For Martin had done everything in his power to keep Governor Dixon from taking the chief executive's chair. In fact, their feud dated back some forty plus years to when they were both young delegates in the General Assembly. But I'd not fully realized the depths of their bitterness until the campaign brought Martin's true sentiments forth.

It quickly became apparent that the campaign held a dual significance to my mentor. Of course, my victory would be the realization of his political ideals, with Martin having finally helped to place a sufficient vision in the Governor's chair. But even more than that, my victory would be to Martin so intensely personal, for it would be the defeat of his long time enemy, a foe viewed as his lesser, but nevertheless one who'd captured the Governor's chair when Martin had not. Sure Martin had long ago spurned the two term control of the Governor's chair opting for the political longevity of the State Comptroller's unlimited terms. Yet all Martin's years of control did little to soothe the burn when his rival leapt above him. For even in his wisdom and foresight Martin, like all of us, had wanted his moment in the sun.

Whether it was campaigning or lobbying Martin had always possessed an abundance of energy but from the moment I agreed to run he attacked this particular campaign with a vengeance. Calling in his political chits and connections he had the framework of our statewide campaign organization formed within the month. In fact, it was only by drawing on Martin's connections that I ever stood a chance. But even to Martin's confessed surprise some of his oldest and most loyal allies declined to support me and it quickly became apparent that the color of the Mayor's chair and the Governor's were two entirely different matters. Still, Governor Dixon quickly began to feel the pressure and before you knew it the state's political machinery had divided into two armed camps even with the election more than a year away.

For my part, I began to piece together a campaign platform for the implementation of my agenda statewide with my chosen path immediately staking out the contrast between myself and my opponent. For in fact, incumbent Governor Miles Milford Dixon, had been elected in 2006 as a backlash to urban politics and governmental control, the state's first Governor from a rural background in the last fifty years.

A well "respected" State Senator from the chicken country of the eastern shore he'd pried himself to the Governor's mansion by relentlessly attacking the past failures of urban social policies and touting a return to "old time family values." As a rural based candidate his initial run to the Governor's office had appeared to be the worst of uphill battles. Yet strangely enough in the end it was votes of the eastern shore's urban flight population increases and frustrated urban voters which placed him in the Governor's chair.

A career politician, Governor Dixon, displayed throughout our campaign, the characteristics that had given him such a long and successful political life. His views could shift like the wind and he was capable of playing voter fears like a maestro. But despite the desires of many of my campaign staff to respond to his dirt in kind both Martin and I agreed that if I were to have any chance of getting my agenda through the legislature, I must enter office with my moral license intact. Thus, we ignored Governor Dixon's mud slinging and focused on presenting my platform in as concise and straight forward a manner as possible.

My campaign speeches, literature, and advertisements all focused on exactly where the resources would come from at both the state and local level and related each step of my platform to the proven successes that had already occurred in the battle for Baltimore. One of Martin's greatest concerns was that our campaign express the vision of my agenda without outstripping the voters capacity to comprehend. For as he continued to point out, when government asks its citizens to change the most difficult task is always making sure they understand why.

Thus, while Governor Dixon continued his attacks we patiently and meticulously presented my agenda to the voters ever on guard for misinterpretation's ugly head. In fact, my campaign staff's preparation was so finely organized that we surprised even ourselves at how well the platform came across. But as happens so often with politics, in the end the decision to walk the high moral ground almost blew up in our faces.

Although I had no respect for Governor Dixon's tactics, I must admit they were effective and he waged a masterful, if lowly, campaign of smear. Inevitably his less than subtle references harkened back to one fundamental difference in our candidacies, that being our race.

As Governor Dixon so frequently put it throughout the campaign, "why should the good people of the state have to pay the price time and time again for the irresponsibility of the few and their pathetic urban blight? For it was a well known fact that the good people of the state were doing just fine and had no need of any governmental big brother check system, particularly interference with their God given and constitutional right to raise their children as they saw fit.

Now of course everyone could agree that those city people needed such restrictions and desperately so. For it was their kind that was causing all the problems in the first place, their families so dysfunctional and in disarray. But the existence of those people's problems in no way meant that the good people of the land required the same. For were the good people responsible for the single mothers, the welfare babies, the broken homes? Did the good people commit the crimes? Clearly the answer was no. Certainly enough had been enough and the time had come for those people to be put back in their place. But by God, let all stand on notice, that they better leave the good people of this state the hell alone."

But in case anyone could have possibly missed his point he made sure to clearly spell it out. Again and again he contrasted our backgrounds making it quite clear, who in his mind, was responsible for society's decay.

"People what in fact is my opponent but a born and bred product of the very same urban blight that's trying to put yet another burden on your already overworked backs. We can't forget my friends that there are two types of people in this state, us the good working people who pay and do for their own and those who do nothing but take. It's not very hard to see which my opponent is with his welfare child record, living his whole life off of government money, government education, and government jobs and now proposing with his fancy reform program that hard working people like us pay the bill once again. In fact people, I'd be overjoyed for anyone to tell me, how a product of the welfare state is ever going to help us fix all the problems they've caused. Hell, it's people like him that screwed everything up in the first place. Anti-family, anti-values, anti-religion, anti-responsibility, anti-work.

Now we all know they've ruined the cities and that a time for change has come. Because my friends if we don't start somewhere there'll be no place left to start. But please people let's not go confusing them with us. Certainly we can all agree they need a firm guiding hand, a sense of discipline they've too long been without. But can anyone honestly tell me that we need the same type of governmental babysitting. I damn well didn't think so.

The point is folks that just because the cities are gone doesn't mean we have to stand by and watch the countryside go too. But sooner or later the good people of this state have to stand up and say enough and folks that time is now. People you simply have to be willing to put your foot down and tell all of them, including my want everyone else to pay for his problems opponent, to stay the hell where they belong. That's what this election is all about folks and that's the way you have to vote."

Just listening to the Governor's campaign rhetoric you got the impression pretty quickly that I was the black face of urban blight, and to be honest, the Governor was so convincing in his speeches that I started to think he actually believed what he said.

But the nerviest part of the Governor's campaign was when he started taking credit for the successes of my Baltimore City reform programs. To hear the Governor talk, I'd been the lazy, money wasting, urban Mayor doing nothing all along and it was only after he'd put his guiding foot down that I'd started to act. For in his version, he'd demanded that I lay down the law in Baltimore or suffer the brunt of his wrath. Needless to say Governor Dixon possessed one very active imagination.

But despite the attacks and fabrications, we tried our best to stay on high ground and when the racially slanted politics burned our ears we simply turned the other cheek. For in all honesty, for those determined to vote with race, there simply wasn't much to be done. The best we could do was ensure that they heard my platform as many times and as clearly as possible. The truth be known, Governor Dixon's attacks probably helped us more then they hurt. For if I'd alienated any one group of voters during my time as Mayor, it was the improverished blacks of my city. For as a rule it was they that had been most impacted by the reform. Yet Governor Dixon's racial tactics only served to make them quickly forget the reasons they thought they hated me and securely line up behind me in defense of our mutual skins.

While the Governor continued to attack my background, I held up my rise from poverty and mayoral track record as the factors which would enable me to lead the state out of its misery. And if the Governor's underlying theme continued to be that the election was about race, ours was that it was an election of civic responsibility, those among us that expected all citizens, no matter what their creed, color or circumstance, to contribute, versus those who did not.

I must admit that we did feel it necessary to stoop to the Governor's level at one point in the campaign. Up until the final month of the campaign, the race had been fairly close separated by only a percentage point or two. But for some reason at this late date, the Governor started to open up a fairly significant lead. Understandably content with the spread Governor Dixon backed out of our scheduled debate figuring he might as well coast into a second term. It was then that Martin came up with the chicken campaign idea.

It was really nothing more than a collection of brief television and radio spots talking about the poultry industry in the Governor's eastern shore political base. The ads then briefly detailed how the Governor had reneged on our planned debate and offered my challenge to debate anytime, anywhere. I suppose the kicker was the close out of each ad calling the Governor the Dixon Chicken and fading out to the sound of chickens clucking. To say the least, the Governor was not pleased for even with all the negative campaigning he'd done the chicken spots still seemed to hit a nerve. Somehow it just always seems to hold true that the folks best at dishing it out aren't very good at taking it.

Well the Governor should have swallowed his pride and stayed in hiding for in the debate his issues avoidance finally caught up with him. Although he tried his best to continue, his anti-urban theme I refused to let him skirt the issues and to be honest when he was forced to directly address the state's problems he didn't have much to say. In addition, the two of us standing up there face to face as equals, completely dispelled his portrayal of me as an ignorant product of the ghetto with the fact that he even felt it necessary to respond to my agenda granting me the very legitimacy he'd worked so hard to deny.

While he attempted to dismiss my positions as ridiculous, just more urban parasite smoke, he continued to fall back on his indirect ethnic finger pointing and after the first few minutes it began to ring quite hollow. For my part, I did my best to punctuate each point with supporting statistics so that by the midpoint of the debate Governor Dixon had become quite flustered. As his frustration grew so did my confidence and I rested securely in the strength of my convictions.

I suppose the climax was my outright denial of the Governor's self professed role in Baltimore's reform and I definitely caught him off guard by directly quoting him from our phone conversations where he'd spoken his true mind. Then, I took the liberty of displaying a chart documenting that all the societal ailments the Governor had been blaming on my so called "kind of people" had increased throughout his term in every political jurisdiction in the state but my Baltimore. The Governor's prolonged silence when I'd finished was a bit embarrassing even for me.

Yet even despite what I believed was my clear victory in the debate I still only narrowly squeaked by in the Democratic primary winning by roughly 10,000 votes out of some 1,200,000 cast. For in the end, despite our best efforts to capture the voters with the issues, the vote had boiled down to a battle between the urban and rural voices of our state with 83% of the rural vote going for Governor Dixon and 61% of the urban vote cast in my favor. It has not been as I'd hoped a vote on the issues, our citizens finally acknowledging society's past failures and demanding a new sense of civic responsibility. Instead it had been an election more than any other of polarization, pitting urban voter against rural, those desperate for a halt to the deterioration against those determined to preserve the status quo.

The results seemed to me not so much a victory as failure for though many of my state's citizens had looked beyond superficiality to substance the exit polls confronted me with one harsh reality. Those voters that had been capable of ignoring my color were in a distinct minority. For the vast majority of citizens both urban and rural, black and white, when push came to shove, never even heard my words but simply voted their skin.

As if the primaries were not disappointing enough my hopes were further dashed by the general election returns against a weak Republican challenger. For when all thought that Governor Dixon was a lock the Republican's efforts were half hearted at best. In fact, my Republican opponent's campaign only truly picked up speed in response to my primary win. Yet even then, in the generally solid Democratic state of Maryland, my challenger pulled in a respectable 37% of the vote, the reason for the unusually large number of registered Democrat defections being all too clear.

I was off to face Annapolis not as I'd hoped with a clear mandate by the citizenry of my state but with a victory tainted by the impact of my skin. The people had not heard my platform not because I didn't make every effort to clearly present it to them but because they chose merely to look instead of listen. Thus, I had no way of knowing whether they supported my vision or doubted it and whether I would lead them or was destined to fail. But as Martin pointed out in his attempts to console me a victory was still a victory despite the voters shortcomings and I should savor the moment before the real work began.

Thus, I tried my best to set aside my disappointment and focus on the future. With Martin chairing my transition team we set about the task of appointing my executive staff and preparing our legislative initiatives for the 2011 session of the General Assembly. As we attended to the thousands of matters which needed attention I simply couldn't believe how fast everything had happened. For it seemed only a few short years ago that I'd proudly accepted my law school diploma. Yet despite the sense of things rapidly spinning out of control I was positive that with Martin and I working together as a team, just like we'd always done, we'd see my vision through the General Assembly. For I'd finally arrived at the point in life I'd been struggling for all along. I was now truly in a position to make the difference. But then Martin went and died.

Chapter 14

It's hard to describe the sense of loss visited upon me by Martin's death. For almost thirty years he'd been the strongest thing in my life, consistent, unbreakable, a base to which I could always turn. Yet now it was as if with his passing so went the last attachment to my youth. My grief was immeasurable and as I flipped my token handful of dirt on his coffin, I knew that a part of me would always lay beside him. For Martin had been there in my darkest hour, Chet's death having left me confused and alone. When I'd had no one and nowhere to turn it was Martin that led me back to the light. Then, when I'd been isolated and alone in my vision it was Martin who believed in me, walking me from vision to reality. How could I help but love him for in all honesty wasn't it Martin, more than any other, who'd made me what I was.

But what did I expect, that he'd live forever? Hadn't he passed eighty-nine years with dignity and grace and seen my vision when all others were blind? Had I any right to expect more? Yet somehow I couldn't imagine going on without him, his strength, his support and before I knew it all of my old fears and inferiorities rushed out from hiding, screaming and taunting that all of my dreams would disappear with his corpse. Oh dear Martin how could you have left me so alone?

Thus, it was in the arms of defeat that I turned from his grave lacking even the courage to cry. Yet it was in the strength of Rachel's arms that I made it to the car and within their security that I passed the night. Then gradually, ever so slowly, as I vented my sorrow in the love of her embrace, it came to me that this was not at all like the day Chet had left me so many years ago. For this time, I was far from alone. Was I not still embraced by my wife and children's shield, the family which I'd so lovingly made, and in fact had Martin really left me at all? For hadn't he trained me well through the years passing his torch to me, steadfast in the belief that I alone could guide society's salvation? Hadn't he in fact organized and run the very campaign which placed me in the Governor's chair? Would I now dishonor his death with the gravest of insults by doubting the very faith he'd placed in me? No. The answer had to be no. For Martin had given me the tools and position, all that was left for me to do was pass our agenda through the legislature. Yet how quickly I found out the task would be easier said then done.

Any illusion I'd had that the task would be easy was quickly dashed as a still embittered Governor Dixon did everything in his power to make my transition to the Governor's chair as difficult as possible. In a surprise to even the most calloused political minds, Governor Dixon spent the remaining days of his term as if he were still campaigning for office constantly on the attack and fanning the legislative fires of resistance to my anticipated initiatives. As is customary, Governor Dixon presented his final budget at the start of the new General Assembly session making a last pitch for his own favored agenda. But then he went one step further taking the opportunity to personally attack my character one last time.

As if that wasn't enough to express his displeasure the Governor and his wife were noticeably absent when it came time for our customary tour of the Governor's mansion. But perhaps the worst snub of all was his blatant refusal to engage in the customary "good luck" handshake upon my being sworn in. Having already used his farewell speech to discuss the accomplishments of his administration without even so much as a single mention of me it was as if he actually believed the mere refusal to acknowledge my presence could somehow make me disappear. Thankfully for all involved the Governor's rudeness extended to his early departure from the inaugural ceremonies, abruptly taking his leave immediately after the swearing in was complete. For once his poor behavior was removed all could refocus on the celebration at hand and actually begin to enjoy it.

Despite the Governor's antics Rachel and I remained in high spirits determined to enjoy the day. After completing my inaugural address the festivities moved from the State House to the Annapolis harbor where we all enjoyed a fine parade, assisted by the fact that it was a beautiful and temperate January day. Then after a quick change the evening concluded with a black tie ball at the Baltimore City Convention Center where as the guests of honor Rachel and I mingled and danced until the early morning hours. Yet I suppose the true culmination of the ceremonies for me was not the State House swearing in as many might expect but the following day when Rachel and I officially took up residence in the Governor's mansion. Because for me personally the realization that I was actually the 62nd Governor of the State of Maryland truly only hit home that first night when I laid my head down to sleep in the house of power.

Perhaps the greatest impact of Martin's death was that now lacking his experience in state politics, I felt it necessary to confide in others. Such reliance seemed somehow so foreign to me for up to this point Martin had always been there to turn to, a trusted how to for each question of my vision, the two of us working together. Yet I was not so naive to recognize that the subtleties of the state bureaucracy and legislature were far more intricate then the government of Baltimore City. Thus, it was with an ominous sense, yet out of desperation, that I turned to the advice of new counselors.

For my part I was in favor of hitting the ground running, pursuing my agenda in as aggressive and vigorous a manner as possible. For although my margin of victory had been slender and blemished by the taint of color politics, the fact remained that I'd been elected to lead the people and that's exactly what I intended to do.

But the calculating experience of my advisors saw things in a different light, pleading with me to reconsider, for in Annapolis they assured me things worked in a different way. I simply had to face the fact that I was a new face in the Governor's mansion, not to mention a dark one at that, and though yes I'd been victorious I had to realize that my aggressive campaign agenda had only narrowly won the day. The State House worked in subtle ways and responded far better to coaxing and compromise than authoritarian threats. Once the ground work was laid, they assured me, then would be the time to strike.

Thus, it was in deference to my advisors that my inaugural speech was of a conciliatory nature. I took great pains to assure the legislature that I fully recognized their power and that their new Governor was not here to demand but for all of us to work together. My first State of the State address followed the suggestions of my advisors as well that of paramount concern was first establishing a dialogue with our opponents and only once sufficient rapport had been developed would we press forward my agenda. In the State House, my counselors advised, patience and caution were a must, for the true accomplishments were always won behind closed doors. Thus, I spoke of our mutual concerns and the common ties which bound us stressing that while there were certainly varying views among us there was no gap so broad as to be irreconcilable.

I have to admit that in contrast to the bitter battles of the campaign it seemed that the strategy of my advisors was working, for I'd been in office some two weeks and, other than Governor Dixon's parting shots, the atmosphere had been nothing but collegiality and smiles. But when the time came to submit my amendments to Governor Dixon's proposed budget, I finally had to put my foot down.

In fact, I was shocked when my own staff members began suggesting that based on anticipated opposition perhaps we were moving too fast, perhaps we should use this session to build rapport and lobby for passage of my agenda the following year. I simply couldn't believe my ears. It wasn't that I was blind to the give and take of the democratic process but here were members of my own camp suggesting that I back down before we even began to fight. That their advice may have been sound thus far I was not prepared to dispute for what was I but a relative novice on the Annapolis scene. But completely backing away from my campaign initiatives, that was something I simply would not do.

Thus, it was over the objections of my supposedly most trusted advisors that we submitted my amended budget to the legislature, my promised prison and youth home initiatives clearly set forth. Then, delivering my budget address before both houses of the General Assembly I reiterated my earlier words stressing our common goals and mutual responsibilities to the citizens of our state. But to the cheers of my supporters and the silence of the opposition I made one thing perfectly clear. I was here for one purpose and one purpose alone and that was to lead the state along the same path set by Baltimore's shining example, where excuses would no longer be tolerated and responsibility demanded. I would deliver as promised to the citizens of this state and I would begin the task starting now.

Any illusions that I'd had of a honeymoon with the legislature ended abruptly then and there. The reaction from my opponents was to say the least hostile and with my supporters being in a distinct minority my office was soon swamped with the fall out from irate legislators and other parties. That the legislative leadership had already made up its mind quickly became apparent as, my fellow Democrats, the Speaker of the House and the President of the Senate paid me a heated visit the day after my budget speech to make sure I was aware of their displeasure.

It was plain that the harsh campaign between myself and Governor Dixon had left a rift in the party and they wanted to make certain that I was well aware of the necessity that I covet their support. They made it clear that, while some might be, they were not in the least impressed with my prior successes and my rapid political rise. For as the elder statesmen in Annapolis, they'd seen many a visionary Governor come and go. In fact, lest I be deceived by my own minor success they felt it their duty, for the good of the party of course, to set me straight. For while as a political newcomer I might have gotten caught up in the public's view of me as a take charge kind of leader they'd come to remind me that such an image was not at all favored by those who viewed the power of their positions as their right.

My visit from the party leadership was disappointing to be sure but by far the greater disappointment was the more subtle objection to my agenda which trailed so softly behind the complaints. For if I'd thought it would disappear with my assumption of office, I'd been vastly deceived. Again and again it whispered to me from beneath unspoken words that no matter how worthy was my agenda and its benefit to our state it would never be adopted, simply because it was mine. But if I'd taken some small comfort in the fact that at least it was never directly voiced the Chairman of the Black Caucus made sure I saw the light. The state's senior black politician's own visit came hot on the heels of the party leadership and he was equally quick to the point.

"Now look Louis, between you and me you know we don't see eye to eye on this thing. I just can't figure out why when a black man finally gets to the Governor's chair the first thing you'd want to do would be to throw a whole lot more of your own people in jail. I mean Louis, can't you see that's just another form of the white man's slavery? But worse than that you want to go ripping little black children from their parent's arms taking us back to the days of the slave auction all over again. Louis, do you want our slavery to go on forever? Honestly, the way you've been acting it's like you're not even up here to look after your own people. Hell, most of the time you don't even act like your black. Alright. Hold up a second. I'm sorry.

Let's just forget about the fact that we don't agree on this thing. But look here. We're the highest ranking blacks in Maryland government and we owe it to ourselves and our people to stick together, to have a unified front. My God Louis, you're the first black Governor this state has seen and I know you can't look me in the eye and tell me you're going to let this opportunity for your people just slip on by. Now look you know I can help you get things done, bring you the votes. I promise you that. But you have to tone it down a bit and make it possible for us to work something out.

But hear me on this Louis. If you think you can do it without us, your brothers and sisters, you got another thing coming. Sure, sure you're sitting in the Governor's chair but don't you think for one minute that makes any difference to these white folks. You gotta realize to most of them you're still nothing but a modern day slave nigger from the ghetto. Understand me, it doesn't matter one bit what you or I think we'll never be a part of them and the sooner you recognize your place the better off we'll all be. I'm sorry Louis. That's just the way it is. So do me a favor and just forget about all this stuff. Because you and I both know that it doesn't matter how good your ideas are or what change they can bring, you simply have to remember that you're always gonna be a black man and that most white folks would sooner die than follow you."

By the time we'd finished I had to admit I'd had more than my fill of racial solidarity for the day, still I held my tongue well aware that I not only needed his support but his vote. But as he walked out the door I couldn't help but think that it was attitudes just like his which continued to extend my people's mental and economic slavery into eternity.

As the days passed the fall out became so intense the majority of my staff went into a full retreat.

"Insufficient mandate," they cried, "insurmountable odds, near certainty of the budgetary ax. Grave risk of political suicide, potential lame duck term. Our only hope to take it slow, develop more political capital, build consensus for a future year."

The prophesies of doom rained upon me and despite words of encouragement from my supporters in the legislature even they had to admit that no matter how we tallied the votes my agenda just didn't seem to have enough.

My state wide prison expansion faced its share of resistance to be sure. Leading the charge were most of the prisoner's rights groups I'd defeated in Baltimore, unwilling to accept their loss as the final say. But their appeals of idealism were to me of not as much concern as the reluctance of my citizenry as a whole. For although the majority of citizens and legislators fully agreed with the severity of the penal system I'd imposed in Baltimore, its urban usage was where they drew the line.

It seemed that all could now agree the majority of urban dwellers were in great need of such stringent measures. For of course it was in the typical city person that the root of society's problems lay. But the countryside was an entirely different matter. For was not the difference between urban and rural like night and day, and if all agreed that the city and its people had deteriorated unchecked for far too long then just as easily all could say that the people of the countryside were still clean and good.

If resistance to applying my prison system statewide was heavy the outrage at my proposed system of statewide youth homes was a storm. How dare I, a product of all that was taking society down, suggest that the good people of the land were not doing enough to rear their own. For it was the likes of me that had brought this fine country down in the first place, always taking and taking, never to give in return. It was my kind, the offspring of lost mothers, trained on urban streets, that plagued society with the crime, the homelessness, the animalistic sex and the drugs. Even if I'd had the good fortune to make it out certainly all recognized that it was my kind, multiplying like so many rats in a cage that had to be stopped before they brought an end to us all.

How dare I suggest that what was necessary for those lost and hopeless masses of the city should ever be applied to the good country people's children as well. For everyone knew it was their children that were the country's last hope, its remaining source of strength to be nurtured and raised to lead. After all wasn't that really the difference between my kind and their's, that they'd always looked after and cared for their own and always would, where my kind cared nothing for their offspring but only for themselves? No wonder I was encountering so much difficulty in the legislature for if I didn't even understand the difference between their kind and mine by now what hope was there that I could ever lead. In fact, just like they'd suspected from the very start, perhaps it would be best for the state, for all of us, if I just went back where I belonged.

Though I'd withstood the storm in Baltimore the battle at the state level was far more complex and the opposition flailed at me from seemingly a thousand directions. Without Martin by my side the task seemed insurmountable. For it was as if I were dealing with the Tower of Babel and try as I might I simply could not keep them focused on the fact that we were all in the same fight and the only way to win it was with us all united as one.

As the session sped forward and I seemed to be getting nowhere it occurred to me that perhaps it was just too soon. Maybe people weren't yet disgusted enough with society's deterioration to start to look ahead. Despite all the misery so readily apparent, the murders, the rapes, the crime, perhaps they required that things grow worse even still. But what shook my confidence the most was that maybe Martin was wrong and I'd really never been the one to lead us after all.

Thus, I must confess as it grew late in the session I became disheartened and standing isolated without Martin's strength the voices of my advisors began to wear me down.

"Haven't we been telling you all along sir that such a confrontational strategy would blow up in your face. Believe us we know the time is simply not yet ripe. Listen to us, heed us, we're on your side sir, supporting your agenda as much as you. We'd never do anything to lead you astray."

Perhaps it had all moved too fast and I'd been left weakened by Martin's passing or despite all I'd been through and all the years, perhaps my childhood uncertainties had finally caught up with me. Perhaps I'd merely become confused or simply just too tired.

But whatever the reason, the pressures from friend and foe alike wore me down and in the end, I heeded the words of my advisors backing away from my initiatives in exchange for the passage of state funding to continue my Baltimore prison annexes and youth home. In fact, I had to battle tooth and nail just for that for more than a few of my opponents fought the funding bill fiercely recognizing that the termination of my successes would pull my already fragile support right out from under me.

The way my supporters and staff celebrated the end of the session you would have thought we'd won a great victory for in their minds the extension of my Baltimore City programs was a notable accomplishment. But in my heart I knew we'd failed miserably just barely holding on to what had already been done and making zero progress on the task which had confronted us. Thus, while the rest of Annapolis engaged in the traditional end of session festivities, I gathered my staff and made sure they were well aware of my disappointment. Although I thanked them for their efforts I took the opportunity to remind them just how horribly we'd failed. For now that the budget for fiscal year 2011 was finalized and the legislative session over the time for our real work had come.

Chapter 15

We immediately went to work in the legislative recess starting with the Legislative Policy Committee which was responsible for creating the next session's agenda. I was not to be deterred that the committee was co-chaired by the President of the Senate and the Speaker of the House who'd already clearly expressed their resistance to my proposals. For in this case I and my advisors for once agreed that if we could not sway the majority leaders to our side we would have little chance of pushing my agenda through the legislature.

I had my staff carefully gather statistics detailing the ailments afflicting our society. But beyond just another repetitive statement of the problems we engaged in the painstaking task of drawing direct correlations between each of my proposed remedies and the elimination of detrimental behavior. The icing on the cake was the statistical proof that for the fourth year in a row Baltimore City was the only jurisdiction in the entire State of Maryland where societal ailments had actually decreased.

Without exception every other Maryland jurisdiction be it township or county, urban or rural, had seen an ever increasing societal deterioration from crime to familial break ups, illiteracy to substance abuse, reduced worker output to infrastructure failure. Thus, from the majority leaders on down not a single representative escaped our efforts as I and my staff undertook a furious lobbying campaign in the corridors of power. Wielding every tool at our disposal our singular purpose was to absolutely convince our elected representatives that the time had come to act and to further delay would only be irreversibly sealing our collective fate.

Yet despite the strength of our efforts, and indisputable statistics in support of my proposals, my plans did not seem to be carrying the day. For as the start of the new legislative session drew near it appeared that we were still no closer to obtaining the necessary votes. It seemed that each time a senator or delegate came to see the light that another would waver reverting to the old way of thought. The most infuriating thing of all was that my compromise of the year before kept coming back to haunt me. Instead of as my advisors had promised, legislators gradually succumbing to the inherent reason of our arguments, a majority of legislators viewed my first year's compromise as evidence of my agenda's weakness. For if I'd not had sufficient faith in my own proposals then why should they. Thus, with the start of the new session upon us it seemed that if anything we were farther away from achieving passage than when we'd started.

It was there in the darkness of the moment as I prepared to deliver my second State of the State address that I finally realized the error of my ways. I had once again fallen prey to the passivity of compromise. Just as in my first year as the Mayor of Baltimore I had again been wooed by the voices of so called reason and so easily persuaded as to what could not be done. For they the defenders of the way things were, so contented in the status quo, ventured no more than the most fleeting of thoughts as to the horror of what was to come.

I'd been trapped yet again, foolishly having believed, that any of them so long entrenched would ever see. Thus, I'd come full circle, aware once again that nothing changed without reason and secure in the fact that if I waited until they finally recognized the threat of our deterioration it would be far too late. It was with recaptured vision that I began my second session with the General Assembly and against the wishes of my advisors that I determined to this time go about things in my own way.

For my part, I opened the new session with what was viewed by many as a rather unpopular address. For although I continued to view the task at hand as a mutual challenge, in the frequently adversarial relationship that exists between legislatures and chief executives, there were many that took my speech for an ultimatum. Yet the truth was, no matter how much they hated to admit it, we were dealing with a problem by far more significant then ourselves. The important thing was not whether they had failed or I, but that we all had.

I addressed them from my heart when I spoke of our desperate need for societal restructuring, not piecemeal but from the ground up. For how could any of us fail to recognize that all that we now enjoyed depended inevitably on the training of our youth. Yet well aware that mere conviction would be insufficient guidance, I spoke to them with the voice of history. For how quickly we'd forgotten the great impact of World War II upon our society, the country entering the war fresh from the throes of economic depression only to exit in a few short years the richest and most powerful nation on earth. Then, delivered directly from the horrors of war, before we had time to blink, the nation was sucked into the post war vacuum of power and suddenly it was our responsibility and ours alone to champion right over wrong, protecting the world from evil.

What arrogance our new found status bred, the nation choosing to believe that such position and power had always been our right, and so quick were we to forget that our country's great strength had grown not through the exercise of rights but through that of responsibilities. Then bubbling up through the freedom that inevitably comes with wealth and power surfaced the first signs of our detached idealism where goals are viewed absent reality's context. Thus, remembering facist oppressions we placed individual rights on a most sacred pedestal, spurred so zealously onward by the threat of the communist bear.

In our ever spiraling idealism, societal context was soon lost as in the name of individuality, well fed intellectuals crushed the collective good. Thus, spurred onward by its controllers, the federal beast held sway imposing its whims across the land, no institution safe from its reach. In sheer wonder at its tax dollar power our government stalked the land demanding codes of societal conduct which even it could not deliver. Society's triparte foundations had no choice but to heed the colossus and no matter how idealistic the judgments accept the commands as supreme.

Thus in order, the authority of the church, the local patriarchs, and then finally, even that of the family fell beneath the onslaught. But in all its arrogant good intentions did our government ever think to fill the void? One need look no farther than the dismal state of our deterioration to see the answer is clearly no. For in our would be protector's rush to so avidly loose our freedoms it never took the time to ponder the result. But what is the good of such liberties if the individual's not trained to use them? For a society lacking the respect of its citizens can only meet one end.

Yet still we as government so idealistically sit refusing even now to admit the inability to train our youth. For to recognize our failure is to admit guilt in society's downfall, it being far easier to keep pointing the finger than ever accept the blame. But in the end, what the State has taken away is its duty to replace, our failure to do so dictating only one possible result.

But whether they heard my words or not I was determined that this time there would be no compromise. I told my supporters right then and there that no matter what deals they were offered I expected them to stand fast. We could not refuse to act yet again. The year before we'd failed the people, none more to blame than I. For where circumstance had required I lead in my weakness I'd merely followed. I simply would not allow that to happen again.

I concluded my address by announcing they'd have my budget package within the week and that it would again include my statewide prison and youth home initiatives. The comparative statistics could not have been more clear that there was a drastic need for both, not just in Baltimore, but across the state. Then, lastly I informed them that as the representatives of the people I expected them to be just that and with the society collapsing around us, that meant one and only one thing, pass the budget as I requested.

As I'd hoped, the strength of my address coupled with the weight of the statistics turned more then a few legislators to my way of thinking. Still, I and my staff continued to lobby throughout the session hammering home again and again that the salvation of our youth made all other issues before the Assembly pale in comparison. For what good was the result of any piece of legislation if the society was literally collapsing around it. But despite all our efforts as the session neared a close it became apparent that my initiatives still lacked the necessary votes.

Then, to my horror just prior to the final budget vote, the Majority leaders and their supporters succeeded in pushing through a series of budget amendments that would not only delete my statewide initiatives but also terminate state assistance to the Baltimore City prison annexes and youth home. Despite our last minute efforts, their budget cuts passed by the slimmest of margins. I simply couldn't believe it. Even with all our efforts, all the hard statistics in support of my proposals, it had made no difference. Instead of focusing on the problem at hand a majority of the legislature had continued to engage in self serving pettiness.

But beyond that, in a gesture of pure personal spite, they'd cut the Baltimore City funding which by even the most cynical of judgments had by this time gained acceptance as money well spent. In short, my opponents had used their powers of budgetary reduction as an all out declaration of war. The lines clearly drawn they left me no option. If it was war they wanted then that's exactly what they'd get.

The intent of my opponent's last minute actions had been to destroy my Baltimore City programs and recess immediately thereafter leaving me with egg on my face and the sounds of their laughter. But while that might have been their intention I quickly developed other plans. I immediately arranged a meeting with the Mayor of Baltimore and his staff and after reviewing their upcoming budget worked out sufficient stop gap funding to keep the prison annexes and youth home operating. Then, I directed my staff to correlate the information I requested by legislative district, which despite their belief that I was committing political suicide, they faithfully carried out. Thus, on the last day of the legislative session when I requested to address both houses of the General Assembly, I was more than ready.

Perhaps my opponents expected to laugh at my anger, perhaps they expected to bask in my frustration or even gloat in my new found humility. But whatever they expected I am certain it was not that I'd address them as individuals. For how easy it always is to find one's safety in numbers never having to face the responsibility of standing alone. Thus, I took a few minutes to express how disappointed I was in my opponents as a group, well noting their self assured smirks as I spoke.

But then as I began to personalize my disappointment the smirks began to change, first to confusion, then surprise, then horror, then rage. Because for each individual that voted against me I not only named them personally as failing the citizens of this state but then proceeded to list the increased crime and school failure statistics in his or her home district for the past year. But even beyond that I read a list of his jurisdiction's victims, the individuals that had actually experienced the assaults, the rapes, the robberies, the domestic and child abuse, the murders, the pain and the fear.

After singling out the first few legislators my intentions were made clear and the majority of the opposition stalked out of the House Chamber unwilling to face my accusations. But though they might run away from me, there was no place to hide for I'd made sure that a full complement of the press was there to witness the proceedings. In fact, my opponents could not have given my message any more power than the news camera footage of their flustered faces beating a hasty retreat. Yet despite their early exit I continued to recite my roll of accountability for the next six hours until eventually only my supporters were left and as I departed to their cheers I knew my point had been made.

But I was not close to being done for the following day, once the General Assembly had recessed, I held a statewide press conference to apologize to the people for my legislative failure and explain to them what I'd done and why. I reminded them of the success which Baltimore had experienced and expressed my disgust that their representatives had cut off Baltimore's prison and youth home funding due to petty political gamesmanship. Then, I beseeched all of my citizens, not just the victims of society's crimes and abuse and deterioration but their parents and spouses, children, siblings and friends as well to rise up in support of, not just me, but of all that was good in our society and tell my opposition just how they felt. But if my opponents thought that they could merely weather the storm, that the rage would burn brightly so soon to fizzle, they were sorely mistaken. For I directed my staff to distribute a weekly roll of accountability to the media and ensure that the information got out.

In fact, my prayers were answered for as my citizens became more aware the infamy of my opponents grew. Teachers, policemen, churchmembers, businessmen, students, fathers and mothers, they all roared with their disgust for once they knew exactly where to address their frustrations there was no limit to their energy. Perhaps the most satisfying thing being that there was no longer any mention of my color. My supporters came out of the wood work, from city to suburb from mountain to farm, with the colors of their skins stretching across the rainbow. In fact, I can't count the number of times I heard comments such as, "You know Governor, now that I've gotten to know you, you're alright. The truth is I guess you're a lot like me. So you go get em Governor."

For apparently for more than a few of my citizens the familiarity of time had gradually diminished the ominous nature of my skin.

As the pressure grew the criticisms and attacks of my opponents diminished for when push came to shove it was clearly evident that they feared the loss of their positions far more than I. In fact, the citizens of our state made things so politically hot for my opponents that eventually I even received a personal visit from my two staunchest adversaries the Speaker of the House and President of the Senate. But on this occasion, unlike meetings of the past, they had come not to demand but plead. But I refused to fall prey again to the same back room dealings so I curtly informed them that my pressure tactics would cease only after I'd received their approving votes.

At the start of my third legislative session I again asked for their cooperation in obtaining our mutual goals. Then I informed them that my upcoming budget request for fiscal year 2013 would, with the exception of spending mandates and population sensitive expenditures, be largely a duplicate of my budget the year before. After addressing other matters of consideration I then concluded the address with my roll of accountability although this time with a noticeable difference. It was drastically shorter. For the months of pressure had turned more than a few opponents into supporters. In fact, it's sufficient to say that those few legislators that remained against me were the victims of either their own stubbornness or that of their chief campaign contributors. Thus, what was to be my final reading of the roll of accountability sounded much more like a list of the condemned than a political pressure tactic.

With my supporters now comprising a distinct legislative majority my proposed budget was approved with little difficulty and a construction schedule outlined for completion of a statewide system of prison annexes and youth homes within the year. For although such a time table at first might have seemed impossible, upon a careful analysis and reallocation of already existing state facilities, what at first seemed unthinkable quickly became quite feasible.

Following the Baltimore model a number of public schools were equipped with the necessary sleeping arrangements and converted to youth homes. In addition, eight state warehouse facilities were converted into prison annexes, with of course again the facilities not quite up to the usual level of prisoner expectations, but more than secure enough to ensure that whoever entered stayed there. But beyond that, with the majority of the legislature behind me, we succeeded in passing the Omnibus Civic Responsibility and Youth Reclamation Act, which far beyond the range of one year's budget, codified a societal agenda for the future. Thus, by the start of my fourth year in office, I had both sufficient prisons and youth homes in place to look the citizens of our state in the eye, including the tainted tenth, and say with firm conviction, that no matter what their class, creed or race all would now be held accountable.

The amazing thing was that as soon as the new facilities were opened, just as in Baltimore City, the prisons and youth homes began to fill. Day after day our troubled citizens passed through their doors until it seemed the facilities would surely burst. But then, also just as in Baltimore City, all of a sudden the flow slowed to a trickle and then it stopped completely. In correlation the crime rates dropped dramatically, the public schools returned to institutions of disciplined learning, and my citizens once again began to take responsibility for their actions and treat others with respect. In fact, the societal changes were so dramatic that many claimed a miracle had been worked.

Naturally, I received a great deal of credit for the success of my policies try as I might to include all those who'd played a part. The public praise and media attention went national with some even heralding me as a social engineer on par with Franklin Delano Roosevelt. But the attention didn't just stop there. For I received a great deal of praise from more than a few Congressmen as well as a personal call and congratulations from the President of the United States himself, Mr. Jay B. Stevens.

Although the extent of praise I received from Washington was entirely unexpected I have to confess that the recognition was not. For since the changes in Baltimore had pushed much of its crime and societal garbage into other parts of Maryland I was not at all surprised that the implementation of my polices in Maryland had a similar effect on surrounding states and even Washington, D.C. itself. Thus, while on the surface Congress and the President congratulated me on my outstanding leadership it was perfectly clear that they were not at all pleased with the spill over affect of my work on their home city.

While all the national attention was enjoyable, a vindication of sorts, it brought about something I'd never dreamed could happen. For shortly after my landslide reelection for a second term as Governor I received an unusual knock at my door. I was surprised to see the head of the Maryland Democratic Party accompanied by the Party's national chairman. But my surprise at their visit was nothing compared to that at the reason why they'd come. Facing the incumbent Republican they seriously believed that the wave of popularity I was riding was the Democratic Party's best chance to take the White House in 2016. To say the least I was shocked. I reacted by telling them that I'd just begun to accomplish what I'd hoped for in my home state. Besides, I'd never even dreamed of making a bid for the presidency and even if I had, at forty-five years old I was damn sure I was nowhere near ready.

For two hours that night they sat in my living room and for every hesitation I expressed they quickly had an answer. Finally, just to stop the world from spinning I promised them I'd think about it and get back to them. Within the week my name started to be mentioned as a possible presidential contender, my party leaders obviously wanting to test the political waters in order to help me decide. To my surprise the public's response was far more accepting than I'd ever thought possible. Still, despite the thrill of even being considered, the burn of previous racial politics was still fresh in my mind and I couldn't help but wonder if things weren't moving far too fast.

But the party chiefs kept calling and enlisted two dozen or more of the most influential Democrats around the country for support. It was all happening so quickly there just didn't seem to be time to think. Then one night in the solitude of my study Martin's voice called out to me. His memory pointed out that although the Republican incumbent had a war hero reputation and was a master of foreign policy, his failed social policies had merely continued the country's decline. The prison systems, welfare programs, crime, poverty, public schools, and the nurturing of our youth had all become increasingly more pathetic until it seemed there was no hope left.

Then it occurred to me, that even though I'd not yet finished in Maryland what was really the point. For even if I succeeded in completely ridding my state of social afflictions and Maryland became a societal shangrila, what then? Was it possible my state could remain indefinitely an island amidst the chaos, its only salvation the possession of sufficient strength to keep the fallen out or resources enough to raise them to an equal plane. But in all honesty was there any hope of that, one tiny state against the multitudes? Then I realized that Martin was right, my work was not nearly done, and necessity demanded that I accept the challenge once again.

Chapter 16

The legislation. What about the legislation? We've all worked so hard, come so very far. It can't stop now. The people couldn't have made it any more clear than the reelection results. Congress has no place left to turn, no way to deny me yet again. This term was going to take us over the top. But more importantly people had started to see the light, finally begun to realize that it's the only way. Yet here I am dying, just giving up, when so much rests on my shoulders.

Sure Vice President Johnson's a good and kind man but who can honestly expect him to push the legislation through, to avoid some watered down compromise. The opposition's going to nibble and pick away at him until they hang him out to dry, the legislation and the dream right beside him. There's just no doubting that in their minds, he is who he is and his voice, no matter how compassionate, is never going to equal the years of my suffering. But how pathetic to think that merely removing my pain from their eyes will permit the redeadening of their conscience.

No Louis, come on, fight the darkness. You can't give up now. I have to keep fighting to live, for Rachel, for my children, for all of us. We're so very close, so close to taking back what we'd lost. Just keep looking at the light Louis. Stay close to the light and you'll be safe. Don't ever let it slip away.

Upon collecting myself from the initial shock, I began to meet with my most trusted friends and advisors, seeking their opinions on a potential presidential bid. The fact was that I didn't have to work very hard to arrange any of the meetings, for once the state and national party chairs had let the word out, people came looking for me in a rush. The news of my potential candidacy spread like wildfire, catapulting directly from the media recognition I'd received for my Maryland success. Yet I would have been a fool not to see that the media attention burned so fast and bright chiefly due to one and only one thing, my dark black skin.

Although there'd already been a number of black candidates for President there had yet to have been any with a realistic chance of winning. Perhaps it was my political experience as Mayor and Governor or my recent success in taming the societal problems of my state, but for whatever reason from the very first the media treated my potential candidacy with the respect of a legitimate bid. But the media wasn't alone. Everywhere I went I was bombarded with inquiries about my intention to run, from staff members to party operatives to citizens on the street, it seemed that everyone was obsessed as to what my decision would be.

In fact, where I'd been expecting my closest friends and advisors to confirm my skepticism, they did just the opposite, agreeing with the party chairs that I was the right man at the right time. Thus, feeling that all of those voters simply couldn't be wrong I arranged another meeting with the Chair of the National Democratic Party to get a few more specifics and explore my options. I was anticipating a very private meeting between myself and a few of the Party's national big wigs but what I got was a full fledged hand pumping pep rally about my bright prospects for the Democratic nomination and how I would personally carry the party back to prominence.

The Party Chair not only showed up with an impressive array of influential Democrats but a short list of national deep pocket donors already prepared to back me. For with my rising popularity and track record they were confident, that even despite the obvious, the Party could ride me to the White House. The last three presidential campaigns had been so disastrous that the Party leadership felt it was time for something drastic. But as enthusiastic as the meeting was, we all acknowledged that for the good of the Party one crucial issue had yet to be addressed. Thus, as I sat surrounded by the inner circle of Party strength the National Chairman made it perfectly clear that it was all of course contingent upon me being able to attract the white vote. They were fully behind me, that is, as long as my color didn't pose a problem, in which case we all understood they'd have to pull the plug.

As always the political grapevine worked at a blinding speed. Thus, I'd acquired some powerful enemies within the Party before I'd even left the room. To say the least the other Democratic hopefuls viewed my potential bid with bitter disgust. They were not only enraged that the Party hierarchy would desert them but to do it for me, a new face on the scene, when they'd all so patiently awaited their turn added insult to the burn.

In short order, I received a number of communications from the other Democratic hopefuls with the obvious reasons why I shouldn't run seemingly numbering in the hundreds. I have to admit that it was probably the calls from the other candidates that finally stifled my doubts and determined I would run. As I patiently listened to their supposedly well thought out agendas my frustration couldn't help but build. For despite their condescension all I heard was more and more of the same, the very same short sighted self serving political arrogance that had brought the country to its current pathetic state. If anything their sermons as to my weaknesses bolstered my faith in my own budding agenda. For where their supposed solutions just piled ever more muck upon the pile, in contrast I began to see that my vision need only be expanded nationwide.

When word was released that I was fully intent on seeking the Democratic nomination the news swept the nation, the powerful combination of my political doctrines and color of interest across the land. As originally feared the additional attention I drew merely for the sake of my skin quickly proved to be a double edged sword. For despite the fact that I had been tacitly annointed by much of the Party leadership the Party immediately began to split upon color lines of those that could truly envision a black face in the White House and those that could not.

Despite being subjected to the disheartening slight of racial politics yet again I immediately set about piecing together my campaign organization. Starting with the base of my trusted staff from two successful gubernatorial bids the campaign spots quickly started to fill with press secretary, issues advisor, director of day to day operations, and political strategist all being occupied with little difficulty. Surrounded by familiar faces I was just starting to feel comfortable when the politics hit the fan.

I'd initially selected one of my oldest political advisors and most trusted friends, John Knott, to be the campaign's National Chairman. In addition, I'd selected another of my old Maryland friends, James Blakely, to serve as Chief Fund Raiser. It was with both of these selections that the National Party chiefs took issue.

Certainly they agreed that John had done an excellent job of directing my reelection campaign for Governor. But they pointed out he had little to no experience in national politics and a presidential campaign, particularly one of the complex nature I was about to engage in, was no place to be learning on the job. Perhaps the worst dose of political reality had to do with their primary reason why John would be a campaign liability and that was his feature that was most in common with mine, his black skin. For certainly I had to understand that a black candidate was threatening enough and I simply couldn't compound the problem by having my primary front man in black face as well.

James was rejected as well for as a strictly local money man they pointed out he had little hope of pulling in the necessary national dollars. Of course, in a presidential campaign dollars was the paramount word and as I was to quickly find out in constant competition with the issues for attention. For how could one hope to bombard and manipulate the public without the requisite cash. If I'd thought the fund raising numbers were outrageous in my campaigns for Governor I was now forced to think again for the cash required for a presidential bid was astronomical. Preliminary estimates were that over the next year my campaign would have to take in a minimum of forty million dollars just to stay in the race, some $200,000 a day, nearly the equal of the President's yearly pay. Therein, I received my first inkling as to our chief executive's power, that so many were willing to pay so much for the mere hope of obtaining his influence.

In fact, as the campaign schedule began to shake out it appeared that I would be attending some 296 fund raising events in the next year making my old Baltimore morning coffee circuit seem a cake walk in comparison. Somehow I couldn't help but wonder what old George Washington, who captured the presidency with his deeds, would have thought. Of course we could all agree there was nothing wrong with my friend James personally. He just wasn't sufficiently connected. In the end, I capitulated to the suggestions of the Party naming two national Party operatives as my campaign chairman and chief fund raiser and relegating John and James to other slots.

My organization now largely in place I was to formally announce my campaign at the Baltimore Hilton on June 1st, 2015. But the truth be known, I almost backed out before I even officially began. In the National Party bosses minds the naming of their operatives to the two chief positions on my campaign staff had just been the first step. For I quickly found out that their intent was not merely to assist my bid for the presidency but assume control of the campaign and turn me into a mouthpiece for their view of the Party's national agenda.

It all came to a boil with the discussion of platform points in my announcement address when it quickly became apparent that my national campaign chairman, Charlie Kline, and I sat on exactly opposite sides of the fence. I was determined to hit the campaign trail running by telling the people exactly what they could expect from my presidency. The exact same method had worked pretty well for me as both Mayor and Governor and I saw no reason to change. Well Charlie near about hit the roof ranting about how this wasn't just small time state politics we were dealing with but the office of President of the United States and I simply had to understand that the crucial thing about any presidential race was that the candidate had to avoid alienating the voters at all costs. Besides, if I didn't realize that I already had one strike against me just by looking in the mirror maybe it would be best to just forget the whole thing.

It seems that my so called "friends" from the National Party had already determined that my reform policies which won people over in the predominantly urbanized and crime filled state of Maryland didn't stand a chance in the American heartland. They figured the only hope I had of taking the White House was if they could tout my urban successes to the heartland while at the same time reassuring them that as President I would never seek to infringe upon their blessed hometown turf. In short, the National Party wanted my popularity but not my policies. Well maybe I wasn't the quickest learner in the world but by now I sure knew enough from my experiences as Mayor and Governor to know when I was being had. So I had Charlie pick up the phone right then and there and place a call to Rick Butters, the Chairman of the Democratic National Party.

When Charlie started to rant again I hushed him up with a single command and then laid it all out straight as an arrow for Rick to see. Why in the hell did they think I'd become so popular in the first place? Surely they could see that if I took office stripped of my vision I might as well not even go. As I clearly told Rick that I was ready to walk, the current in the room confirmed for me that they thought they needed me far more than I needed them.

Sure Rick still gave me his speech, Charlie bobbing his head in agreement, about how I was deceiving myself if I didn't realize that my policies would play for city blacks but never for rural whites. He even tried a little guilt trip about how he couldn't believe I'd take this attitude after all they'd done for me. But I'd already clearly drawn the line and both of them knew there'd be no backing down. Still, just before the receiver clicked off Rick took one last shot.

"We'll back you through Iowa Louis but you better damn well remember you're out on your own on this one and I'll not let the Party be dragged along with you. If you fall you fall alone."

By the time I officially entered the race the field was already crowded. With five other candidates it promised to be a hotly contested campaign. But the early backing I'd received from the party chieftans along with the strong and well organized efforts of my campaign staff quickly put the others on notice that I was far more than a long shot. In fact, my national name recognition as the urban saviour coupled with the fact that each of the two front runners had already failed in past Democratic nomination bids made it apparent that even despite my color I had realistic potential. Nevertheless with Rick's ultimatum still ringing in our ears Charlie and I turned our eyes to the Iowa caucases well aware that I needed a strong showing to even stay alive.

I campaigned with a passion nationwide. But as the Iowa caucuses neared while the other candidates split time amongst the various states on the primary trial I practically lived in Iowa. I was well aware that if I captured a significant percentage of their heartland vote it would automatically send a stamp of approval to rural whites in the rest of the country. Day after day we travelled the snow splattered highways with me speaking to anyone who was willing to listen. Then, we'd return to our convoy of cars and busses and drive someplace else seldom getting to bed before two in the morning. Yet for all the acceptance and open ears I encountered inevitably there were also the doors slammed in my face and the irrational rejections from that winter land of white.

But the premature pollsters were proven wrong as the Iowa results came in and to the amazement of all I not only captured a significant percentage of the vote but finished third less than fifteen percentage points behind the front runner. The late night thumbs up call from Rick Butters sent us directly to New Hampshire where the campaigning culminated in a five way candidate debate with only Governor Davis of New York, the front runner, declining in light of his signifigant lead.

If there was a crucial point of the primaries it would have to have been the New Hampshire debate. For while at first the crowd seemed cold toward me, by the midpoint they warmed and my post debate reception drew by far the most enthusiastic crowd. As many people approvingly told me I was the only candidate to specifically state my plans, at that early date my opponents all opting for Charlie Kline's oft expressed rule of presidential campaigning, "avoid alienating the voters at all costs."

Well apparently the straight talking citizens of New Hampshire loved my approach and I actually placed second in the six way contest with twenty-four percent of the vote. Governor Davis captured his second win taking thirty-one percent and Harlan Johnson, the Senator from Texas, carried eighteen. Needless to say the decision by Governor Davis to skip the debate was not well received by the people of New Hampshire.

After the New Hampshire results three candidates dropped out turning it into a three way race between Governor Davis, Senator Johnson and myself. But despite my strong showings in both Iowa and New Hampshire there was a sense that the the nation was still skeptically holding its breath, few willing to state it outwardly but all thinking the same, that my success had been just a fluke. Yet at least there was one noticeable impact from my early postings. Both Charlie Kline and Rick Butters stopped trying to convince me to back off my agenda and began urging me to just keep doing whatever it was I was doing.

Despite the overall sense of skepticism I continued to post strong showings and though I had my share of losses I continued to pile up convention delegates at a rate on par with Governor Davis. The end result was that Senator Johnson dropped out of the race after Super Tuesday the strength of his showing in his home state of Texas not nearly convincing enough for him to continue. If anything Senator Johnson's exit worked to my favor and my margins of victory increased particularly in the more urbanized states such as Ohio, Illinois, and California. Yet one nagging fact still remained clear. Although our polling efforts encountered general approval of my platform the election results were never as one sided as the issues polls indicated. In the end, we were finally forced to admit that the average voter's reluctance to reject my color in public was having a significant impact once the voting booth curtains closed.

Nevertheless, despite all the skepticism, by the last week in May it became obvious that I would total a sufficient number of convention delegates to take the nomination. It was then that Governor Davis and his supporters began calling for an "open convention." The numbers were such that the only chance to defeat me was for Governor Davis to induce some of the delegates I'd already won to vote differently at the convention from the way their people had instructed them at home. But while the term "open convention" sounded democratic and the mere excitement of it acted as a form of attraction, in reality it was anything but. For it would allow the convention delegates to ignore the results of their state elections and free them to negotiate on their own. In reality it would turn it into a "brokered" convention where the final decision would be made by secret trading for delegate votes in the convention hall's private rooms.

My supporters within the party hit the roof, for if there was any circumstance which would permit the ugly influence of racial politics to taint the results, it was just such an open convention format. But despite our best efforts to pressure Governor Davis he refused to back down. The Governor persisted in holding up the banner of party fairness as a shield when in reality his only concern was that he avoid the stigma of becoming a two time loser at any cost, even if the party had to go down in the national election as a result.

Despite my rage at his tactics, I fully recognized the party split which might occur if he continued his chosen path and after consulting with Rick and Charlie I determined that everyone's interests would best be served if I could effect a reconciliation. Thus, in an attempt to soothe our differences I met with the Governor in private and suggested we serve on the same ticket if he would consider being Vice President.

Well for the life of me I guess the stress of the campaign had just been to much for him, because he broke into a rage which almost forced me to physically restrain him, expletives and insults flying fast and furious. My surprise at his reaction was such that to this day I can't recall much of what he said with the exception of those last words which followed him out the door.

"How dare you think that I'd ever serve beneath the likes of you."

I guess for my part I just couldn't believe that a man capable of behaving in such a manner could ever have envisioned himself in the White House in the first place.

Forced to take the bad news back to my camp, I met with my staff and we determined that Governor Davis might want to take himself down and the Party right along with him. But we certainly weren't going to let him do it without a fight. Thus, I immediately arranged a meeting with Senator Johnson from Texas to discuss the nomination and platform as well as the upcoming general election. Over the course of a six hour dialogue we both found out that we had by far more in common than we ever could have believed possible in the battle mentality of our respective campaigns.

After excusing myself to confer with Charlie and Rick the three of us quickly reached unanimous agreement. Senator Harlan Johnson was the absolutely best choice to be my running mate as Vice-President. He was viewed by the public as fairly moderate, he could help us capture his electoral rich home state of Texas, and he had twelve plus years of congressional experience to balance the fact that I would be a newcomer on Capital Hill. But as our hands clasped with his hearty acceptance, one simple but necessary qualification he brought to our ticket stood out perhaps more than any other. Senator Johnson was white.

With Senator Johnson safely on board I was simply amazed that we ever could have considered Governor Davis in the first place, it being hard to imagine more different personalities than these two respective men. But I guess it just goes to show again that politics sometimes almost makes strange bedfellows.

We went immediately to work, with Senator Johnson stepping right in sync, contacting convention delegates both to announce my running mate and to convince them to vote down the proposed open convention format. With over four thousand delegates it was to say the least a monumental task. Harlan and I naturally focused on the most influential of the delegates, that is those with the clout to sway other votes. The end results of our last minute phone campaign were better than we'd hoped for and the question of an open convention soon became nothing more than a bad dream.

Nevertheless, Governor Davis refused to lay down using his speaking opportunity during the platform debates to launch a final personal attack on my character. In fact, the utter vulgarity of his last ditch effort, which he'd so hoped would irreparably split the party and destroy any chance I had in the general election, only served to unify much of the bad blood. For even those who for so long had believed me to be their enemy were horrified by the display. In the end, Governor Davis was even shouted off the convention floor, the roar growing so loud even the microphones couldn't make him heard. I suppose, ever so appropriately, the Governor left the hall in disgust.

The final vote was taken the following day and the next evening I went to Madison Square Garden to accept the Democratic Presidential Nomination. I'm told that the night of my acceptance was literally cause for rejoicing by Republican strategists across the country for not only had we the Democrats nominated a presidential candidate amidst a huge party split and controversy, but a black one at that. Come to think of it, as we started in working on the general election campaign, I'm not so sure that most people didn't agree with them.

Chapter 17

Perhaps the Republicans were right, for the post convention polls placed my incumbent opponent with a lead of some twenty-one percentage points. But if the Republicans saw fit to giggle about a second term already won, my staff and I looked for the silver lining, that at the very least when election day came the people would be able to clearly distinguish between the two of us. For there could not have been a greater difference between myself and the man I faced.

President Jason Baines Stevens was the son of one of our last surviving World War II heroes, his father a decorated veteran of Iwo Jima and Guadalcanal. After the war his father had returned to America's great wealth and promise and rode the tide of her economic success to a vast fortune in the Pacific Basin trade.

Like his father before him young Jay began in the military, although with Jay things were slightly different. Instead of being drafted Jay received an appointment to West Point, the senior Senator from California being one of his father's "closest" friends. But just as his father before him Jay rose to the challenge, naturally finishing high in his class, a tribute to his lineage. Then, as a Captain in the Army he fought with distinction in the Gulf War. Victory was all the sweeter because Jay, like many, viewed it as the long awaited return to American power, particularly after the disappointments of Vietnam so many wished to forget.

As his father did before him Jay came home a hero but chose politics over business as a more direct route to power. His father's money and connections behind him Jay's political rise was meteoric and he recited the family mantra all the while, as to how men like they had always made America great. For Jay, like his father, truly believed in America's revival and that returning the nation to their guidance was all that was required.

First a seat in Congress, then the vacant Senate seat of his father's retiring friend, until at last, in 2012, their years of effort bore fruit and father and son brought home their coveted presidential prize. Then, just as he'd done in the House and Senate, his presidency preached the nation's greatness while attacking with a vengeance those he deemed fit to blame. His power of persuasion was immense for he'd trained and practiced well. Thus, the majority basked securely in the strength of his mantra trusting it to purge the evils which marred their streets and days. For through the years Jay had learned one thing so very well that it had long ceased to be necessary for America's leaders to actually live their creeds, when credibility could be had for mere lip service just as well.

Perhaps the Republicans were right to laugh at my bid, I ranting on so about America's inevitable demise, the bothersome antithesis of their champion. After all who could expect anything less in the polarization that America'd become, so far apart and different we'd really all become the same. Black face, white face, yellow and brown, each now so utterly concerned with itself there was no room left for the other. But what better contest to bring forth our nation's supreme leader than the two of us toe to toe. One white face, one black, one the self professed champion of all that had been good against the other, I the prophet of all that had gone bad. Go ahead then. Bring on the challenge, for after all wasn't it every American citizen's paramount right, first and foremost, to be entertained?

Before the dust and hoopla of the convention had even settled we'd begun assessing the latest polls and our approach to the general election. After reviewing the nationwide voter reports the meeting's mood was somber but determined. The truth is, it was hard not to be a little down coming directly from the convention's euphoria smack into another uphill climb. But even though the polls showed we had a lot of ground to make up there was still room for optimism.

After all, it's natural for the incumbent to start with a lead, particularly when the challenger was as relatively unknown on the national scene as I. But the bad thing about starting off way ahead is there's always plenty of room to fall and if anything I'd just started to come out of the political closet. For in a few short months, I'd bested two well known national political figures and gone a long way toward unifying a party that seemed hell bent on committing election day suicide. Not to mention the fact that I'd come through a volatile primary, if anything more credible and popular than when I'd started, while President Stevens had yet to answer word one of campaign heat.

Beyond that our greatest cause for optimism was the fact the polls showed a much higher percentage than usual of undecided voters. The percentage of uncommitted voters in most states was close to thirty percent, more than enough to swing the election even in President Stevens' electorally rich home state of California. In fact, when I say most states, there was one exception, that being my home state of Maryland where I had an overwhelming twenty-eight percent lead in the polls with only five percent undecided. Thus, while at first glance the polls looked disappointing we were well aware there was plenty of room for movement and thus our general attitude could best be described as "hungry" as we set about plotting campaign strategy.

Despite the presence of some positive signs all of us agreed, this time even Charlie Kline and Rick Butters, that our best shot was to keep the campaign as substantive and issue based as possible. For it went without saying that just as it had in the primaries, the color issue would inevitably come. We decided our most effective strategy would be to treat the color issue as if it didn't even exist, forcing our opponents to risk alienating color blind voters should they sink to racial politics. For my part, I would continue to follow up on my straight talking campaign of the primaries fully intent on convincing those that might fear my skin that I had absolutely nothing to hide and clearly setting forth the reasons behind my agenda for all to see. It was my hope that the sincerity and honesty of my speeches would prove to all that

I was fully competent and, that based on my record and that alone, I deserved their vote, even despite the nature of my skin.

Thus, a crucial part of our strategy involved having as many debates as possible with President Stevens to clearly define for the voters the contrast in our policies. But if our camp had come to the decision that a series of debates and an issues campaign would be to our advantage then President Steven's political advisors had reached the exact opposite conclusion. They rejected all of our overtures to debate without even the slightest consideration and where I addressed each speech directly to the issues President Stevens campaigned on a platform of style.

Unable to engage my opponent directly, we began our final run through the southern states with Virginia, planning to work our way through the entire southern region before starting our western campaign. Everything went as smoothly as can be expected until September 4th when I reached Jackson, Mississippi, where I was scheduled to speak from the courthouse steps that very afternoon.

But when I arrived Josh Reynolds, my events organizer, pulled me aside in a panic and informed me that a group of some one hundred Klansmen had received a permit to march at the time of my speech. Josh said he'd tried his best to have local officials prohibit the march but that we were bucking directly against the free speech clause and asked me whether I wanted to postpone my speech or cancel. Well I was shocked he'd even suggest a change, but after I collected myself I told him to just make sure the microphone system had enough volume.

Naturally, the press had gotten wind of it so the open space in front of the courthouse was jam packed. Still, I began my address at 3:00 p.m. sharp as scheduled and sure enough at about 3:10 here came a group of at least a hundred hooded Klansmen, with police escort, marching up the street. The rest of the audience obviously became quite agitated but nevertheless, I continued with my speech calmly addressing the points I'd intended.

David L. Dukes

When the Klansmen came as close as the outer fringe of the crowd would permit they began to chant a mixture of derogatory comments and racial slurs. The gathering quickly began to work itself into a frenzy both sides exchanging insults and converging toward the police separation line. To say the least it appeared that a riot was imminent. It was at that point that I motioned for Josh to turn up the mike volume until my voice cracked out like thunder and I said, "People, my dear people. I truly appreciate the fact that you came to hear me speak and I do assure you that you'll be able to hear. Now please ignore the children as I'd like to continue my address."

Well the crowd hushed for an instant and then went wild with laughter and applause before finally redirecting their attention toward me. The Klansman continued to chant but were drowned out by the thunder of my words and as for me, I took the interruption personally, so I continued to speak for another two hours until the Klansman became bored and went home. Personally I was amazed their attention span lasted that long.

The day's affect on the campaign was like a shot in the arm as I was heralded around the country for my strength and composure under pressure. The press made such a big deal of my performance it even forced President Stevens to publicly condemn the "vile racist behavior" of the Klansmen and praise my fortitude. But the best part was I took a leap in the polls closing to within thirteen points of President Stevens.

Yet despite my leap in the polls President Stevens still skirted any sort of candidate interchange. He was content to let his associates attack me while he remained out of harms way. And attack me they did. In the eyes of the conservative religious and political groups I had become the great inner city black satan fully intent on manipulating the powers of their government and tax dollars to break up their cherished families, steal their children away from them and indoctrinate their young with all of the sins and evils that our urban Sodom and Gomorrahs could muster. For to hear them speak my agenda was the reincarnation of the Hitler and Communist youth programs all rolled into one.

A steady diet of such propaganda made it easy to recall my first campaign for Governor and remember that I'd been in exactly this position once before. But to me one of the few beautiful things of American politics has always been that no matter who you are or what your status one fact of campaigning holds eternally true. You can run but you can't hide. Thus, I determined that if the President refused to engage me I would simply hold the debate by myself.

From that point on I never missed an opportunity to contrast the President's platform with my own, hammering home to the public again and again the distinction between his style and my substance, his vague statements and my specifics. Thus, where President Stevens touted his political experience over mine I noted that he'd never governed anywhere but on "the Hill" and that while his home city of Washington, D.C. and state of California were enduring ever increasing societal decay my home city and state were flourishing for the first time since World War II.

Where he praised the success of his administration's economic policies I pointed out that over the last two years Baltimore and Maryland were the only two political jurisdictions in the country to have actually decreased the costs of their public schools and public safety, by far and away the two most costly governmental expenditures. Then, finally to his assertion that during his presidency Americans had enjoyed an unparalleled "lifestyle" and "quality of life" I publicly questioned, "how is it that we as Americans enjoy President Stevens' so called world's best "quality of life" when we fear to even walk our own streets."

If anything the President became more and more withdrawn under my assault as if all he hoped for was to simply ride out the tide. But by mid-October the combination of my direct accusations and his refusal to respond had gained me another seven points in the polls. In fact, we'd closed to within six points with, from my camp's view, the best thing being that most polls still showed a whopping twenty-two percent undecided.

The numbers obviously became too close for my opponent's comfort because as the campaign reached the home stretch we finally received an agreement to debate. The debate was to be held in San Francisco the week before election day and after a great deal of preparation I came in fully loaded. The truth is, the feeling it was do or die was no help to my nerves and though I was well prepared I just prayed that I'd get through the first five minutes. But to my surprise as the two of us shook hands at the start it was President Stevens who was the more ill at ease and I have to admit his discomfort did a hell of a lot for my composure.

The debate was no more than a repeat of all the issues I'd been campaigning so hard on the past months with one notable exception, President Stevens was now in the hot seat with no place to hide. The more he stumbled the stronger I became to the point where a few times I even interrupted his miscues to fill in the fact or statistic he was searching for. At the midpoint break I could see advisors swarming about him like so many piranhas as it was obvious to everyone involved that the President was in real trouble.

That's when the President reached for what he believed to be his trump card and in the following series of direct candidate to candidate questions he took his best shot. Briefly prefacing his question by reciting all the demonic characteristics his campaign had attributed to me he asked, "If my agenda wouldn't just be stepping into yet another great "black hole" with the real intent behind my program being nothing more than to ask the good people of this country to keep forever training the children of those too lazy to care. For when would I admit to the American people and myself that it was me and my kind, so intent on breaking up the American family, that was bringing society to its knees?"

The audience drew an audible gasp at his attack and though I knew he was trying to suck me in I refused to back away.

"Mr. Stevens," I said, "I certainly would agree with you that my skin is black and yours white. I believe it's plainly evident for all to see. But what's not plainly evident to me is why you and your administration have been so content with merely pointing out who's to blame for our country's problems. Actually sir, it's kind of ironic that you who so proudly speaks of your strong family background and father would portray me as the anti-family demon. For if you'd actually listened to any of my words these past months you'd know that above all else I stand for the protection and restoration of the American family as our sole salvation. In fact, I would have thought that you among all people with all the privileges and benefits of your strong family life would have been the first to reach out to me, and as you say, my kind, in recognition that you've always had the one thing that we've so desperately wanted, a family and father.

But all that aside, the truth is that personally I don't care who's to blame because I don't figure that to be part of the job description as President of the United States. I say to you sir and to the American people that if elected I'll have one and only one thing in mind and that's not pointing out the problems, it's fixing them."

The President's plan for the second half of the debate lost its steam then and there and he literally melted on stage. His fire gone, the remainder of the debate passed as merely a rather bland session of Q and A, with everyone aware of just who had emerged as the victor.

By the weekend the polls indicated that we were pretty much dead even so in the final few days I moved as rapidly as possible to all the key places I could reach, frantically making a last ditch effort to swing the undecided vote. The excitement of the crowds rose to a feverish pitch with me seemingly shaking hands from dawn to midnight. Then, after my final cross country swing Rachel and I returned to Baltimore for election day to await the people's decision. After casting my vote, I went directly to our suite at the Baltimore Hilton where Rachel, the kids and I and a small group of my closest friends and advisors awaited the returns.

The early returns from the exit polls showed that we were running a very tight race. Thus, we all settled down for what we anticipated to be a nerve wracking night. But as the count progressed I started to gradually build a small lead and by 10:00 p.m. it became apparent that President Stevens was in serious trouble. Although I was not to receive his concession call until early the next morning, by 2:00 a.m. it was obvious to everyone what the final result would be.

When I entered our campaign headquarters a half hour later I was shocked by the cheers, for due to the lateness of the hour, I'd expected the majority of my supporters to have already gone home. But if anything the crowd had grown and the hall was packed with such whooping and hollering it sounded as if we'd won a war. The final margin of victory failed to give me the popular mandate that I'd hoped for. But as I stood at the podium surveying the crowd, I couldn't have had a greater feeling of accomplishment. The ever present dread throughout the race was that I'd never be able to pull the white vote, yet here my supporters stood before me in equal numbers of black and white.

As I looked out upon them it was of the paler skins that I was most proud. For unlike many of my brothers and sisters who attributed their success solely to contributions by their own kind, I fully recognized that it was only the acceptance of those quiet white faces which had granted me the honor to serve as the forty-sixth President of the United States.

Chapter 18

Just before noon on January 20, 2017, Rachel and I were picked up from Blair House, the Washington guest house for visiting heads of state, and driven through the White House gates. Jason and Lisa Stevens were waiting for us and, by tradition, he and I got in one car and Rachel and Mrs. Stevens in another for the drive to the inaugural ceremonies. As we drove up Pennsylvania Avenue the President and I were seated side by side, but despite my attempts at conversation, he uttered nary a word refusing even to look me in the eye.

In fact, his behavior was just as it had been a few days before when Rachel and I had gone to the White House to see the rooms where we'd be living for the first time. We'd been looking forward to the Stevens giving us a tour of the family quarters, one first couple to another, but they turned us over to the White House staff almost as soon as we'd arrived and beat a hasty retreat. I suppose that Rachel and I could have taken this as an insult but after Governor Dixon's poor performance at my first gubernatorial inauguration our skins had thickened and we'd become accustomed to expecting the worst.

The inauguration was being held on the west side of the Capitol and hundreds of thousands of people were already waiting, stretched as far as the eye could see. The press, as usual, had already been making a big deal out of the fact that the inaugural crowd was by far the biggest ever. For aside from the normal compliment of interested citizens and onlookers the crowd had grown ten fold with the mass arrival of black citizens from across the country, for whom my inauguration represented so much.

In the distance, standing watch above the people, was the shining white column of the Washington Monument. Then beyond it, at the far end of the Mall the Lincoln Memorial, inside of which sat the bronze skinned statue of Abraham, a monument to me so very special. First Harlan was sworn in as Vice President. Then I placed my own hand upon the bible to swear my oath. It was all so very hard to take in and I muttered the oath in a trance like state finding it simply unbelievable that a child of the welfare state could have ever become President of the United States.

Because it had been the central focus of my campaign and in my mind the reason for my entire political career, I devoted a good deal of my address to the nation's youth. I noted that as the country had become ever more enamored with its own grandiose power we'd devoted less attention to those little tasks which nurture children into citizens. Then, I restated my long held conviction that in the idealistic name of progress our government had usurped the people's power, permitting our cancers to grow while at the same time forbidding the common citizen from stamping them out. But now that decay had finally reared its ugly head it wasn't enough for big government merely to return the people's control. For if a lofty government of idealism had taken our power away then a righteous government of reality must halt the decay and give our power back. As the newly elected head of the governmental beast, I pledged then and there to do just that.

Yet as I spoke gazing out on that sea of blackness I wondered if even they could truly see my vision. For it seemed the only real point of interest was not my platform but my skin. First black President. First black President. First black President. Again and again and again until I almost had to scream. All the black skins so congratulating, always winking as if it were our own special secret and all the white skins so slyly whispering just how well they understood. Why couldn't they all simply understand I was no different from any of them and that all I really wanted was just to be like everyone else. But then again maybe it was all the excitement and I was giving it more thought than it was worth or perhaps I was just too sensitive. After all, did John F. Kennedy ever hear about anything at the start but his

Catholicism or youth and if it didn't bother him who was I to be so different?

For that matter, what's wrong with acknowledging people's differences anyway. I'd be a idiot to think my individualities or anyone else's could ever go completely unnoticed. Only a fool could ever believe that people are truly equal, failing to recognize the fat or thin, tall or short, smart or dumb, or strong or weak. Besides, if the good Lord didn't want us to see the differences wouldn't he have made us all the same? Or if it's Charlie Darwin's science that's preferred, then God made us different for a reason, to give the frailness that is our species more strength through diversity, a better chance to survive in the beautiful but hostile world in which he placed us. In fact, how can anyone help but see that a man's strength in one environment becomes his weakness in the next.

All that's necessary is that we use both the instincts and reasoning we've been given to further our own adaptation. In fact, it's pretty basic to see that any society's only hope to survive is by rewarding characteristics that enhance the collective good and striving to eliminate those that don't. Yet never can we forget, throughout this constant struggle, that these differences in each of us are man's greatest source of strength.

My inaugural address ended the ceremonies and we went into the Capitol for lunch with the members of Congress and other invited guests. After lunch we rode back to Pennsylvania Avenue and from a pavilion set up on the White House front lawn reviewed a fine inaugural parade. Originally, I wanted to follow Jimmy Carter's idea and walk from the Capitol to the White House shaking a few hands along the way. I guess I'd just wanted to feel like I was one of the people, part of the people, my people.

But the idea was nixed by my Secret Service detail as far too dangerous with all the crazies out there, particularly on inauguration day. So I capitulated to the concerns of my security detail having become accustomed to their watchful eye ever since my first big primary win. For in fact my Secret Service detail was assigned immediately after New Hampshire with everyone quite aware of the added threat my skin color posed. Yet as I rode down Pennsylvania Avenue waving from the back of my armored limousine I couldn't help but taste the bitter irony. Here I'd finally reached the highest office in the land yet was still forced to hide from the ignorance of those who hated my skin.

When the parade finally ended Rachel and I walked together alone toward the White House and though we'd known for some time that the moment would come nothing could have prepared us for the emotion of entering our new home. We walked through the front door entering what is known as the State Floor, being the part of the White House that's open to public tours, and then took an elevator to the second floor where the two of us would be living. As the elevator doors closed behind us we stood in a huge, long hall with a high ceiling that extended almost the full length of the White House. Through an archway on the west side of the hall we could see our new living room and as we walked down the hallway it was quite easy to get swept away.

In a daze I tried to imagine the sound of the footsteps and voices of those who'd lived here before. Roosevelt, Truman, Kennedy, and especially Lincoln, the emancipator of my ancestors, his bedroom still furnished exactly as it was when he lived here. Next to his bedroom sat the Grand Treaty Room, its walls lined with historic treaties and other documents, including the Emancipation Proclamation. Then, adjoining the magnificent center hallway was the formal living room, a thirty by forty foot oval room which opened onto the Truman balcony.

Then as I was about to be overwhelmed by the sheer majesty of it all I caught myself and remembered why I was here. For the people had called on me to deliver my vision and distractions I simply could not permit. I excused myself from Rachel after telling her how much I loved her in a hug and followed a Secret Service agent to the Oval Office. As soon as I entered the security agents closed the doors and I was alone. Sitting there at my desk I reviewed my life to date focusing long and hard on both the blessings and the pain. For I had finally reached a summit from which I could go no higher. My success or failure and society's hope would come from the chair in which I now sat or not at all. At peace in my isolation I offered a prayer to God for assistance and gave silent thanks to Chet and Martin. Then my internal strength reassured I went to dress for the evening's inaugural festivities. The media could report what it liked as I was going to fully enjoy the moment, for with the dawn the real work would at last begin.

Rachel and I adjusted more easily to life in the White House than we ever could have imagined, for after the initial shock wore off, we fell right in to treating it as our home. Nevertheless, acutely aware of the level of scrutiny we were under and wanting as little distraction from my domestic agenda as possible, we decided that the less changes we made in the day to day routine of the White House, the better. However, I did make one simple change.

Since the start of the campaign it seemed that I was constantly surrounded by a press of people seldom able to have even a single moment alone. Then, on the first day in our new home I found that the security men were all around me even to the point of opening each door as I approached it. Well I certainly realized the need for security precautions but I hadn't come all this way from the chains of slavery and poverty to feel caged in my own home. Thus, from that moment on I directed the security personnel to stay at a distance while I was in my living and working area so I could finally have some peace.

One of the well known facts of the presidency is that the First Lady receives a great deal of attention. While First Ladies through the years have chosen various paths from totally avoiding public life to continuing their roles as wives and mothers, participating in Washington society life, or even actively involving themselves in the administration's agenda, one thing was certain that Rachel would be under the public microscope from the start. In fact, from the earliest days of the campaign, the potential for Rachel to become the first black First

Lady of America had received nearly as much attention as my own candidacy.

However, exactly as she'd been doing since the day I first met her, through my time as Mayor, Governor, and then President, she handled it all with grace and style. For through the years it was always Rachel more than any other who was by my side. Others seemed to come and go but there was no denying that she'd always been my right hand woman, my counselor, my strength, my love, and I had no doubt that as we faced this new challenge together, she would continue to be by my side, in all her strength and wisdom, until the day I died.

During those first weeks I shook hands with literally thousands of people greeting governors, local officials, business executives, members of Congress, military personnel, the diplomatic corp and many others. It seemed that everyone wanted to meet the new man in town and the interest of foreign governments was far more urgent than with any president of recent memory. Around the world my election was viewed with a mixture of elation and unease. The darker skins of the world tended to view my election as the true end of European colonialism with a descendent of former slaves rising to the most powerful office on earth being a sure sign that the equality of man had finally triumphed. Racial and ethnic realities around the world being what they are, it would have been naive not to recognize that more than a few in the world community viewed my rise as a threat, the darkness of my skin perceived as ominous for a myriad number of reasons.

Being such a novelty I received requests for state visits in record numbers with some sixty-seven nations extending invitations in my first thirty days. Perhaps the biggest surprise was that, with the exception of Algeria and Lybia, every nation on the African continent invited me to come. But however I was viewed the reaction was the same. Peoples and nations the world over collectively held their breath and awaited what America's first black president would do with so much power.

Perhaps to the chagrin of many, I chose Africa for my first foreign visit, with the implications of my decision sparking much speculation and debate. But in the final analysis my choice had no great geopolitical signifigance. For our nation's political interests required as part of my duties that I eventually visit much of the world. Thus in recognition that I had to start somewhere I chose the continent of my roots.

Of course, my four nation swing of Africa included the crucial states of Egypt, Nigeria, and South Africa. But in deference to our country's past I also made one less strategic stop. In fact, my brief two day visit to Ghana had far greater impact on me than I ever could have imagined. For though I was well aware of the history I'd be seeing, I had no idea just how hard it would hit home.

My tour of the slave trade ruins was for me the most ghastly of rememberances, the screams and suffering of long lost ancestors beckoning horribly from the silence. In fact, it was terribly hard to draw myself away, almost as if my mere lingering could somehow wipe away their pain. But my hosts were far more interested in discussing their foreign aid package so I was ushered from the ruins, wined and dined, until all felt the time was just right. It was then and only then that their request for more money came. Thanking them for their hospitality I returned my by then standard reply that such matters of course required appropriate channels with all things coming in time.

Yet, as much as the slave ruins affected me, the King's final question struck me far more. He confessed to me in fact that he'd been wanting to ask me since I first arrived but had only just then developed the nerve.

"You see President Hayes the one thing I've always wanted to know, particularly since so many of our fellow Africans were sent to slavery from these very shores, is why after all the progress you American blacks have made do you still insist on calling each other nigger?"

After struggling to find a response I had to admit that I really didn't know the answer and that, "only a small minority of us do so" rang quite hollow as a reply. As we lifted off from Africa I stared back at the coast of my origin but the miles left me only to wonder if I'd ever be known for being anything but black.

The international attention was all well and good but I had come to this office with one primary purpose in mind. Above all else I was determined that before my watch was done the country would be started on the long road back to civic responsibility. Throughout the campaign I'd hammered home my vision for restoring American society utilizing the same principles that had achieved such dramatic success in Baltimore and Maryland. In the election the people had spoken choosing my agenda with their collective voice. Now it was my responsibility to see that I implemented just that choice.

To accomplish this goal I set about assembling my White House staff the morning after the election. Beginning with the political family that had served me so well as Governor and in my campaign for the presidency I began to sift through the names from which I'd select my executive staff. Chief of Staff, Press Secretary, Chief Congressional Liaison, Legislative Coordinator, Legal Counsel and Assistant to the President for National Security Affairs were just a few of the many key positions to be filled. As many of us had worked together for years there was a certain trust and comfort as I began to see familiar faces fill out my staff but with an eye toward the group's relative inexperience in Washington I also made certain to balance out the staff with a healthy number of Washington insiders.

As with my personal staff I chose my cabinet members and other officials with great care. For though I did not have the luxury of prior relationships with all of my choices, I selected them from among proven leaders with strong reputations for expertise and character. The Secretaries of State, Education, Treasury, Defense, Interior, Agriculture, Commerce, Labor, Health, Education and Welfare, Housing and Urban

Development and Transportation, Energy, the Attorney General, National Security Advisor and Director of the Office of Management and Budget would complete the collection of advisors I'd come to rely on so much.

The most disappointing aspect of my staff selection was the fact that the press constantly scrutinized my actions in terms of race, even going so far during the appointment process to engage in such idiotic speculations as the "Black White House Staff" and the "Colored Cabinet." Honestly, sometimes it seemed as if there was no level to which the press wouldn't stoop to sell a few advertisements. But all said and done, other than my own skin, the composition of my administration ended up being for the most part just like any other presidency of recent memory. Just the same I made personally sure that every member of my staff was fully aware before they came on board that I was going to conduct my administration not as a black president but as "The President" and none of them better forget it.

Despite the strain inherent in selecting the staff responsible for guiding me through all the myriad tasks of my presidency I'd have to say that my most difficult appointment by far came in my fourth month in office. It was then that Chief Justice Milner died. In recent history the composition of the Court had been amazingly stable, not having received a new appointee since 1999. Thus, as if a Supreme Court nomination wasn't newsworthy enough as a life long appointment to the most autonomous branch of government, the scrutiny was heightened by the fact that I would be appointing the first Supreme Court Justice of the new millennium.

I began the process by asking the Attorney General, Bob Richter, to narrow the search for potential candidates. Within the month we had a short list of respected jurists each of whom appeared to possess both the legal intellect and judicial integrity to fill the job. But then as with seemingly everything else in my presidency the discussion turned to color with each segment of the population loudly shouting its reasons as to why one of their own should be selected.

David L. Dukes

Naturally, many black citizens felt, that as one of their own, I'd appoint a black solidifying the legal gains which had come so hard for my people. For in the majority of the black community's mind it seemed that anything less could only be viewed as a sell out. Then, there were the white males who firmly believed that one black on the court was already enough and with two women currently sitting the only logical solution was white and male. Beyond that there were other minority groups, abortion activists, both pro and con, feminists, gays, lesbians, church groups and every other conceivable societal grouping of people from the most radical to the most extreme.

As our search narrowed, I personally interviewed the top seven candidates, paying no mind to their societal grouping and finding them all to be well qualified. But as the time for my decision neared I found the cacaphony of conflicting advice literally no help at all. I still clearly recall that as I was pondering Lincoln's sacrifice on my first official visit to Ford's Theatre the answer suddenly just popped into my head. So in the end I selected Alvin Gonzalez of the Texas Court of Appeals. For in truth, if the Court already had five white males, two white females and a black male I saw no reason why the nation's Hispanic citizens at eighteen percent of the population shouldn't have a justice on the court as well.

In fact, the biggest surprise of the whole process was that after all the public racial hoopla, the Senate offered next to no resistance to my selection, going no further than some behind the scenes groans. The country having long since become used to the Senate's political cruxifiction of every Supreme Court nominee, I guess the public was just as surprised as I. I guess it just goes to show that where matters of race are concerned people are seldom, if ever, rational. But despite the fact that my Supreme Court appointment failed to become a racial stone throw I was still haunted by the fear that inevitably the sole defining quality of my presidency would be the color of my skin.

Although the appointment process and piecing together my administration was an immense task we finished in time to meet as a full cabinet and plan our first days in Washington. In fact, my advisors and I had been fleshing out our legislative goals since the day after the election. Thus, with my administration in place and a well defined agenda we began the task of implementing our plans the morning after the inauguration. But while my staff and I looked forward to the upcoming session of Congress with great optimism, the Republican majority in both Houses had entirely different ideas.

The Republican congressional leadership made it clear from their post election comments that their view of the election results was quite different than our own. For while we viewed my victory as a call to implement my agenda they attributed my narrow margin of victory to the people's indecision. To the political animals that roamed the Hill, public uncertainty meant one and only one thing, a license for Congress to do as it pleased.

Despite my campaign pledge to accomplish my goals or go down fighting I fully recognized the necessity to work with my colleagues on the Hill. Thus, I took the initiative right after election day, first meeting with Maryland's congressional delegation then branching out to fellow Democrats, the Black Caucus, and finally my Republican opponents. In fact, much of the transition period was devoted to discussing with as many legislators as possible the multitude of issues that would confront my presidency. Then, in turn I met with the Foreign Relations Committees of both the Senate and House, the committees on HEW, Defense, Taxation, and as many other key legislators as I could reasonably schedule.

Though most of the meetings seemed to go fairly well it quickly became obvious that the entrenched political animals that stalked the Hill were not nearly as impressed with their new chief executive as I'd hoped. More than a few of the top leaders felt they were far more deserving of the Oval Office than I, and the party splits that had surfaced in the Democratic primaries certainly didn't serve to help my cause. In addition, my early congressional relations suffered due to the fact that I'd so emphasized the power of the people in my campaign, proudly touting my use of their power in the State of Maryland and Baltimore. Well if there was one thing that irked my friends on the Hill more than anything else, be they elephant or donkey, it was the threat of their chief executive doing an end run around their authority and going directly to the people.

Perhaps the most disappointing thing was that the overwhelming Republican majority viewed themselves as the true visionaries having just passed yet another crime package in the prior session. The seventh such attempt in the last twelve years, it was plain for all but Congress to see that they were merely adding more of the same, failing even to keep pace with our deterioration much less digging out of the hole, any hope at resurrection obscured through their compromise. But if one thing holds true, no self professed visionary ever likes another leaping beyond him, particularly when it's the new kid on the block. Thus, through all the plesantries, smiles, and backslaps I could feel my opponents tensing, well aware that it was their prelude to attack.

We fully realized from the start that pushing my programs through Congress would require the support of virtually all of the Democratic minority as well as a substantial number of Republicans. Thus, many of my more seasoned Washington political advisors started to suggest that I begin my legislative initiative with a more compromising approach using my first State of the Union Address to find common ground between myself and those that opposed my agenda. But I well remembered travelling that road with the Maryland legislature and the dismal results it brought.

I was determined not to make the same mistake again and stood resolute in my conviction that Baltimore's and Maryland's success must be applied across our great land. For over the years I'd seen president after president campaign with sincerity and vigor, fully believing that when his time came in the seat of power, he'd truly accomplish all he foresaw. But inevitably chief after chief wilted before our bureaucratic and legislative maze, succumbing to the falsity of compromise. But I'd sworn upon my faith and love for this great country that I'd sooner die than capitulate.

Thus, as the Republican speaker announced my State of the Union Address, I made my way through the packed House Chamber, shaking hands and exchanging smiles. Then, standing there at the podium I gazed on those before me, such a small gathering to represent our nation's great multitudes and power. Before me stood the full House and Senate, the Supreme Court, my Cabinet, the Joint Chiefs of Staff and the Ambassadors of many foreign nations. Then to my rear, still standing, the Speaker and the Vice President as well with all patiently waiting to see what my words would impart.

Yet as I began my address the Chamber was eerily quiet. Strangely absent were the partisan whoops and hisses as if by virtue of being "the first" I was treading more sacred ground. Despite my surprise, I moved forward discussing the broad range of issues and dilemmas which our great nation currently faced. In order I addressed our ever present deficit, the domestic and global economy, social security, health care, the continued reduction of a wasteful governmental bureaucracy, international peace and terrorism, and nuclear proliferation.

Then, twenty-five minutes into my address I paused, taking time to put on my glasses and beginning with the Vice President and the Speaker in turn, I briefly stared into the eyes of as many people in that Chamber as possible. For more than ten minutes, in complete silence, I stared our country's government in the face. Then, when I'd finally finished I continued my address starting with these words, "But none of that makes one bit of difference if we continue to do nothing for our children."

Their attention gathered I then proceeded to lay out the general outline of my administration's chief legislative initiative, the Civic Responsibility and Youth Reclamation Act, and pledged that a complete legislative package would be sent to Congress within ninety days. Beginning with my proposed budget for Fiscal Year 2017, my administration would pursue one goal of paramount importance and priority and that was the salvation of our country's youth. For as they went so would go the rest of us and as their lives went so would go the life of our country. But I reminded them that I was not here to point fingers at any class or group for the time for finger pointing and blame had long since passed. There was a challenge to be met, a challenge to be faced not by some, but by all of us.

Lest they believe I was merely uttering political rhetoric I briefly conveyed to them the feelings of respect I'd had since childhood for some of our nation's great leaders, including our first President George Washington, the original "Father of His Country." For exactly what this country needed was a return to a system of beneficial patriarchs where the strong possessed the authority to guide and care for the weak and the weak possessed the faith that they'd be cared for. Where local citizens actually possessed the authority and therein the motivation to care about their towns, counties, and streets.

Thus, my own children already grown, and in keeping with President Washington's sterling example of deeds over words, I would continue my role as a patriarch setting an example for all to see. Then, to the cheers of the Chamber I introduced the two foster care boys, one black and one white, which Rachel and I had adopted, and announced that they'd live as our children not only at the White House for the next four years but under our roof forever after wherever it was.

To my surprise Democrats and Republicans alike vigorously applauded at the end of my address for most, including myself, had expected harsh attacks from my opponents on both sides of the aisle. Thus, as I made my way out of the Chamber I enjoyed a gauntlet of congratulations and hand shakes and I couldn't help but think that I was finally seeing the light at the end of the tunnel. However, as I was to soon find out the spirit of good will and collegiality that day was merely the quiet before the storm.

I don't quite remember exactly who told me but I believe it was the day after I delivered my first State of the Union Address that I received the news of Reggie's death. Apparently he'd passed away shortly after I was inaugurated and in all of the excitement and confusion of occupying the White House the news had just taken an unusually long time to reach me. Inquiring about the funeral arrangements, I was informed that he'd had an indigent burial, having already been cremated at the expense of the state, for there'd been no attempt made to claim his remains.

His mother already deceased, I sent condolences to his sisters and those of his children that I could track down. But I don't believe my efforts met with much success. As of the six letters I sent out I failed to receive any reply. But I suppose if his closest relations didn't even care enough to look after his remains my expressions of grief for my life long friend would have had little meaning. Thus, as I reflected back upon the life of the only brother I'd ever had, there just wasn't much for me to do but cry.

Chapter 19

Despite the somewhat frantic atmosphere of the transition period, and the immense anticipation and excitement of beginning my presidency, after a few weeks Rachel and I settled down more or less to a White House routine that would carry on throughout my presidency. For my part, I generally arose early, around six a.m., arriving at the Oval Office by six-thirty. I'd begin my day with a light breakfast and black coffee, the morning newspapers, and the overnight report from the Secretary of State. Generally, I read the Secretary's report first because in its brief two or three pages it encapsulated those world events and issues of the last twenty-four hours deemed most significant by the State Department.

My first scheduled meeting in the Oval Office each day was with my National Security Advisor, Edward Langdon, where he would give me my daily briefing from the intelligence community. In fact, I would generally see Edward several times a day depending on the circumstances. But in times of crises, he was either by my side or coordinating meetings with my Cabinet officers and other leaders in the permanently secured and isolated compartment on the floor below the Oval Office known as the White House Situation Room.

The National Security Advisor's Intelligence Report brought to me each morning was a top secret report distributed to only five people: the President, Vice President, Secretaries of State and Defense, and the National Security Advisor. Ed and I would discuss the report and other foreign affairs and defense developments and frequently I would consult the Secretary of State or Secretary of Defense during Ed's presentation, all of us trying our best to stay one step ahead of a rapidly and ever changing world.

At eight, there was generally a meeting with the Vice President and my top staff people to review our current agenda and discuss any new problems that might have come up. Then, several times a week I'd arrange a breakfast or lunch meeting with the leaders of Congress or other influential visitors which I felt might aid the progress of my legislative agenda. My regular appointment schedule usually began around eight-thirty with meetings ranging in length from a few minutes to several hours. Cabinet members, staff people, foreign dignitaries, Congressmen, local officials, federal administrators, state dinners, receptions, public events, personal appearances, political supporters and personal visitors. I doubt if anyone could ever truly imagine the number of persons seeking an audience with our nation's Chief Executive.

Finally, between appointments I addressed the flood of paperwork that could not be avoided. In the beginning, I was receiving upwards of sixty documents a day on my desk, ranging from brief pieces of correspondence to special reports on the range of issues with many pages of detailed analysis. There was absolutely no way that one set of eyes could absorb it all. Thus, it took several weeks of discussion with my staff to develop a workable system of screening and abbreviation by which my reading load could be cut down to a bearable level.

Due to the extremely confrontational nature of both the primaries and the general election I decided to meet with my Cabinet weekly from the start of the term. For if there was to be any chance for our success I felt that my administration must operate as a unit as much as possible and to do that I must get a personal sense of each of my key advisors' own responsibilities. It's amazing, for instance, to see how all of us sitting around the Cabinet table were so interrelated in the grand beast that had become the Federal bureaucracy, the connections permeating throughout the various levels of the many governmental agencies and departments. But more importantly than me getting to know them I wanted them all to have an early opportunity to get to personally know me. For if they had any superficial notions about me or my presidency I wanted to make absolutely sure they checked them at the door.

One interesting note is that various staff members and aids kept showing up at our first couple of meetings, as it was a great symbol of prestige for others to meet at the Cabinet level. The meetings became so unwieldy that I finally directed that only Cabinet level officials could attend. I wanted to make sure that all of us understood just how interdependent we were and the necessity that we operate as a team. Almost without exception, the members of my administration served both myself and their government with loyalty and distinction, my administration experiencing one of the lowest turnover rates for staff appointments in history. But as I became more accustomed to my job I came to realize that in those first few weeks I'd somewhat deceived my Cabinet members for in the final analysis it would not be the group of us that faced the country's most difficult decisions together, that responsibility would fall to me alone.

When I used my initial State of the Union Address to declare my Civic Responsibility and Youth Reclamation Program my administration's number one priority, it was impossible for me to imagine the bloody legislative battles that would come. For even though I had stepped directly into the fire to implement my programs in both Baltimore and at the state level in Maryland, at the time I had no idea just how very hot Washington could get. My bitter four year battle with Congress would practically consume my entire first term but despite all the frustrations there was never a moment when I didn't consider the implementation of my Civic Responsibility and Youth Reclamation Act to be my administration's paramount goal.

As I was sworn in on January 20th, 2017, our country faced two problems of chief importance. First, the ever declining lack of personal responsibility which the average citizen was prepared to take not only for himself but for the greater community at large. It was clearly evident that the nation's level of personal accountability had been ever decreasing since the end of World

War II, with the average citizen looking increasingly more to big government as a cure all while at the same time developing an ever decreasing level of respect for government's capacity to get the job done.

Second, that the steady deterioration of our society had made it nearly impossible to nurture the nation's children into productive, responsible future citizens. The country desperately needed a comprehensive program that sought, not to dictate to but to work in conjunction with, the average citizen to purge the negative taints that had ruled the towns and streets of our society for far too long. But circumstance demanded that we as a society finally acknowledge that stepping in at sixteen, twelve, eight, or even six years of age was far too late. We simply had to admit that our society could no longer continue without the imposition of a structured system for nurturing our youth.

I and my advisors were firmly convinced that our agenda must be presented to Congress in one well balanced and comprehensive legislative package if there were to be any chance of success. Yet in drafting the legislation we came to realize just how many aspects of the Federal bureaucracy my agenda involved, not to mention the fact that the organizational structure of Congress was simply ill equipped to address a single subject so sweeping in scope. As the time came to send our legislative package to Capitol Hill I was shocked to find that congressional procedure dictated that the legislation would have to be considered by as many as fourteen committees and subcommittees in the House of Representatives alone. In addition, the rules of the Senate dictated that it would be considering at least four separate bills simultaneously. Well aware of the potential threat this quagmire posed my legislative aids and congressional supporters made a valiant effort to streamline the legislative process. But their efforts were to no avail for the Republican majority in both houses certainly knew that they controlled the rules and the committees and were fully intent on exercising their control.

I was well aware that to push my legislation package through Congress I would need the votes of a substantial number of Republicans not to mention virtually all of the Democrats. But it quickly became apparent that the surprisingly pleasant reception I'd received at my State of the Union Address was not a sign of things to come. The majority of the Republicans were still fuming over my election victory and viewed a crushing defeat of my key legislative initiative as the perfect opportunity to extract their revenge.

Their task was made all the easier by the fact that many of them passionately and philosophically disagreed with my initiative. For the campaign had made abundantly clear that I was viewed by more than a few as the epitome of everything bad in the country with my legislative agenda being merely an extension of myself. And though the manner of speech was generally subtle the message was clear. Many of them truly believed the country's decline had been brought about solely by the nation's blacks and their inability to assimilate and become productive members of the society. Now just because my people couldn't nurture their own, I wanted to destroy the family life of all those who could. But the days of the welfare state had long since ended and in their minds I'd simply have to recognize that if my people couldn't care for themselves they'd simply have to suffer.

Beyond the Republicans came the opponents from my own party, sad to say the majority of them from the one source I'd believed I would receive the most support, the Black Caucus. For in their minds it had always been the whites that had ripped the black family apart whether slavery or poverty the result was still the same. Now here I came exposing my true color intent on putting more black men in jail and stealing little black babies from good black parents once again. It wasn't enough I had to act white. No I had to go, just like the white man had always done ever since he first saw the African shore, trying to take one of the few freedoms my people had left, to rear their children as their own.

206

Yet whether they were Democrat or Republican, black or white, for all their finger pointing they refused to see that it was their congressional predecessors, and they as perpetuators, that had stolen from black and white alike. So enamored were they by their majesty they'd usurped the power of those they were sent to protect, imposing such lofty standards that in time we all became confused, no longer clear as to what was right and wrong. Yet for all their wisdom and foresight it was their own short comings to which they stayed blind.

Nevertheless, recognizing the uphill climb I borrowed a page from FDR and took directly to the media in hopes that the public's support would help to carry the day. Thus, I began a series of speaking engagements, both from the White House and around the country, trying to bolster as much support for my initiative as possible. It felt almost as if I'd been elected and took office merely to start another campaign. Still, generally my overtures were well received as citizen concern swung more and more in favor of personal safety than freedom. For though not all agreed on the method the public was unanimous at least that something had to be done.

Throughout the winter and early spring my aids and congressional allies continued to flesh out a comprehensive agenda until on my April 4th birthday, the anniversary of Martin Luther King's death, I addressed the nation on prime time network TV. I carefully laid out the specifics of my Civic Responsibility and Youth Reclamation Program sending the complete legislative package to Congress the very same day. Through the remainder of the spring and early summer we continued our lobbying effort with both Congress and the American public. But by mid-summer our comprehensive package had been chopped into six different bills in the House and four in the Senate. It seemed that literally every legislator had a different view and I honestly felt fortunate at times that we were not facing 535 separate legislative initiatives.

By the end of August the weight of Republican gavels had bogged down the legislation in committee with my opponents on both sides of the aisle smiling away. As October and the end of the session neared it became clear that my legislative initiative had collapsed. Congress adjourned without passing a single piece of the proposed legislation, with in fact, not even a single aspect of my agenda making it out of the Republican controlled committees. In fact, the only related bill receiving passage was a moderate increase in the prior year's Federal Crime Fighting Assistance to States package. To say the least, my disappointment was immense, for despite having had a strong first session on other pending domestic issues everyone knew that the Civic Responsibility and Youth Reclamation Act had been my keynote legislation.

Despite my disappointment at the loss, one reassuring fact came out of my legislative battles with Congress in 2017. As the confrontation and harsh words increased on both sides I had the privilege of finally becoming the subject of the Washington cartoonists. For throughout the campaign and my first months in office they'd declined to touch me as if I were somehow too delicate to withstand such critiques. Most Presidents would have been overjoyed at such anonymity, whatever the reason, but for me it was yet another reminder that in the public's mind I'd still not been fully accepted.

Perhaps my favorite cartoon was the one depicting me as George Washington in colonial dress entitled "Father of His Country." In this cartoon the Republican Speaker of the House lay awaiting a spanking with his bare bottom upturned over my knee and the majority leader of the Senate waiting fearfully next in line. But the cartoon that stirred the most controversy was one done by a popular black cartoonist depicting me as a wisened white bearded old Uncle Tom on a rocking chair kindly lecturing the "Children of Congress" at my feet. As can be imagined the "Uncle Tom" usage ignited a fair amount of public outcry. But for my part I didn't mind the cartoons, no matter how raw, for they merely represented that people were finally starting to pay at least as much attention to my policies as my skin.

Chapter 20

The grim warnings from my political advisors began immediately at the close of the session, that by continuing to tie my presidency to a single agenda I risked completely incapacitating my administration. The Presidency, they advised, was the mightiest office in the land with one of its most powerful tools being the aura that when the President spoke, people listened. In my advisors opinion I could not afford to exhaust my remaining political clout by being ignored in the next congressional session yet again. I would turn into a President without voice, my words dissipating with the wind. I simply had to understand that Washington was compromise and restructure my agenda to first gain achievable victories, gaining momentum for a future push. Yet as I mulled over my advisors pleas for political reasonableness I simply refused to believe that I'd come so far to hit the proverbial wall.

My opponents were having a field day with the end of session media, seemingly waiting in line to praise their legislative success. But as I scanned the nation's news media one underlying theme continued to ring home. My opponents may have viewed themselves as victors and I as the vanquished but to the American public neither their Congress or Chief Executive had won or lost. The true loss had been their own. Yet again their leaders had squabbled and bickered but the streets were still unsafe, public schools a joke and civic pride nonexistent.

Our nationwide polls brought home the same conclusion time and time again, that those we supposedly represented cared nothing of our Washington power or how we got the job done. Their sole concern was the results. For the one thing that infuriated our citizens most was that yet another year had passed, their society ever sinking, and their so called leaders had failed to act again. Perhaps the worst of all was that while their

President spoke openly of his disappointed failure, his Congressional opponents hailed the stagnation as a great victory.

Despite the fact that much was directed at me I was comforted by the public's disgust. Thus, I spurned the advice of my politicos and set my staff to the task of tending the public's dissatisfaction. Apparently, I'd not been the only one eyeing public opinion, for as Congress convened in 2018, my opponents seemed dramatically less hostile. Still, having dealt with my esteemed colleagues before, I was not the least bit deceived, particularly since I was quite aware they were facing an election year.

But with Congress now fully intent on proving its worth to the voters, my legislation was again sponsored and reassigned to the appropriate committees. Then, to my amazement, and a great deal of Congressional self praise, over the next two months the House actually brought an omnibus version of my legislative package to the floor. But as my allies in the House had forewarned it was in no way a cause for celebration. For the revised version of my legislation was nothing more than a slightly beefed up version of the Crime Fighting Assistance To States Legislation they'd passed two years before. My dejection was immense for only two months into the session I could very well see how it would be a mere repetition of the prior year's failure.

It was in the early morning hours of February 28th, when it seemed that things could not get bleaker, that I received a request for an emergency meeting from my National Security Advisor Edward Langdon. As I made my way to the Oval Office I knew something big was up for it was the first emergency meeting Ed had requested in the fourteen months that I'd been President. I couldn't help but feel a sense of energized excitement, for though I realized it might be some potentially awful event, I had to admit I'd often dreamed of being in just such a situation at the presidential controls. But though I'd already attended my first G-7 Economic Summit and made state visits to Africa and Russia nothing could have prepared me for what Edward laid before me.

Ed was waiting for me in the Oval Office his face a mask of worry and concern. He quickly laid out the facts based on the most up to date intelligence and just as quickly my eagerness to face a world crisis turned to dread and the desire for anyone to take my place in the hot seat. For Edward informed me that in the last twenty-four hours our intelligence operatives in Iran had started to pick up some very worrisome rumors.

The primary concern was that a group of Iranian fundamentalists had potentially acquired a nuclear warhead. The rumors were all the more alarming because our intelligence agencies had recently lost track of a shipment of Russian nuclear warheads being relocated from one base to another. But as if that weren't all bad enough Edward pulled out an N.S.C. memorandum from some two months before which tracked the movements of two highly advanced Chinese built mobile ballistic missiles up to the point where they'd disappeared somewhere close to Iranian territory.

The implications from piecing the facts together were horrid enough but the situation was made far more nerve wracking by the fact that despite our best intelligence efforts we were still largely in the dark. My dismay quickly turned to anger as a worst case scenario shot through my brain and I have to confess that Edward bore the brunt of my initial rage. I demanded to know how in the hell all of this could have possibly happened and I was just now hearing about it. But after struggling to calm myself I quickly came to the question of real importance. Just what was there that we could do about it.

Edward dove into his briefing and by 9:00 a.m. we'd pretty much covered the situation, so after scheduling an update meeting for 4:00 that afternoon Edward left to do what he did best. For my part, I moved on to attending to the hundreds of daily matters that are involved with being the chief executive of the world's most powerful nation. But as I turned my attention to other matters, sitting in arguably the most powerful chair in the world, I was plagued by a sickly feeling of impotence and just how many questions lay unanswered. The rest of my day was occupied with my regular appointment schedule and paperwork. But in all honesty, it all seemed trivial in comparison to what we potentially faced, and despite my best efforts to give each matter my undivided attention, inevitably my eyes watched the clock, willing it to reach 4:00.

I held the 4:00 meeting in the White House Situation Room with Edward, the Director of the CIA, Bob Wilson, Vice President Johnson, the Secretaries of State and Defense and the Joint Chiefs of Staff. The room was crowded and tense as we set to work reviewing the available information. Military status reports, satellite and ground site photographs, shared intelligence from other countries, and a seeming mountain of reports from our own intelligence agencies, it was an impressive array of information. Yet one fact rang clear. Despite the situation's potential gravity and the vast array of resources available to the people in that room the only thing that could be said with any certainty was that we were still far from in the know. As the meeting broke up I offered a silent prayer that if such a wide range of intelligence resources was still so uninformed that the old adage of no news is good news would somehow carry the day.

By the next day the situation had turned from dismal speculation to ever worsening reality as a reliable ground operative indeed confirmed that at least one Russian nuclear warhead had been diverted from its transport convoy. Unfortunately, our man on the ground could not confirm whether or not the warheads in question had all been resecured and the fact that Russian security troops had shot all the hijackers dead only added to the uncertainty.

Better safe than sorry we continued to work under a worst case assumption that Russian warheads and Chinese missiles might somehow both fall into Iranian hands. In fact, my intelligence briefing early that morning only served to make the potentialities of such a scenario all the more horrific. For it was well known that the Chinese had long engaged in dubious technology exchanges with practically anyone who'd pay the price. China's late twentieth century technology exchanges with both Pakistan and Iran were only two of the many examples. For as China's previous transfer of short range ballistic missiles to Pakistan had indicated, China was generally far more concerned with influence and profit than world safety. But if the Chinese did not seem as concerned about nuclear proliferation as we might have hoped, even more scary was the potential ease with which they could flood the world with nuclear arms.

Perhaps we were partially to blame, for in the 1990's our own military and nuclear weapons laboratories had begun studying precision low yield weapons designs or "mininukes." The research had continued under a Joint Chiefs of Staff Doctrine which stated that lower yield nuclear weapons might be a useful battlefield alternative. Utilizing our Star Wars missile defense systems technology it had been no large leap to mount nuclear warheads on these small highly concealable and mobile missiles. Of course, not wanting to fall behind, the Russians developed their own line of "mininuke" missiles and as General Barker of the Air Force so bluntly put it at the briefing, "If we and the Russians can do it I wouldn't bet the farm the Chinese can't."

My military advisors then went on to inform me that indeed the warheads in question could conceivably be adapted for Chinese missiles assuming the requisite expertise. It seemed that the more information I received the bleaker the picture looked. Even though we were operating on worst case assumptions I took some solace that it had yet to be confirmed that either Russian warheads or Chinese missiles had made it to Iranian hands or that even if they had that the Iranians were in any way capable of putting the two together. But despite this small glimmer of hope one thing was for damn sure. We'd better find out quickly or it might just be too late.

With each passing hour the waiting grew ever more tense but despite our best efforts by the end of the second day we were still getting nowhere fast. As usual, the Chinese were a closed book denying any transfer had occurred even when confronted with photographs of the missiles being loaded on the plane. The source of the missiles a dead end, we concentrated the bulk of our efforts on Iran, focusing all available intelligence resources, both technological and human, on the suspected destination. Still, not wanting to alert the Iranians just yet our probes were necessarily restricted to the most cautious of inquiries. But despite the intensity of our efforts no new leads appeared.

In fact, the one place we were the most optimistic of receiving assistance from also turned up dry in both official and unofficial channels. But whether it was the embarrassment of yet another nuclear incident, the fact that they feared jeopardizing their own recovery efforts, or just plain resentment at what they perceived to be more of our meddling the Russians refused to talk as well. They even refused to say whether any of their warheads were in fact missing.

Due to the extreme urgency of the situation and what I felt to be my own personal rapport with the Russian President Nicolai Dobrin I decided to pursue a more direct effort. For during my first year visit to Moscow it seemed that not only were President Dobrin and I quite capable of communicating on affairs of state but on a personal level as well. In fact, during my three day visit we'd made great progress on the trade and economic aid relationship which existed between our two countries as well as voicing our basic agreement on the world strategic roles of our respective nations. But beyond our agreement as to the roles and responsibilities of our respective countries President Dobrin had seemed intent on reaching out to me to bind our nations not only at the diplomatic level but on the basis of our personal friendship as well.

I have to admit that going into the Summit I had my own preconceived stereotypes about the Russian people and in the back of my mind carried the notion that the people of the cold white north would have a natural prejudice against my skin. In fact, I'd been well briefed on the propensity of Russian leaders to use American race relations as a negotiating tool, choosing to view America as if its race relations had been frozen forever in a time long past.

But things couldn't have been more untrue. I was received with the warmest of receptions, President Dobrin going out of his way to arrange for several private one on one sessions and taking the extremely rare step of waiving away the interpreters and speaking to me in English. In fact, the singularly most impressive thing about my entire visit was just how open and well informed he was about the dynamics of race in 21st century American society. As our talks progressed I found myself wishing that my fellow Americans could be even half as racially pragmatic as this foreigner from the north. For it was obvious to both of us that we clearly understood the difference between past and present.

The visit was ended, to the horror of both of our delegations and to my delight, with President Dobrin taking the liberty of skipping the traditional vodka toast and serving us both Black Russians instead, after which I was treated to the friendliest of Russian bear hugs. Yet what heartened me the most as I directed my staff to contact President Dobrin via the Moscow Hotline, was the seemingly mutual concern we'd shared during my visit on the issue of nuclear proliferation. For it appeared that both of us clearly agreed that the world's current status regarding the matter was far too unstable and that the best hope lay in the nuclear authority of our two nations working together toward a safer world.

But the man on the Mo Link was far different than the one I'd toasted in Moscow. His response text repeatedly insisted that no Russian warheads were missing. In fact, he even went so far as to say that if some rogue state had by some chance acquired a nuclear warhead the matter was no concern or responsibility of the Russian people. I simply couldn't believe what I was seeing and in an extremely undiplomatic fit of anger I tersely communicated to my counterpart that the Russian bear better wake from hibernation because if he didn't come out of his cave soon it might just be too late.

Unfortunately my bravado approach turned out to be not only ineffective but entirely unnecessary. Because in a videotaped BBC broadcast aired the very next day a shocked world listened to a calmly fanatical religious zealot demand that all "infidels" leave the "Lands of Islam" in seven days or face the fires of hell. Firmly planted in his demented mind was that the holy "Lands of Islam" had only been tainted in the first place due to oil driven greed. Aided by false worshipping puppets, like the Saudis, the white devils had continued to defile and contaminate the holy purity of Islam. But he and his brothers of the truly faithful had finally had enough and the white devils of Washington and Moscow must now respect the holy lines he'd drawn in the sand. His demand was clear. Leave the "Lands of Islam" in seven days or face true hell on earth.

His rhetoric complete he went on to map out the geographic boundaries of his holy claim and explain how the detonation of his nuclear warheads over the rich oil fields of both Saudi Arabia and Azerbaijan near southern Russia would touch off the very fires of hell. In fact, to him it seemed to make no difference that millions might suffer, for his focus was singular and unyielding. Whether the infidels left voluntarily or in flames the effect would be the same, Islam's holy lands would be purged and cleansed forever.

As I watched the tape again and again staring down those hateful eyes I couldn't help but wonder how many just like him our world had seen. In fact, it seemed to me somewhat miraculous that with his kind freely stalking our streets that so many of us could still love each other at all. But perhaps for me his message was all the more foreboding as he concluded his address by warning me, "the Great White Satan" personally that my interference would be my death.

At the conclusion of his address the world moved quickly from shock and disbelief to panic. Well remembering the Gulf War oil fires of 91', I directed the State Department to issue an advisory to all U.S. nationals in the region and assist in their immediate evacuation. Naturally, the other inhabitants of the threatened areas were beside themselves with fear and hundreds of thousands of refugees were instantly on the move. Yet the truth be known, there really wasn't much point to their panicked attempts at flight, for the vast oil fields that were their nations really left nowhere to hide.

Of course, I was immediately swamped by the calls of many nations, the oil states first in line, the question on everyone's lips being just exactly what was I going to do. But as bad as our worse case scenarios had been they soon turned to grisly reality. For less than two hours after the videotape aired I received a Mo Link telex from President Dobrin informing me that based on updated information the Russians were in fact missing two theatre nuclear warheads. He even went so far as to state that it was highly likely the warheads had ended up in Iranian hands and suggested an immediate pooling of U. S. and Russian intelligence resources in an attempt to track down and eliminate the threat. Frankly, it all seemed like just another bad international spy novel but since there really wasn't much time for reflection I directed that our respective intelligence services begin coordinating within the hour.

I immediately called another full meeting of the National Security Council. For the situation was rapidly expanding requiring a comprehensive review of our most up to date information and options. As my top advisors gathered in the White House Situation Room the atmosphere was businesslike but tense to say the least. In fact, we'd picked up our first break when British intelligence traced the delivery of the videotape to a known member of the Iranian financed and supported Islamic Jihad. Unfortunately, the bad news was that this particular member belonged to one of the most radical and dangerous factions of the Jihad well known for the willingness to risk anything and everything in the name of their god. But when directly confronted the Iranian government denied any involvement claiming the whole business was just another Western fabrication to discredit their holy state. Still, just in case we had any ideas they issued the usual holy war threats should I, the Great White Satan, in any way infringe on their territory.

Despite the Iranian's denial my military advisors pointed out that by naming their targets our terrorists had at least been good enough to provide their general location. Since the maximum range of the Chinese missiles they'd potentially acquired was five hundred miles it was merely necessary to chart range circles around their targets. Thus, the good news was we quickly narrowed down their potential positions to a very short list. The bad news being that their most likely location was the rugged and remote mountains of west central Iran. As our unsuccessful searches for Iraqi Scuds in the Gulf War had proven finding such missiles could be like searching for the proverbial needle in the haystack. Still, I tried my best to remain objective as I listened to the range of our diplomatic, economic, and military options. But as the toll of potential death and destruction mounted I developed a sense of frustrated rage at these senseless and hateful fanatics.

Our diplomatic and economic relations with the Iranians having long since been at zero my options in those areas were naturally few. Thus, it was our military options which received the bulk of consideration. From search and destroy missions to retaliatory bombings to outright invasion my military and intelligence advisors detailed a broad range of actions. But as our options were laid out before me it became increasingly apparent that all led down the road to death.

The intelligence services of many nations were continuing to probe for information even as we spoke. But the cold fact still was that to this point we were not completely certain the terrorists even had any warheads or missiles much less if they were actually capable of putting the two together and carrying out their threat. It was then that the sickening thought crossed my mind that perhaps it was all a cruel bluff. But whether the terrorists were in fact bluffing or not one thing was certain, we simply could not afford to take the chance.

Yet what was I to do? Should I authorize the recommended low level reconnaissance flights and put American lives at risk? Perhaps I should go one step further and order the insertion of reconnaissance ground teams deep inside Iranian territory, their mission to comb thousands of square miles for an objective that might not even exist. Then, there was the most dramatic option of all, a full scale invasion with tens of thousands of American troops conducting their search in a hostile land at the risk of a protracted war with Iran and perhaps the entire Muslim world. But even should I choose such an option what hope was there for success in so little time?

Still, when everything around me screamed for action perhaps the best course was merely to be patient and wait, relying on our high tech missile interceptors to finally earn their keep. But even should our missiles be up to the task, what of the thousands of American servicemen such a defense would require to be floating in the Gulf and the potential for them to be trapped in a vast radioactive tub? For truly what was really the point of it all? Was I really willing to risk so many American lives for the sake of another's oil?

Yet a decision had to be made and quickly, the responsibility for me alone. I had to decide who would live and who would die and hope their lives would not be forfeit in vain. As I wrestled with my misery I pondered what could have ever made such fanatical terrorists and all the while I wondered if my hatred could ever equal their own. But after all wasn't it man's eternal contrast that his brain's complexities could create such beauty and hate, his one great challenge forever being to guard himself from his brother.

In the end, I opted for what seemed to be the most reasonable course. I ordered a battle group from the Sixth Fleet, complete with our full range of missile interceptors, to the Persian Gulf. Their orders were clear, use all of their available firepower and shoot any missiles down. Then, I and President Dobrin publicly issued a joint ultimatum demanding that the Iranian government locate and produce the missing warheads within twenty-four hours or rest assured that we would. In addition, we informed the Iranians that should any attack originate from their territory that the Iranian government and people would be held fully responsible as with any other act of war and that full reprisals would most certainly and swiftly be carried out. Sadly the Iranians still refused to cooperate their only response being a repetition of their holy war threats should we in any way encroach on their lands.

Thus, with four days to the deadline I directed that our low level reconnaissance flights begin informing the Iranians of our purpose and warning them that any attempt to obstruct our search effort would be considered an act of war. To the amazement of many, including myself, the Iranians made no attempt whatsoever to interfere, seemingly content to let us search as we liked. For their part, the Russians dispatched upwards of twenty thousand troops to the Iranian border complete with all the missile intercept capabilities they could muster. But despite the frantic nature of our joint intelligence efforts and the blanket of our aerial search with twelve hours to go there were still no warheads or missiles to be found.

The situation demanded that I exert all the influence and strength I could muster from the most powerful office in the world. All of America's diplomatic, economic, and military forces lay marshalled ready to respond to my command. But there I sat seemingly powerless. I'd tried everything I could think of to do and now with time running out ever so rapidly I was left only to wait and pray.

Chapter 21

The detonation occurred at aproximately 5:00 a.m. our time the following morning, the fundamentalist's greed bought technology not quite up to their holy war ambitions. The world will never know exactly what happened. Whether they'd actually attempted to launch and experienced a misfire or whether something had simply gone wrong on the ground will be forever unknown for the only people capable of divulging the facts were obliterated in a flash. But whatever happened, one thing is certain. Our hateful zealots were rewarded with their holy fire and maybe even died happy, at long last content in the arms of their martyrdom.

Perhaps the only fact that could be clearly determined is that the size of the blast assured that both warheads had been detonated. But unfortunately, for those of us that wanted no part of their hell on earth, the fall out was tremendous. Originating at the detonation point high in the Zagros Mountains of West Central Iran, it cut a hundred mile wide path of destruction carrying as far north as Volograd Russia. The analysts say that even though the warheads were considered "mininukes" the radioactive fallout was four times the scale of Hiroshima and that only the grace of prevailing winds prevented far wider destruction. But if the rest of the world could consider itself so very lucky in avoiding the horror, those in its path were all the more cursed absorbing the full force of its wrath.

To many's mind the carnage in Iran was so justly well deserved, for the rational world had long since tired of one nation's constant hate. Yet to my way of thinking I couldn't help but pity those Iranians who'd not been involved, so many forced to bear the cost for the hatred of so few. But though I personally wished to help those thousands of Iranian innocents, the geopolitical realities demanded that on their suffering I turn my back.

While circumstances would not permit me to alleviate the Iranian's suffering, southern Russia on the other hand was an entirely different matter. For even though some advocated our inaction as befitting the Russian's earlier denial I could take no other course but to aid those so in need. Thus, I immediately extended my offer to President Dobrin to use all our available resources in assisting their efforts of relief. Yet the truth is my offer came from less than a unified front for their were more than a few of my advisors and military counselors who viewed such generosity with grave resistance. Even in the face of such horror the prevailing view seemed to be that the less our nuclear expertise made it into Russian hands the better. But my own camp's protests fell on deaf ears and with President Dobrin's permission the first of our military emergency clean up teams began arriving in twenty-four hours.

It's impossible to know how many lives the brave efforts of our soldiers saved. Perhaps the best indicator would be the feelings of accomplishment and joy our own troops expressed on their return home. For although our clean up teams had great praise for the Russian's efforts to save their own, it was also our on site technicians who best saw how ill prepared the Russian's were to handle such a holocaust. Of course, the real victim count will only become clear in the decades ahead for such a killer once unleashed is above all so very patient. But one fact became certain, which is that the cooperative efforts of our peoples insured that countless Russians would live to love another day.

For my part, I was proclaimed a humanitarian and hero the world over, touted not only for my composure in the face of crisis but my compassion in the face of need. Yet, despite all the praise I couldn't forget that all my powers had failed to locate the warheads and that in the end only God's winds had truly restrained their devastation. Still, within three weeks I'd gone from an impotent President who was the laughing stock of Congress to a national and international hero.

My popularity both at home and abroad soared. The result was that quite a few members of Congress seemed to have a change of heart, now quite unwilling to go on record as slighting the public's new found hero, particularly in an election year. After all shouldn't a President that can save the world at least be given a chance to resolve our domestic problems?

The net result was that by July 15 the House narrowly passed a Civic Responsibility and Youth Reclamation Act that virtually mirrored my original proposal. By August 5th the Senate had moved three separate bills onto the floor for debate as well, the text from two of which combined incorporated the primary points of my agenda. I found it hard to believe but at long last it seemed we were finally in sight of the goal. I'm afraid it was then that I made my worst political blunder.

When the success of our joint relief effort made it clear just how very well we could work with the Russians under certain circumstances it naturally led me to question why it wasn't a more full time arrangement. To my mind the whole tragic incident would have been avoided if we just could have worked together from the start. Yet our years of mutual mistrust had prevented an effective joint effort until it was far too late. Thus, I called a special National Security Council meeting to inquire as to the feasibility of incorporating the Russians into a more effective nuclear nonproliferation intelligence exchange treaty.

Despite his refusal to cooperate at the start of the crisis, I believed that President Dobrin and I still agreed that as the world's only two nuclear superpowers our countries must join together for any global nonproliferation policy to truly work. Yet, as President Dobrin had so candidly confided to me after the detonation not all those of influence in his country shared such a viewpoint. In fact, I could certainly empathize well aware that Russia-U.S. cooperation was seen as less than desirable by more than a few in my own camp.

The National Security Council debate on my proposal was heated to say the least with my Secretary of Defense, John Trainor, eventually even going so far as to resign in protest. But after fully discussing the range of technological and national security issues the majority of my advisors agreed, that under the right circumstances, such an arrangement could be beneficial to both of our countries, and of course world safety. Naturally, in the course of our deliberations we consulted with the appropriate members of Congress, their comments running the gamut from enthusiastic approval to aggressive rejection. In the end, based on what I believed to be sufficient support, I gave the order to go ahead convinced that once the grisly details of southern Russia were fully known that even the most skeptical would come around.

The problem was that although the world had been under a global Non-Proliferation Treaty since 1968, with some 175 of the world's nations participating, it was still far from sufficient. For as the steady increase in nuclear weapons related incidents since the NPT's inception had shown the nature of man is such that even in the face of his own potential extermination many are still unable to control their greed.

But even beyond man's self serving nature, logistical realities dictated that no mass group of 175 would ever be capable of a timely response to rogue nuclear threats. To me it seemed so readily apparent that the solution lay, if only for this purpose, in the union of our two great nations. For if the two superpowers could not work toward man's common good in the face of their own destruction what right did we have to demand rationality of others?

In fact, I'd originally envisioned the treaty as a complete joining of the nonproliferation intelligence efforts of the world's nuclear states. For although the intentions of the world's existing Non-Proliferation Treaty were fine and good, its capacity to achieve its goal was remote. The reality was that with so many parties involved no one was completely forthcoming with their intelligence data. Thus, the supposedly protective web of shared nonproliferation information disintegrated into largely an every man for himself free for all. But just as the Iranian Nuclear Crisis had shown for any nonproliferation effort to stand a chance its intelligence practices must not be limited to exchange in the face of crisis but operate in an ongoing systematic daily cooperative effort.

But the Chinese, still smarting from our accusations in the Iranian Nuclear Crisis, were less than receptive to our overtures. Although their comments were subtle it was quite clear they wanted nothing to do with the Russian bear. In fact, it had taken quite a bit of effort on my part to get President Dobrin to even consider including the Chinese in the first place, for the suspicions generated by their vast mutual border had been too long held to wipe away. Of far greater disappointment, was the Russian's rejection of our nuclear European allies as potential treaty signatories. For from Napoleon to Hitler it seems that Russian memories of continental invasion were far too vivid to ever forget. Yet if anything, our European allies were equally opposed to exchanging intelligence with the Russians for they viewed their nuclear capabilities as the only thing holding the forces of the Bear at bay.

But beyond the objections of the world's reigning nuclear states we also had to contend with those nations not in the nuclear club. For from the first inklings of my proposed treaty the negative fall out from the world's non nuclear states was immense. The idea that the nuclear states should be privy to information they were not was to them completely abhorent and as many pointed out the insecurity would only add further fuel to the "have nots" race to obtain nuclear arms.

By far the greatest dilemna was simply keeping people focused on the distinction between the exchange of nonproliferation intelligence for the good of all humanity and intelligence related to more self serving interests. But where opposition to a pact exclusively between the world's nuclear states was rampant, there was by far less objection to a strictly bilateral treaty between the U.S. and Russia. The geopolitical reality was that our two countries had long since been accepted as a sort of planetary patriarchs with the breadth of our respective nuclear arsenals putting us in a class by ourselves.

Where the jealousies and competitions of many nations came into play on other issues all could agree that the less the U.S. and Russia had to fear the safer the world would be.

But if one thing holds true, it's that competition between equals is generally the fiercest. Thus, as the treaty process moved steadily forward domestic concern grew. My advisors began to warn of cold war paranoias alive and well, with more than a few in the Senate viewing the treaty as a betrayal of our NATO allies and a grave threat to national security. I must confess, I was somewhat blind to the concerns of my advisors. I simply found it hard to believe that the very same group of Senators who'd just finished so applauding my actions in a catastrophic world nuclear incident could now turn full circle and oppose a treaty which would so surely help prevent a reoccurrence. So despite the building current of opposition our negotiation teams moved forward at a blistering pace, neither I nor President Dobrin willing to let such a historic opportunity slip by.

By late August the negotiating teams had for the most part wrapped up the text of the treaty leaving just a few final points of contention for President Dobrin and I to sign off on. In fact, at my invitation, President Dobrin even agreed to a Washington signing in light of my prior year's visit to Moscow. Despite an underlying atmosphere of protest the Washington Summit went far better than even the most optimistic of us could have hoped.

The wrap up negotiations flowed quite smoothly with the only major sticking point being the effective date of the treaty. President Dobrin's thinking was that such an unprecedented level of U.S.-Russian cooperation should be justly acknowledged by the representatives of the American people, and thus preferred to wait until Senate ratification to make the treaty effective. I took the liberty of pointing out to President Dobrin that it only took thirty-four Senators to block a treaty, also noting that the custom and prior practice of our two countries had carried out the terms of many treaties without Senate ratification. But on this point President Dobrin wouldn't budge, expressing his desire that our treaty be thus binding and protect many a future generation from each of our countries.

Since we'd come so very far I signed as he wished at the time having no doubt that the Senate would ratify the treaty in turn. After handing our respective copies of the signed treaty documents to one another, we shook hands enthusiatically, and to the delight of the many onlookers concluded the ceremony with a warm Russian embrace. Walking away from the signing ceremony I felt the warmest sense of cooperation and that what we'd accomplished was truly a step forward for humanity.

I immediately forwarded the treaty to the Senate for ratification, anxious to begin implementing its terms at the soonest possible date. It's the one decision that I truly regret. For I realized too late that my advisors were right and I never should have dropped the treaty into the middle of the Senate's debate on my reform legislation. Perhaps I'd just been so preoccupied all along with getting the Russians to sign that I'd been blind to the fact that my biggest problem lay in my own backyard. I have to admit that the Senate did take immediate action, although not of the kind I'd hoped and the very next day they voted to postpone debate on my reform package in order to further scrutinize the treaty's implications.

Although somewhat shocked by the Senate's foot dragging, we nevertheless mounted a furious lobbying campaign encompassing numerous speeches, news interviews, and private Senatorial briefings. Unfortunately the Senate's minority contingent of Cold War holdovers continued to gain support as the treaty debate progressed. For it was far easier for reelection seeking Senators to convey their "political character and strength" through well publicized outdated rhetoric than by the more anonymous act of merely voting for something to benefit all mankind. As the opposition's numbers approached the thirty-four votes necessary to block the treaty's passage, I was even presented with a number of drastic amendments to my reform legislation which they sought to barter in exchange for the treaty's ratification. But I'd simply come too far to be turned back yet again.

Thus, I determined with my Senate supporters that rather than have the treaty defeated outright or settle for a watered down version of my reform package we'd leave the treaty in the Senate Foreign Relations Committee enabling us to keep its provisions intact. In retaliation the minority opposition stalled further action on my reform legislation until the end of the session, thus frustrating my hopes once again. Needless to say my disappointment was immense. For not only had Congress had the opportunity to finally act on my domestic reform package, but also approve a treaty which would signifigantly further world peace and safety. Yet once again, those that were empowered to represent and protect the welfare of the people had instead been more concerned with protecting their own.

But if Congress had been wise to heed the people's dissatisfaction at the beginning of the session it would have been wiser still to follow through. For though my opponents viewed their actions as fully justified, the American public disagreed whole heartedly and with an outlet for their frustrations readily available in the form of the midterm elections of 2018 the people made sure their displeasure was known. Unfortunately for those legislators that had finally seen the light, it was deemed too little too late and the voters in their desire to clean house orchestrated the largest political turn around since the midterm elections of 1994. When the dust had finally settled, 18 Republicans had lost their seats in the Senate and an amazing 106 Republicans in the House, leaving me with a strong Democratic majority in both houses. The feeling throughout my administration and among my congressional allies was one of overwhelming euphoria. For the sweeping midterm results seemed if not a sign from heaven then at least a sign from the voters that my agenda would finally become law.

As my third session with Congress got under way the Senate set the tone by immediately turning their attention to my Nuclear Nonproliferation Intelligence Exchange Treaty, conducting a mere two weeks of debate and ratifying it before the new session was twenty days old. Not to be outdone at the same time my supporters in both houses were reintroducing my legislative package for the third time and pushing it through the maze of committees. Riding the wave of legislative enthusiasm bills moved through both houses at break neck speed. Still, well remembering prior disappointments, I cautioned my staff members and congressional allies against overconfidence urging everyone to exert their maximum efforts.

Despite my apprehensions both houses finished their committee work by mid July with the real surprise being that only one bill arrived on the floor of each house for debate. The rare singular focus of both houses represented by far our best chance for passage to date, and even though a signifigant amount of opposition grumbled behind the scenes I took heart in the fact that the combination of the House and Senate bills incorporated substantially all aspects of my reform package.

By September 15th each bill had received passage in its respective house and they were forwarded to a conference committee to try and work out a compromise between the two different versions. It was in the conference committee that the first real opposition began to surface. For even though the midterm elections had replaced Republicans with Democrats the same old objections were being voiced. All agreed that something must be done but no one saw the training of our children as the paramount answer.

Whether conservative or liberal, Republican or Democrat it seemed to make no difference. All were reluctant to in any way curtail individual rights in the name of the collective good, particularly where the parenting of our nation's youth was concerned. In the end, it was a tooth and nail battle to push a bill of any meaningful signifigance through the conference committee, the single greatest point of contention being that the nation's youth were not in nearly so much jeopardy as I claimed. Still, despite growing opposition, by December 1st we succeeded in sending a final bill to the full House and Senate for a vote.

With my own reelection year rapidly bearing down upon me I was painfully aware that this was the final push. I spent every available minute on the phones or in meetings with Congressmen lobbying for the passage of my legislation. Then, a week before the vote I made a televised broadcast to the nation explaining yet again just exactly why I believed such drastic measures were necessary. In addition, I asked the people to ring the phones off the hooks in the days before the vote to make sure Congress understood their views. Then on the evening before the final vote I was granted my request to speak before a joint session of Congress.

As I made my way into the packed House Chamber I walked not alone but with my own four children in tow. Then, staring out on the people's representatives I spoke to them of the security, nurturing, and love which I'd tried so hard to provide for my children. I spoke of the worries, joys, and pain as parents that many of us in the room knew so well. But beyond speaking of my children's lives under my care, I asked my two adopted children to step forward and while holding them in my arms detailed the social horrors they'd been forced to endure in life before they'd become mine. I told of their exposure to drug abuse, alcoholism, crime, violence, sexual abuse, hysteria, malnutrition, and many other deprivations of both the body and mind.

Then I gave each of my adopted children a kiss and right then and there told each of the five hundred and thirty-five people responsible for guiding our society just how much I understood my children's pain. For even now after so many years I was still so very much aware that I'd been one of them in my youth and always would be. The insecurity, the frustration, the loneliness, I'd known it all and nothing could ever remove it. For all said and done it was and always would be a part of me.

I wanted so much at this moment standing there as the nation's president and chief executive to bring all the strength and force of my will to bear. But there as all the memories rushed down upon me, despite all my attempts to hold them back, my tears began to flow. First one, then another, until their path became a river and as I stood before that gathering of my nation's leaders I completely broke down and cried.

All four of my children immediately surrounded me in a protective circle, and after a few minutes of their loving support I was able to collect myself and began to speak again. I told of just how I'd been saved by the guidance of Chet and Martin where my own creators had left only a void. In fact, it was in memory of Chet and Martin's love that Rachel and I had stepped into the lives of our own two adopted children in hopes of giving them what they'd never had but so richly deserved.

Then, in the strongest voice I could muster, I asked our country's representatives. But what of the others? What of the thousands, the millions of lost children which roamed our streets each day without guidance, without futures, without love. If we, the elected leaders of the nation, the appointed patriarchs, failed to shepherd them what hope was there for their fate? I concluded my address to the Chamber's shocked silence by asking for their votes and telling them if they wouldn't do it for those millions of pathetic lost children at the very least they should do it for their own. For if we as a society continued to remain blind to those lost we'd all inevitably become a part of them.

The following morning I arose early and was back working the phones by 7:00. I spent the whole day calling Congressmen but by late afternoon the dismal results were in. We lost in the Senate by only three votes and in the House by twenty-four. In the end, our nation's leaders simply refused to believe that the cornerstone of our society, the children, were in sufficient jeopardy to warrant action. In the final analysis, I was defeated once again by the incessant call for rights, rights, rights. Leaving me only to wonder if we continued to refuse to talk about reponsibilities just how soon would it be before we had no rights left.

I suppose if a bright side could be found it was that the vote was so very close. Still, well recognizing that I was facing an election year I realized that another attempt in the next year's session would be futile. Thus, the next day I called a full meeting of my staff members to make it clear that I would definitely be seeking a second term. I assured them that I wasn't nearly done yet and had just started to fight. Then I thanked them for their efforts and concluded by reminding them that there was still plenty of work to be done for we had an election to win.

Chapter 22

"Ok there's the entrance to shock trauma. Here we go."

"Hang in there Louis, we made it baby."

"Now ma'am please just stick with us. We're going directly to surgery. The doctors are already waiting."

"Just stay with me honey. We're almost home."

"No. No. Hold it. Bring the stretcher around to his head so we can get a better shoulder lift. Ok ready, lift. That's right steady now. Good strap him down and let's move."

Sweet Jesus, turn down the lights. Doesn't anybody ever pay attention to the patient for Christ's sake? At least slow it down a bit you're gonna break me in two before the doctors ever get a chance to look at me. Oh Jeez, I think I'm gonna be sick. Somebody pull off this mask. Don't let me get sick, not now. Rachel, where are you honey? Don't you go leaving me now. Not now that they can patch up whatever the problem is and I'll be good as new. Modern medicine, hell, they can do practically anything now a days. I'm gonna be just fine. Rachel? Where are you Rachel?

"Come on, come on. Hey nurse. Where's the surgery team? They were supposed to be cranked up and ready to go."

"They're scrubbing right now Agent Meyers. They'll be out as soon as he's prepped and the x-rays are up."

"What in the hell are they still scrubbing for. They're supposed to be ready to go."

"I'm sorry Agent Meyers but you'll just have to step back and let us handle things, unless you're intent on slowing things down."

"Yeah I'm stepping back alright. But you better get a move on or it's your ass."

"Clear him to the table. One, two, lift."

Jeez people, people, I'm not a sack of potatoes here. Take it easy. No. Not, Jesus not the clothes. Some Commander In Chief lying under these bright lights hanging out for all to see. At least pull up a sheet or something. Turn down those lights. I can't see a damn thing. No not the mask again. Not yet. Dammit I can't see with this thing on. Rachel honey where'd you go? Rachel don't leave me. Please don't leave me here alone.

"What is it Agent Meyers? What's going on?"

"Nothing for you to worry about ma'am. You just concentrate on him and leave the rest to me."

"I believe I've already made myself clear Agent Meyers. My husband's in here fighting for his life. Now if something's going on we have a right to know. Now what is it?"

"Yes ma'am. Alright. It's some more information on the girl that shot him. Seems her father and your husband were a couple of childhood friends that kind of went their separate ways. Apparently she hasn't seen your husband in person since she was four or so. Never even had much contact with her father after five. But since then she's gone the typical unwed teen mother route, had a couple of babies, ended up on welfare, drug problems, some domestic abuse, the whole bit. Well long story short, the State of Maryland finally took her kids away from her and placed them in a state run home under the authority of the legislation your husband implemented when he was Governor. She blames your husband for taking her babies away, so she shot him."

"No. No that can't be. That's insane."

"I'm sorry ma'am. That's why I didn't want to tell you. There's just all kind of crazies out there. Why don't we pray for him together ma'am, just you and me."

"What...oh. Yes...yes I'd like that. Yes let's pray together. It's all just gone so crazy."

Honey you're so right. That's insane. How could Boncy possibly blame me? Doesn't she understand it was her inaugural party as much as mine? Didn't she realize why I worked so hard all these years? Couldn't she even see that I'd come back for my own, to take her and her babies and all those lost little children just like them away from the misery forever?

How could she blame me? Did I send her to bed hungry or beat her in my frustrated rage? Am I the one that vented my yearnings on her innocent, childish form? Did I give her the booze, the drugs, or keep her home from school? Did I keep pushing all the filth on her body, her mind, locking her away with no choice but to scream? Was it I that ignored her cries?

How could she blame me for her children? Did I make her pregnant, force her take the drugs? Did I force her out of school, quit her jobs, fill her days with nothing? How in the hell could she blame me? Despite her past, all her misery, all the grief, did she have nothing whatsoever to do with the fall? Dammit why am I to blame? For if she's so free of responsibility why not me, why not all of us?

How dare she demand I bear responsibility for her failure. How dare she point the gun at my head instead of her own. The hell with her and hers to place such righteous blame. Why did I ever even go back to them in the first place? How could I have been so blind to what they really are? For have they changed one bit in all these years, these centuries? Have they yet to even make any effort at all? For just like time, isn't their kind eternal, their existence as constant as the sun or the stars? How could I have ever been so blind? But enough is enough. No more. No they're not my people, not now, not ever. I guess they never have been. But Lord why did it take me so very long to realize?

Wait. Hold on a second that's ok. You can leave the lights on. They're a pain but it's sure a lot better than sitting here in the dark. Rachel? Where'd you go honey? I can't see you anymore. Meyers? Tell them to turn the lights back on. Where'd everybody go? You can't tell me I'm supposed to be left unattended in this condition. What's the hell's going on here? Let's get diagnosing or operating or something. For Christ sake this is the President of the United States you're talking about. Rachel? Rachel honey are you there? Rachel? If you're there please come to me. Please come where I can see you. Honey I can't see a damn thing. It's all so deep, so dark, so black.

April 4, 2021. Today the nation celebrated the birthday of Louis Jefferson Hayes, the forty-sixth President of the United States, with President Harlan B. Johnson declaring the day to be a national holiday. President Johnson described former President Hayes as a visionary on the scale of Martin Luther King and John Fitzgerald Kennedy, noting that it was only through the devoted and tireless efforts of President Hayes that the Federal Civic Responsibility and Youth Reclamation Act ever achieved passage. President Johnson went on to say that in the end President Hayes gave the supreme sacrifice of his life to create a better and promising future for our children, for our families, and for all of us, the true shame being that he couldn't live to see his dream become reality.

THE END

Previews of Other 1ˢᵗ Books By David L. Dukes

THE LAST WHITE SOLDIER

Chapter 1

U. S. AIR FORCE ICBM BASE, PLEASURE, MONTANA

Sitting alone in the eerie silence of the missile control room, Colonel Norman B. Granger calmly checked his watch and took another sip of water. For that was about all there was left for him to do, unless of course, he finally received an order to launch. Yet somehow, even now, he found it hard to believe that any of this was really happening. But then the enemy's acetylene torch began gnawing at the control room door again and he knew that it was all very much for real.

Hidden deep within the American heartland, his missile base was supposed to have been impregnable. For the base was safely nestled among the nation's vast northern plains, endless miles of flowing brown grasses completely absorbing it with their whispering sighs. Whether it be the hot dry summers or the brutal icy winds of winter, its isolation was always total and complete, the only real company being the ever present stars of clear and untainted western skies.

As if the base's sheer isolation wasn't enough to keep its weapons safe, it was constructed using state of the art technology, its security system the world's cutting edge. The missiles were protected by twenty foot thick concrete hardened silos and the control bunker itself lay deep beneath the ground. The base was even capable of absorbing a direct hit from an enemy nuclear attack and still rising from beneath the ashes to launch a counterassault. For as the country's last line of defense, the base had been built to withstand the enemy's worst.

But who in their worst nightmare would have ever expected this. That anyone would dare to carry out such a commando raid so deep inside American soil. Even now the Colonel couldn't help but admire the sheer nerve of it. Imagine confronting the world's most deadly weapons with mere foot soldiers attacking on the ground.

Yet the assault had been perfectly timed to coincide with the base's shift change, the guards taken completely by surprise. Before anyone knew what was happening, their outside perimeter had been breached and only seconds later the enemy had forced its way inside. All so fast he simply had to believe that the enemy had been aided by an inside source. But what difference did that make now. The time for worrying about internal security leaks was already long since past.

Once the complex had been breached, the base personnel's years of sitting behind computer terminals was simply no match for the enemy's well trained assault force, the end result being, that the battle for the inside of the complex was necessarily short and sweet. In fact, as the last living defenders, he and Captain Thomas J. Murphy had just barely managed to shut themselves off in the launch control room. Tom giving his life on the threshold rather than ever let the enemy inside.

Glancing back at the control room's double steel door, the Colonel saw the first flash of bright orange sparks, the hot blue blade of the enemy's torch racing hungrily to complete its first cut. Yet as he swept his eyes across the rest of the control room, he still couldn't help but feel a surge of pride. For even now, cut off and isolated, he stood ready and waiting to see his mission through.

The room was a maze of operations panels and monitors, all linked to a central core. For each in their own way contributed to a single purpose, that being to empower the launch control panel at which he now sat. Spread out before him sat three rows of twenty lights each, blankly staring up at him just like so many impassive eyes. They appeared to be no more than so many unlit Christmas lights, patiently awaiting their time to shine. But the harsh truth was that each group of three lights represented a Lancer Mark 4 Missile, the nation's latest and most deadly means by which it could make war. Carrying thirty Kilotons of explosive force a piece, each missile had six independently targetable warheads, more than enough in the nuclear age to make over a hundred foreign cities burn.

Checking the perimeter warning system, the Colonel was relieved to see that the enemy hadn't breached any of the missile silos yet. Yet though the missiles themselves were still safe, even there he knew it was just a matter of time. But where in the hell was the counterassault response team. It had already been over two hours since he'd signalled news of the attack. At the very least, the National Strategic Weapons Command Center at Cheyenne Mountain should have figured out a way to break through the enemy's jamming frequencies by now. Yet still the radio spoke only in indecipherable static, any hope of communicating with the outside world completely cut off. The most frustrating thing of all being that the unimposing little black box responsible for delivering his encoded launch orders still just merely sat there silent and cold.

Here he sat surrounded by the world's most superior technology. Given the proper launch codes, even he alone, just one man, was capable of sending the most powerful weapons in the world into action. All it would take would be the pushing of a few buttons and the turning of two keys. Yet in all their planning and high tech wizardry, no one had ever thought to prepare for an enemy that was capable of jamming their communications system from right on top of their very door step.

But no. It couldn't just end like this. What about all his years of training? What about all those years spent working his way up to become a commanding officer of some of the nation's most powerful weapons? Then the constant state of readiness, the endless isolation, waiting year after year to finally be called upon to serve. It couldn't have just all been for nothing. For even though he knew his best years had already come and gone, his once sandy blonde hair long since becoming flecked with gray. He was still a soldier, first and last, still patiently waiting to execute the mission for which he'd been trained. But time was running out. It was running out fast and still the order hadn't come.

No. Not like this. No. It simply couldn't happen like this. The counterassault team would be here any minute. Any minute now he'd hear the sound of friendly fire blazing away just outside the control room door, blazing away with a vengeance to fight its way through to rescue him. But even if he didn't, at the very least, somehow Cheyenne Mountain would find a way to break through the jamming frequencies. Somehow Cheyenne Mountain would find a way to reach him. He just had to keep right on doing what he'd done all of these years, just stay calm and be ready to answer when duty called. All he had to do was just hold out until help came.

But as the Colonel turned back toward the door, all he could hear was the sound of the enemy's torch. Hissing and spitting, it continued to cut, cutting its way through hard steel so that the enemy could finally get to him. The funny thing was that he still found it hard to believe that all of this could have happened in such a short time. But then again, hadn't everything happened so quickly? Hadn't it all just moved so fast, right from the very start?

THE ZEBRA CONFESSIONS

Chapter 1

Hissing softly, the .22 caliber bullet slapped rudely into the back of the old man's head. Gray hair and withered brown scalp quickly parted as the projectile punched past the bone to tunnel a meandering path through the soft tissue inside. The force of its velocity mostly spent, the bullet failed to break through the opposite side of the skull. Instead, the now misshapen lump of metal exhausted its remaining energy cartwheeling lazily about in the less resistant tissue of the brain. Like a stone, the old man dropped face first to the pavement, blood gurgling across the shoulders of his black thousand dollar suit. The Most Honorable Reverend Martin Muhammad was dead.

The Most Honorable Reverend Martin Muhammad had been an old man. Exactly how old no one quite knew. For ever since he'd passed his seventieth year the New Nation had refused to acknowledge his age. In fact, the last decade had seen a great deal of propaganda effort at convincing people that the Most Honorable Reverend Martin Muhammad was a good deal younger than his appearance led one to believe, with some of his more ignorant followers now even believing, that as the newly chosen prophet of Allah, he had ceased aging altogether. But in reality, he was an old man no different than any other, merely struggling to the point of his dying breath to hang on to the power and wealth which the years of his labor had created.

Over sixty years he'd been in "the business", from the ghetto storefront temple days of Elijah Muhammad and Malcolm X through the stagnation of Warith Muhammad and Louie Farrakhan. Through it all he'd remained faithful, first to the bad seed of Elijah Muhammad and then to the second rate night club singer called Calypso Gene. For even though he'd seen from the very start that they lacked the insight and intelligence to ever pose a serious challenge to the entrenched power of whitey, he'd patiently bided his time, learning from their foolish mistakes while he grew strong.

He was well aware that in their eternal ignorance they'd never realize what was so clear for all to see. The only path to a truly lasting segregation was not from outside the "System" but from within. He'd known all along that first his people must rise throughout the System's ranks to occupy true positions of power. Then and only then, would the time come to bring whitey's tainted little world crashing down.

Thus, through the years he'd listened ever so patiently to the rantings of the others, the teachings of these self professed leaders of men no more than the sound of dogs barking. Then, when the Nation's dissension and apathy finally reached its peak, at last it was his time to strike. And despite all of their threats, and eventually even their pleadings, it was then that he separated, welcoming the dissatisfied followers of his mentors.

Following the plan which he'd so painstakingly compiled through the years, he built his New Nation of Afro-Islam into a multibillion dollar a year business, his flock increasing in leaps and bounds from the lure of the almighty dollar. Leveraging off the revenues of his New Nation Security Concepts, Inc. he'd moved in turn into books, cosmetics, music, and clothing, and once cash flow permitted, eventually even built the New Nation of Afro-Islam planned communities and universities.

Yet despite the strain of the building years, he still fought off the sell out practices of his predecessors. In fact, he even reformed the very roots of Islamic doctrine so as to completely eliminate the Arabic taint of his people's original enslavers. Yes, let the world's fools be sucked in by Malcolm's sell out kaleidoscope of racial harmony, ignorantly denying the unparalleled greatness of the black man. For he and his flock the time had finally come and they would never, ever again, be manipulated by the treachery and lies of the lighter races.

It had required all of his cunning. For he was no longer dealing with the ignorant ghetto negroes of Elijah Muhammad, and the media continued to sweep away his flock's blinders as fast as he could build them. Of course he'd had to overhaul Elijah's outdated doctrine as well. Not even the most ignorant could still be expected to believe that whites were the genetic creation of an ancient black scientist seeking vengance against Allah. But his energy was boundless, for he was nuturing and protecting the only thing he'd ever had. Tirelessly he worked, ever staying one step ahead of the ignorant sheep which comprised his New Nation, for well he knew that nothing was ever achieved without struggle.

Like all old men he constantly had to guard against those younger, so eagerly coveting what was his. For like hungry jackals they circled him, teeth sharp and awaiting the time when they could pounce. Perhaps he should have died some other way, maybe peacefully in bed, his greatest worry a bloated belly full of gas. Yet like many old men the Most Honorable Reverend Martin Muhammad had simply outstayed his welcome. For he had something that others desperately wanted and had simply outlived his ability to protect it. So as the late afternoon sun looked on, the Most Honorable Reverend Martin Muhammad lay face down on the pavement, blood and brain tissue bubbling out of his skull like a dolphin's blowhole spray.

As the old man fell, Cecil Muhammad quickly glanced at the building from where he knew the shot had come. From an upstairs window, the briefest flash of black skin met his eye before the assassin began his retreat. Yet as Cecil pictured the assassin rushing down the stairs, happily tallying the reward for his services, a cold sneer crossed his lips. For the thought reminded him of his third son Mustafa, already waiting for the assassin at the safe house, loaded gun in hand. Idiot assassin, just like a dog on a leash, blindly, always blindly, following another's command.

Yet Cecil Muhammad knew what it was to follow as well. In fact, he'd been following the Most Honorable Reverend Martin

Muhammad for almost fifty years to this day. For it had been Martin who swept dirty little Cecil off that street corner so many years ago and renamed him. It had been Martin who fed and clothed him, educated him, instructed him in finance and manipulation, and most importantly of all, it had been Martin who taught him about desire.

In the early years, Cecil had been nothing more than a watchdog. For hours he'd stood faithfully outside the bedroom door, ignoring the slaps and moans as Martin exercised his privileges with yet another of the sister faithful. But as the years passed and the Most Honorable Reverend Martin Muhammad rose through the Nation's ranks, he pulled Cecil right along with him, gradually transforming Cecil from the wayward street youth he'd once found into one of the Nation's most trusted soldiers.

But then came the separation, and like so many others Cecil was forced to choose. So naturally he'd followed the man who raised him, unwilling to forsake so many years of his mentor's trust. Yet his loyalty was well rewarded, as the Most Honorable Reverend Martin Muhammad immediately pulled him into the inner most circle of the fledgling New Nation.

Then over time, as the New Nation grew and other advisors and lieutenants died off or fell out of favor, the gap between them narrowed even more. For twenty years Cecil followed Martin, for forty years and more, and then one day, to Martin's surprise, when he turned around to seek counsel there was only Cecil by his side. Cecil of all those years, Cecil like a son. The only person Martin had ever been able to truly trust. It was then, in the weakness of old age, in his desire to ease long shouldered burdens, that Martin forgot his single greatest conviction. No matter how hard things got, no matter how tough the road, never, ever, trust anyone.

For a while Cecil was satisfied. No move was made without him. He had only to wait and upon the Most Honorable Reverend Martin Muhammad's death, the New Nation was as good as his. But there was one big problem. Martin wouldn't die. Seventy years old, eighty, and more, Martin lived on. Cecil's own flesh became wrinkled, his once jet black hair became gray, and his bitterness grew with each passing year. The fire, once started, quickly grew into rage and Cecil's daily prayers began to focus solely on the expedient death of his mentor. But still, Martin refused to relinquish his spindly grip upon life and the reins of the New Nation. Finally, his patience at its limit and confidence in his own longevity long since broken, Cecil had ordered the deed.

As the body fell, two guards dropped to the side of their fallen master while the rest scanned their surroundings with panicked eyes. Instantly, weapons appeared in tense black hands, fanning the street in frustrated targetless arcs. Excited voices shouted out, both giving and seeking directions all at once. For anything was better than to remain simply idle and helpless, powerless to stem the flow of their master's blood. Ticking off the seconds in his head, Cecil watched the frenzied commotion with wary eyes until finally satisfied that no one else had seen what he knew, he breathed a long and deep sigh of relief.

In the seeming timelessness of the moment, Cecil couldn't help but notice the fine black suits of the bodyguards. For he could well remember the days when the Nation's soldiers had marched in their Goodwill and charity store specials. But in those days, just as now, the quality of their uniforms had been of secondary importance. For everyone from Adolph Hitler to the Boy Scouts knew that uniformity brought unity and with unity came strength.

In fact, it had been Martin who'd demanded that they keep their dark suits and bow ties even after the separation, insisting that they had as much right to their established identity as anyone. Besides, as Martin pointed out, their identity was their product and only a fool would mess with a good thing.

As Cecil studied the garb of the frantic men before him, he had to admit, that thanks to Martin, business had been very good through the years indeed, and like all successful businesses their employees had enjoyed the trickle down of profits. In fact, these elite of the New Nation's soldiers were the fashion models of bodyguards, five hundred dollar suits with all the accessories outfitting each and every one. Little wonder if even the price of their underwear couldn't pay a poor man's rent. Scanning their strained faces it left Cecil to ponder which was of more immediate concern to them anyway, the death of their master or its affect on their privileges. Then it occurred to him, that there was probably at least one young Cecil in the group if not more, and from now on he'd have to be very, very careful indeed.

Deciding that enough time had passed, Cecil then summoned up his most enraged tone and jabbing forth a trembling finger of judgment he pointed in the opposite direction of the assassin's flight. Bolstered by the years of oratory practice his voice swept across the guards with the righteous lash of vengeance.

"There he goes. Around that corner. I saw the devil who did this. It was a white man."

Like dogs freed from the leash the guards leapt forward in a frenzy, their thoughts of failure instantly converted to the blinding rage of the hunt. Yet as the footsteps of the others quickly faded into the distance, two of them stayed faithfully behind to attend the lifeless form of their leader. Cecil Muhammad hid his eyes as he knelt next to the body, his back shuddering with practiced sobs of grief. And though the remaining guards kept a respectful distance, they were still forced to wipe back their tears, so moved were they by Cecil's open expression of love for The Most Honorable Reverend Martin Muhammad.

About the Author

David L. Dukes is a novelist, attorney, and observer of humanity. A graduate of both Duke University and the Duke University School of Law, he was engaged in the practice of law until the memories from his days in Afghanistan and Columbia, South America led him to take up the writer's pen. Yet he doesn't write merely to record his observations but to project their significance into the future.

Printed in the United States
749000004B

9 780759 665651